PRAISE FOR THREE COINS

"Ah Ying's story transported me to another time and another place. I was enthralled with the story of Three Coins and the weaving together of the historical facts. Kudos!

"I also believe that all of our lives are connected. As said in Flower Drum Song, "A Hundred Million Miracles Are Happening Everyday"

Nancy Kwan
Actress – "Flower Drum Song"

"Congratulations! What a fascinating story. It is one of the many untold stories of women who endured and built the foundation of Chinese American families that continue to be the fabric of American Society. Three Coins is one of the few books that actually is from the point of view of the woman rescued and how she managed to take control of her life--not a story from the rescuer's perspective. One chapter flows into the next as the author weaves the stories into a historical context. Great job!"

Doreen Der-Mcleod
Executive Director Donaldina Cameron House 2001-2009

"Ah Ying is a woman after my own heart. She is feisty and smart. Definitely got a mind of her own. And once she decides what she wants, she goes for it. She's so different from the stereotypical docile, filial Chinese daughter. What a good read!"

Sue Lee
Executive Director Chinese Historical Society of America
2004 - 2017

“A wonderful story! The author has a very clever way of weaving together historical facts and fiction. I love the way he takes an old photo and makes it come alive within the story. I found some parts, like Ah Ying’s escape from the tong men and the family's experience after the earthquake and fire of '06, really gripping! Reading Three Coins was very enjoyable. Good job!”

Gregory Ng Kimm
Genealogist and researcher of Chinese American history

"I never knew my grandmother. Russell Low writes with such vivid descriptions of Ah Ying's life and his detailed in-depth story made me feel as if I know this courageous young woman. His writing style is very intimate and active so you are completely engaged in this exciting, dramatic novel. It's beautiful.

Arabella Hong-Young
Singer, Actress, Author, Teacher
"Flower Drum Song"

THREE COINS

A Young Girl's Story of Kidnappings, Slavery, and Romance In 19th Century America

Russell N. Low

Russell N. Low

Cover photograph by Thomas Houseworth, The Christian Stairway c. 1886. Courtesy of the Kimm Family Collection.

Chinese Coins Jiaqing 1796-1820 (middle) and Daoguang 1820-1850. Courtesy of Alexander Akin.

All photographs and artwork, unless otherwise indicated, are in the Public Domain.
ISBN: 9781796601343

DEDICATIONS

This work is dedicated to Margaret Culbertson,who set Ah Ying free, and to Rose Low and Grace Lee and to all the others, who encouraged me to keep the past alive.

CONTENTS

PREFACE

Three Coins recreates the world of Tong Yan Gai, or Chinatown, before the turn of the twentieth century. The Chinese population in San Francisco grew from only a handful before 1850 to 25,000, or 8.6%, of the city's population, by 1890. Along with this rapid growth came many social and political problems. A series of legislations passed by the United States Congress reflected the growing anti-Chinese sentiment, as the Chinese were perceived as an economic and social threat. The Page Act of 1875 banned Chinese women from immigrating the United States. The Chinese Exclusion Act of 1882 prohibited the immigration of all Chinese laborers to the United States. The ban was renewed in 1892 with the Geary Act, which also required registration of all Chinese, and was made permanent ten years later.

Because of the Exclusion Act, the Chinese population in San Francisco declined from 25,000 in 1890 to 14,000 in 1900, with an eventual further decline to less than 8,000 by 1920.

What remained was a predominantly all male bachelor

society in Tong Yan Gai. There were twenty men to every one woman. The illegal importation of Chinese women and girls, to serve as prostitutes and child domestic servants, developed and flourished in this environment. The Presbyterian and Methodist Churches in San Francisco took an active role in rescuing trafficked Chinese women and girls, establishing Mission Homes to house and educate them.

Two of these Mission Homes are shown in Arnold Genthe's iconic 1906 photograph looking down Sacramento Street after the infamous San Francisco earthquake. The photo shows both the beginning and the ending of the story of Three Coins. It depicts the moment of destruction of the old world of Tong Yan Gai, and it also reveals a secret from the past.

In Genthe's photograph, the new Presbyterian Mission Home at 920 Sacramento Street is easily recognized on the left, but the building on the right with its brick wall collapsed into the street has never been identified. The building with the collapsed front wall is the original Presbyterian Misson Home at 933 Sacramento Street where Ah Ying lived with her sisters. One can see the distinctive brick archways in the three-story building with its collapsed front wall. They are the same building. This building served as the Presbyterian Mission Home from 1877 until 1893.

Examining this and a second photograph Genthe took that morning allows a look into the rooms where girls rescued from slavery and prostitution lived with Margaret Culbertson, who ran the Presbyterian Mission Home. If those walls could speak, they would tell the stories of these hundreds of girls. The Mission Home was only the beginning of their new life in America. Their lives continued beyond their rescue as they married and started families.

These young Chinese women were independent and bold, and above all else knew how to survive. They became pillars of strength for their families and for the newly emerging Chinese American society. Three Coins shares the story of one of Margaret Culbertson's girls, Tom Gew Ying, or Ah Ying, following her life for 26 years from her village in Southern China to the streets of San Francisco.

Arnold Genthe understood the significance of his photograph, even commenting on the collapsed building in his autobiography:

"Of the pictures I had made during the fire, there are several, I believe, that will be of lasting interest. There is particularly the one scene that I recorded the morning of the first day of the fire [along Sacramento Street, looking toward the Bay] which shows, in a pictorially effective composition, the results of the earthquake, the beginning of the fire and the attitude of the people. On the right is a house, the front of which had collapsed into the street. The occupants are sitting on chairs calmly watching the approach of the fire. Groups of people are standing in the street, motionless, gazing at the clouds of smoke. When the fire crept up close, they would just move up a block. It is hard to believe that such a scene actually occurred in the way the photograph represents it."

Genthe captured this surreal moment for eternity, but he also captured a peek into the world of Ah Ying and the girls of the Presbyterian Mission Home.

BEAR
PHOTO
SF 387

ACKNOWLEDGMENTS

Researching and writing Three Coins was a journey that would not have been possible without the kind assistance and encouragement of so many people. Foremost, Doreen Der-Mcleod, Executive Director of Donaldina Cameron House 2001 – 2009, was instrumental in locating the original entry in the Registry of the Presbyterian Occidental Board Mission Home. The details provided in these records brought to life the true story of my great grandmother Tom Gew Ying.

Two individuals were key in illuminating Chinese American history and culture. Grace Lee, the 102-year-old granddaughter of Chin Shee, shared her tremendous depth of knowledge and supplied the Gin Family photos. Gregory Kimm, a great grandson of Ah Ying's sister Ah Mooie, shared his extensive research into the Occidental Mission Home and generously provided the Kimm family photos including "The Christian Stairway." Greg's editing added authenticity to the manuscript by providing the Cantonese translations of the Chinese words used in THREE COINS. Robert Low, the great-great grandson of Ah Ying, was instrumental in his review and thoughtful revisions of the manuscript.

The photographers and artists whose work brings Ah Ying's story to life must be acknowledged and appreciated for their vision. Ah Ying's friend Isaiah West Taber, Arnold Genthe, Thomas Houseworth, Charles Weidner, Alfred Hart, and artists Robert Blum, Charles Graham, and Jake Lee helped to recreate the world of San Francisco's Chinatown from 1880-1906. I am indebted to the Chinese Historical Society of America for allowing me to reproduce Jake Lee's paintings to illustrate THREE COINS.

Finally, Vivian Shen of the Guangzhou Overseas Chinese Affairs Office, arranged my 2016 return visit to the ancestral villages in Toishan where my great-grand parents' story began 180 years ago.

PROLOGUE

Grandma Hong's Visit – Salem 1920

Gwunde's face was plastered against the screen door of the family home on 13th Street in Salem, Oregon. It had been ten minutes since Mama had told him that Grandma was coming to visit him, but it felt like he had been waiting here for hours. Finally, unable to contain himself, Gwunde swung open the door, stormed out onto the wooden porch and hopped down the two rickety steps into the yard. The bright Salem sun warmed his face as he kicked the leaves and ran around and around the small front yard. Gwunde spotted his favorite cherry tree and scrambled to the top far above the streets of Salem. From his lookout he would see Grandma coming a mile away! He knew she was coming from Oakland by train and watched for the smoke announcing her arrival.

Suddenly, he spotted an old black Model T coming towards the house. The car pulled up and a young man got out, ran around the car and opened the door. Grandma Hong, dressed in black as usual, stepped out of the car. Her hair was pulled back tightly, revealing a high forehead and kind eyes. Clambering down the tree, Gwunde ran up to Grandma grabbed her gown and spun her around and around.

"Hello, Grandma! I have been waiting for you for days!"

"*Neih hou*[1], Gwunde. Slow down before we fall!" smiled Grandma at her four-year-old grandson.

"Come on Grandma! Sit here and tell me a story!" begged Gwunde as he pulled her towards the old wooden chair in the front yard.

"Alright, but just a quick story before I find your mother and all of your brothers and sisters."

The two sat on the chair with Gwunde climbing up onto the armrest. Uncle Kim stood in front with his ever-present camera in hand. Grandma reached into her pocket and took out a cluster of red grapes and a small paring knife. She patiently began to peel each grape and handed them to her grandson who eagerly devoured the treats.

"Thank you, Grandma, but tell me the story please!"

"Try to speak Chinese, Gwunde. Say, *Do jeh!* for thank you."

"*Do jeh!* Grandma," offered Gwunde tentatively. "That's all the Chinese I know!"

Grandma sighed fairly certain that Gwunde was telling the truth. He was a handful, but she loved him. He reminded her of her Gee Sung.

"Look this way!" ordered Kim pointing his camera in their direction. "No, over here, Gwunde! Take your finger out of your mouth!"

"Just take the photo, Kim. He's impossible!"

With a snap the photo and the moment with Grandma and Gwunde was preserved for all time.

The screen door opened slowly with a creak, and Mei Gil, Gwunde's older sister, stepped onto the porch.

"Hello, Grandma!"

"Chinese, please! Say *Neih hou*!" instructed Grandma.

[2]

"OK, *Neih hou*, Grandma! Can I sit on the chair with you and Gwunde?" asked Mei Gil politely.

"Of course. You are a good girl. Sit here on my right. Gwunde, sit still!"

Kim raised his camera and snapped another photo in the early Salem morning sun just as Gwunde spotted a crow in his favorite cherry tree.

"Now I will tell you a Chinese proverb so you will understand my story.

When drinking water, you must think of its source, so you do not forget its origin.

In other words, you must know where you come from."

Mei Gil, with her hands folded in her lap, waited patiently for Grandma to begin. Gwunde, squirming around on the chair, hoped it would be an adventure story.

"Please hurry, Grandma. I can't wait any longer."

"I will tell you a story about dragon boats, slaves, highbinders and kidnappings. This is where you come from."

Gwunde's eyes grew big with anticipation. Now she had his complete attention.

CHAPTER 1

Kidnapped 1880

I remember opening my eyes and seeing the dancing light on the dirt floor as the early morning sun filtered through the open window. The leaves of the fig tree outside our home rustled in the already warm breeze making the sunlight dance on the floor. Each morning from my mat in the corner of the room I watched the light playing with the leaves, so I knew it wouldn't last. It was time to rise and find Baba. This was the day he promised to take me to see the dragon boats.

It was the fifth day of the fifth month of the Chinese Lunar calendar, Saturday June 12, 1880, the day of the Tuen Ng Festival. Mama told me the story of the famous patriotic poet Wut Yuan from the Kingdom of Choh, who drowned himself in the Mit Loh River rather than see his country conquered by the State of Qin. Fishermen searched for his body sailing their boats down the river. The villagers threw eggs and *joong* into the river to attract fish, so they would not destroy his body. Every year the people honored the story of Qu Yuan during the Dragon Boat Festival.

I heard Mama cooking breakfast in the kitchen. The aroma of the steaming *joong* was overpowering. I quickly dressed, brushed my hair and teeth and joined Mama in the kitchen.

"*Jou sahn*[3], little one. Sit down and have breakfast,"

I watched as mama opened the lid of the bamboo steamer and placed the steaming *joong*[4] on the table. The sticky rice wrapped in bamboo was a rare treat. I loved the bean paste and egg yolk filling hiding in the mound of yellow sticky rice. Food in the village was not plentiful following the poor harvest last year. Our family's new baby boy, little Ah Choy, was a joy, but I knew Mama worried about how to feed another mouth as he grew older.

I eagerly waited for Mama to place the steaming *joong* on my plate, and then I hurriedly unwrapped the bamboo leaves, revealing the sticky delicacy.

"Thank you, Mama. I will save some for dai dai."

"No, today this is all for you, my little Ah Ying[5]."

I was surprised. I always had to share food with my little brother. Inhaling the smell of the rice, I was unable to wait any longer. I took a piece with my chop stick and gently placed it in my mouth, savoring the taste so it would last a little longer.

"Ah Ying, I have packed two more joong, flat bread, pickles, and a boiled egg for you to take on the trip with Baba," said Mama, as she neatly wrapped the food in a cloth.

"I will be home for dinner Mama. Why do I need to take all that food?"

Ignoring my question, Mama took out a perfume pouch and a five-color silk thread. She gently took my hand and tied the five color silk thread around my wrist.

"What is this Mama?"

"Shush! You must not speak while I am placing this on your wrist or the magical healing powers will not protect you," cautioned Mama in a whisper.

She finished tying the silk thread on my wrist and draped the perfume pouch around my neck, patting it for good measure. She then took out three Chinese coins and handed them to me.

"When you cross over the water, throw these three coins into the water to protect you on your journey."

"I won't need these coins, Mama. I am just going with Baba to see the dragon boats today."

"Just promise me you will do as I say!"

I looked at my mother's face and saw the tears in her eyes before mama quickly turned away.

"Promise me you will be good, Ah Ying."

"Yes, of course, mama. Don't cry. I won't be gone long."

Mama handed me the bundle of food tied in a cloth and then opened the package and slipped in a toothbrush and new washcloth. "Now go and find your father. He is waiting for you down by the well. He will take you to see the dragon boat festival, Ah Ying."

Taking the package, I replied, "Thank you, Mama, I will be good and will keep the coins safe until I need them to cross a river."

I then hurried out the door in search of Baba and the dragon boats. Walking through Bok Sar village I saw the familiar three rows of houses facing east with the school at the tail of the village. Secretly I wanted to learn to read and write, but only the boys went to school. I often hid outside the school and listened to the boys reciting their lessons. In fact, I knew the precepts of Confucius better than the younger boys but dared not repeat them aloud. Today the building was quiet, as the village was preparing for the festival. As I passed the fishpond, I spotted Baba waiting for me by the village well.

"*Neih hou*, Baba!" shouted Ah Ying as she ran down the dirt path to her father.

Baba looked up and smiled weakly at his daughter trying to hide the pain in his heart.

"*Neih hou*, my little Ah Ying!"

Ah Ying took her father's hand and pulled him along the path towards the river.

"Hurry, Baba! We will miss the start of the dragon boat race! I want to see the pretty boats up close."

Baba followed behind his always-energetic daughter as they walked through the fields being planted with beans and squash. Their family worked ten mou[6] of farmland, but the harvest had been poor last year, and the ground was dry again this year with not enough rain. *Fui Sing* the one-legged rain god must be displeased with their village, for it had not rained in months. The scorching sun was only part way up the sky, but the heat was already building. It would be another stifling day in Toishan.

"Baba, I will help you in the fields this season. I can dig, and hoe, and manure the crops, and harvest the crops just like last year," announced Ah Ying proudly as they passed the family farm.

"Yes, my little Ah Ying. You are my best helper," mumbled Baba absently without even glancing at the farmland or his daughter.

As they approached the festival, Ah Ying broke free and ran down to the water's edge. The races had started! The men strained to pull the dragon boats through the water with their paddles keeping time to the beat of the drum on each boat. Ah Ying loved to watch the boats gliding through the water, imagining the heart of the dragon beating with each beat of the drum.

"Look, Baba! Our boat is in the lead!"

The men from their village practiced all year for this one day of racing. Working long hours in the fields gave them strength, but today it was the spirit of the ancestors that pulled their boat to the front of the pack.

"We're winning, Baba!"

"Shush! Don't be so proud, Ah Ying," whispered Baba to his excited daughter.

"I am sorry, Baba, but we have never won the race before! We have to follow the boats!"

Ah Ying pulled Baba along past the vendors selling every imaginable type of delicious food. The wood burning stoves were glowing with red embers keeping the steamed food warm, but Ah Ying hardly noticed as she ran towards the finish of the race. Breaking through the crowds along the shore, Ah Ying spotted their boat.

"We are still in the lead, Baba!"

But Baba was not looking at the race. He pulled Ah Ying close and held her tightly looking at the daughter that had been his joy for the past nine years.

"Be good, my little Ah Ying and remember your family."

With those words he turned away not wishing to see what was about to happen.

Ah Ying turned to see her father walking away.

"Baba, you are missing the race! Where are you going?"

Suddenly, Ah Ying's world was dim. She felt a sponge held over her face that smelled sweet and bitter. Her head was spinning and she felt weak. Now she could not see. Ah Ying fought for air and struggled against the arms holding her down. But she grew weaker and the sounds of the race were now gone. All that remained was darkness.

CHAPTER 2

In the Belly of the Beast

Ah Ying slowly woke from her deep sleep in a strange place. Her head was groggy. It was dark and humid and noisy, with the rhythmic sound of an engine not far away. Her hands were tied, and there was a something over her head. She struggled to free her hands and wiggled her wrists out of the binding. Tearing the sack from her head, she gasped when she saw the outlines of dozens of women and children around her, huddled together in the dark.

"Where am I? Where is my Baba? I shouldn't be here!" whimpered Ah Ying to anyone who might help her.

She waited for a reply, but there was only the sound of the engine and a vibration that shook the entire room.

A woman next to her finally replied, "Forget your family. They do not exist. You are alone and going to Gum Saan[7]. Get used to the dark. We will be in the belly of this ship for two months."

Now Ah Ying was truly afraid. Not of the darkness, but of the unknown. How could she be alone? Her Baba must be frantically searching for her.

"I know Baba is coming to get me! He must have lost me along the river. He will be here soon," pleaded Ah Ying.

She had heard tales of the White devils in Gum Saan and wanted nothing to do with these pale ghosts.

"You are alone. Your Baba sold you to Wong Shee. They did not want you, and she promised to take you to Gum Saan to stay with a rich family. You should be happy for your good fortune."

The truth of Ah Ying's plight was slowly becoming clear. She had been kidnapped, and this evil woman was sent to confuse her with lies.

"I don't believe you! My Baba would never sell me. I am his Ah Ying. He needs me to take care of the family," said Ah Ying in a voice more certain than she felt inside.

The only reply was the sound of the engine and the vibration, which she reasoned must be from a paddle wheel. Wasn't it just last week that she had seen a steamship in the harbor? She had pestered Baba until he explained to her how its great wheels churned up the water with the strength of a hundred dragon boat crews. But Baba was gone, and Ah Ying was truly alone for the first time in her life. She covered her face, and her arms began to shake. Soon her whole body was shuddering as she sobbed uncontrollably.

In the darkness Ah Ying felt a hand on her shoulder.

"Shhh! Don't cry. You are not alone. We are all going to Gum Saan. I will be your friend," said a soothing voice.

Ah Ying lifted her tear-streaked face to see a pretty young girl only a bit older than she. A small crowd of women and children had gathered around her. Still shaking, she took a deep breath,

"I am sorry….."

"Don't be sorry," interrupted the young girl. "My name is Sing Yee. I am traveling to Gum Saan to marry my husband Gin Lun Gee. He is an herbalist."

Ah Ying looked at the young girl in surprise, "But you are too young to marry! You can't be more than thirteen years old."

"Well actually, I will not marry for several years, but I have been promised. Once my parents agreed to the marriage, he sent money for the bride price and for my passage to Gum Saan. When I am married my name will be Chin Shee, but for now, you can call me Sing Yee. What is your name?"

"I am Tom Ah Ying. I don't understand what is happening.

Why am I going to Gum Saan on this ship?"

"Wong Shee is the woman who bought you, and she is taking you Gum Saan to work for a rich family," offered Sing Yee. "She has several girls your age onboard."

Ah Ying's heart sank as she realized she had been sold to be a servant, a slave, a *mui tsai*. She didn't know exactly what was in store, but it couldn't be good.

"Will I be a *baak haak chai*?"[8] She knew of this life of shame and would rather die right now on this ship.

"Oh no, you are much too young. You will be a household servant for some rich Chinese family," explained Sing Yee.

Ah Ying was considering her prospects when an old Chinese woman approached her in the darkness.

"You, sit down over here! I am Wong Shee, your new master! You will obey me!"

Ah Ying did not much like being told where to sit by some stranger.

"Why should I listen to you? You are not my mother or father!"

"I bought you from your father for eighty dollars. Now I own you, and you will obey me! Come over here!"

Ah Ying approached the old woman tentatively and then stopped short for good measure. She remained, standing silently glaring at the old Chinese woman.

I will not obey you! she thought.

The old woman reached out and grabbed Ah Ying roughly by her tunic and pulled her down onto the wooden seat with a strength that surprised Ah Ying.

"I said to sit! If you expect to eat on this voyage, you will learn to obey me!"

"Where are my parents? Why did you kidnap me?"

"Your parents sold you to me and I am taking you to Gum Saan. You will live with a rich merchant family in Dai Fow[9]. You should thank me for my kindness!" the old woman sneered.

"I will thank you when you take me home to Bok Sar Village," exclaimed Ah Ying defiantly.

"You will learn not to be so proud. It is a long voyage, and you will need to eat something more than the slop the White man will serve you. You are no more than a dog to him."

After some time, Ah Ying learned to control her anger so that she could eat and sleep in peace. Inside she was still angry with Wong Shee and with Baba for not protecting her, but she found that remaining silent was the best way to deal with the old woman.

The steerage deck compartment for women and children was located at the bottom of the ship. The low seven-foot ceiling made the compartment seem more cramped. It was always dark, and the small space was crowded and unsanitary. It was crammed with double-deck wooden bunks lined up in the direction of the ship, with one row on each side and a third row down the middle of the compartment. Each bunk was supposed to hold five persons. Mattresses stuffed with straw soon became infested with lice and bed bugs. Flies were everywhere.

Wong Shee's promise of good Cantonese food if she behaved was a little more than a lie, and she was offered only a small handful of rice. To survive, Ah Ying ate what she could stomach of the White devil's food, choking it down with her eyes squeezed shut and her nose pinched tight. In the morning there was oatmeal, coffee, hard bread, and butter. In the evening there was watery soup with some unrecognizable meat or fish served from a slop bucket.

As the trip wore on, the food became laced with weevils and other bugs, which she desperately tried to pick out with her chopsticks before forcing down the watery mush. After several weeks at sea below deck, the stench and heat were unbearable. The constant rocking of the boat and its seasick human cargo added to the discomfort and smell.

One day, the hatch finally opened and the intensely bright daylight streamed into the dark hold, momentarily blinding the women and children. Even though she could barely see, Ah Ying was still the first in line to go up on deck. She climbed the varnished wooden ladder and peered out from the hatch that led topside. The intense sunlight was painful but welcome relief from the darkness below deck. She inhaled the salty air deeply. After being imprisoned in the fetid bowels of steerage, the fresh sea breeze and ocean spray on her face was intoxicating.

Feeling for the coins in her pocket, Ah Ying recalled her Mama's instructions. She ran over to the rail and hurled them into space. She watched them glint in the sunlight as they hung in the air for a brief eternity before falling into the surging whitecaps that rose up as if to accept the humble offering.

"There, now I have satisfied my Mama's wishes, and I should be safe from Gong Gong the evil water god for a little while."

Wong Shee approached, and sat down next to Ah Ying.

"When we arrive in Dai Fow the Custom House official will question you. You will tell them that you are my daughter, and that we are going to see your father who is a merchant. His name is Fong Wy. He owns a dry goods store on Washington Street. Can you remember this? If you fail this test, they will feed you to the sharks in the bay!"

Unsure of what to believe, but none too fond of sharks, Ah Ying set about memorizing Wong Shee's newest lies. As she rehearsed, she gazed up at the tall masts and white billowing sails, where young boys not much older than herself climbed the rigging. She peered over the side of the boat and traced the foamy white path that sprouted like a kite's tail from the steadily churning paddle wheel. She could hear and smell the engine room, where an enormous metal monster devoured coal by the shovel-full, breathing blasts of steam and clawing its way relentlessly forward – dragging her ever closer to an uncertain yet unavoidable fate. By the time they finally arrived in Dai Fow weeks later, even Ah Ying was beginning to believe the lies of her new life in Gum Saan.

[10]

CHAPTER 3

Life of a *Mui Tsai* in Dai Fow

"Ah Ying, get up off the floor, you lazy girl!" screamed her owner. "Why aren't you finished scrubbing the kitchen?"

Ah Ying dropped the scrub brush and instinctively reached for her leg. But it was a second too late. She saw the blur from the corner of her eye and heard the sickening slap of the switch striking her flesh. The searing pain enveloped her and she curled up in the corner as her owner struck her legs repeatedly.

"Aiya! You, useless girl! I will teach you not to be lazy!" as she raised the bloody stick again and again.

When the screaming finally stopped, there was only silence and the panting of her owner. Curled up under the table, Ah Ying slowly opened her teary eyes and rubbed her throbbing leg, black and blue from the constant beatings.

"Yes, Tai Tai![11] I can work faster. Please don't hit me again," pleaded little Ah Ying, as she fearfully eyed the bloody stick and the woman's chubby face, red with rage and heaving from the exertion.

"Scrub that floor! It is as filthy as your worthless soul. And pick up the baby. It needs to be fed now!"

[12]

Ah Ying looked at the fat screaming infant, picked him up and placed him on her back as she returned to her work. She hated the child but felt sorry for him for having such a miserable and cruel mother. Returning to her chores, she silently prayed to any god who might be listening for deliverance from this life as a *mui tsai*.

Left alone to her work scrubbing the floors, Ah Ying murmured, "Don't worry little one. Your parents are rich, but they have no heart and are soulless and evil. You will have to be strong to live among these people."

She did not really hate the baby but despised the privileged life that he represented and the cruel way his parents mistreated their servants. She was only nine-years- old but could remember a time when she was free and happy with her own family in China. Dai Fow was cold and lonely and so very far from her home. Someday she would escape from this life as a servant. For now, she only wanted to survive the day without another beating.

Little Ah Ying's days were long. She started work at 7a.m., and some days had to work right on until 2 o'clock in the morning. She was expected to cook, clean the home, and take care of the baby boy. Emptying the slop buckets was the chore she dreaded the most. The whole family owned her and the whole family beat her to their hearts content. If the rice was not cooked to perfection or if she could not get the baby to stop crying, Ah Ying was whipped, or her head was banged against the wall, or her face was scratched with the long claw-like nails of her owner. When they tired of these forms of cruelty they beat her with a stick or inflicted burns with a hot iron. This torture was so common that Ah Ying swore she would one day escape before she died in this wretched house.

◆ ◆ ◆

As the months turned into years, Ah Ying learned how to avoid most of the beatings. She was submissive and obedient to her owners, but Ah Ying felt a growing defiance as she plotted her escape from this miserable life. When she was a young teenager, she was allowed some freedom to leave the house on errands for the family. She loved these trips through the streets of Chinatown. She memorized every street. Dupont Gai[13] was her favorite. She knew all the stores and smiled at the shopkeepers. She envied the young children that played freely on the streets and alleys. The sights and smells of Chinatown reminded her daily of her home in Bok Sar. She rarely ventured as far as Sacramento Street but had heard of the Jesus House that rescued young girls and had once seen the missionary ladies shopping in a store. *If only they could see me. I am right here*, she thought.

[14]

Ah Ying's only friend was Sue Lee, a girl her own age, who was a *mui tsai* for another rich Chinese merchant family that lived in the same building on Jackson Street. The two sometimes went to the market to buy food for the family. The pots of steaming food were so large and heavy that they literally dragged them home. The aroma of the delicious food was almost too much to bear for the starving girls, who would only be fed the leftover scraps after their fat owners feasted.

"Hello, Sue Lee," chimed Ah Ying as she spotted her friend leaving her apartment. "Are you going to pick up dinner for your owners?"

"Yes, of course. They never seem to stop eating!"

Both girls had infants strapped to their backs, which was the unmistakable sign of a *mui tsai* in Chinatown.

"Come, we can walk together and take turns carrying the heavy food back home," said Ah Ying hoping for some company.

The girls walked uphill on Jackson Street towards Dupont Gai. At Bartlett Alley[15] they passed the Royal Chinese Theater at 622 Jackson Street where they paused to watch the actors and musicians arriving for the evening performance. They turned left at Dupont and walked uphill past Washington and Clay Streets where they found the Hang Far Low restaurant that prepared their family's meals. The rich aroma of steaming Chinese food filled their nostrils but not their empty stomachs. At home they could dream of delicious meals but would be lucky to be given a little rice and bean sprouts.

The girls waited inside the restaurant, inspecting the red and gold Chinese decorations that they knew by heart. Ah Ying loved the ornate carved lantern hanging from the ceiling with its pretty red tassels. The familiar sizzling and stirring noises came from the kitchen. Finally, the kitchen door swung open followed by a man with trays of steaming food.

"*Neih hou*, Uncle Chan!" chimed both girls in unison.

"*Jou sahn*, Ah Ying and Sue Lee! Have you eaten?" Not waiting for their reply, Uncle Chan placed on the table the two bowls of noodles he had prepared for his young friends. "Sik faan!"[16]

"*Do jeh*, Uncle Chan!" The girls quickly sat down, picked up their chopsticks and hungrily feasted on the delicious noodles.

When they finished, Uncle Chan loaded up each girl with five bamboo containers stuffed with food for their owners. "Be careful! Don't trip and spill the food!"

"*Joi Gin*[17], Uncle Chan," chimed the smiling girls from behind their heavy loads of food. "We will be careful. See you next time!"

The crowd of Chinese men dressed in their dark trousers, tunics, and black hats smiled at the girls but did not offer to help them with their heavy loads of food. They knew better than to interfere. The girls' owners were wealthy and powerful people with close ties to the highbinders, who would deal harshly with anyone that threatened their property. Any man with such poor judgment would be left dead in a Chinatown alley.

As the girls carried their heavy food baskets along Dupont towards Jackson Street, Ah Ying had a brilliant idea.

"Maybe we can eat all the food and then run away and hide out in Portsmouth Square! Or maybe we can stow away on a ship at the Pacific Mail Dock and go back home to China!"

"We can't possibly eat all this food, and what would we do with these babies?"

"Well, let's take the babies to the Jesus House and then stowaway on a ship. I know the way to the waterfront, the mah ta'ow. I watched the wagons bringing the Chinese men up Kearny Street from the docks at the end of 3rd Street. I talked to the driver. He said it's not far. We could run there in a few minutes!" exclaimed Ah Ying as her plan of escape took shape in her mind.

Sue Lee's eyes grew large as she looked at her friend and realized she was serious, "You must be crazy! They will catch us and beat us until we are dead!"

"It would be better than being their slave."

"Maybe you're right. Last night I heard my owner talking about selling me to a brothel to be a *baak haak chai* and buying a younger *mui tsai*."

Both girls were silent as they considered what awaited them in Dai Fow's houses of shame.

Ah Ying shuddered, "Sue Lee, we have to act now. We have been talking about escaping for years. This may be our only chance."

Without a further word, the girls turned around and headed

south on Dupont Gai towards Sacramento Street. Ah Ying looked to her left and saw the horse-drawn wagon coming up Kearny carrying the newly arrived Chinese men and their belongings from the steamers at the Pacific Mail Dock.

Smelling her freedom, Ah Ying forgot about the babies. She grabbed Sue Lee's hand and started running down Kearny Street, tracing the wagon's path back to the docks.

"Hurry, Sue Lee!" she exclaimed breathlessly.

Just as they drew within sight of the docks, a pair of large hands grabbed them from behind, stopping both girls dead in their tracks.

"Where are you girls going?" demanded a deep voice.

Ah Ying turned around and saw a hairy, White policeman with a bushy mustache and a round, black hat.

"We are running away to the docks! Please let us go!" pleaded Ah Ying.

"You are stealing these babies as well I see!"

"No! Please let us go! We need to escape before our owners sell us to be *baak haak chai*," implored Sue Lee.

But Officer Mahoney would not help the girls. In fact, he was paid by the Tongs to look the other way when violations–or much worse–occurred in Chinatown. He took the girls back to 611 Jackson Street, where their owners feigned great concern for the girls' well-being and thanked Officer Mahoney for his kindness.

Once inside, Ah Ying's owners came at her with a vengeance.

"You want to run away, you ungrateful worthless girl! And you were stealing our baby to sell! You will pay for your disobedience!"

The man held Ah Ying down with her face smashed into the table, while his evil wife heated up an iron tong. They stripped back her gown, exposing her skin. When the iron was glowing red hot, the evil matron came at Ah Ying and plunged the iron into her back.

Ah Ying screamed at the searing pain and then blacked out.

The last thing she remembered was the smell of her burning flesh. Sue Lee's fate in the house next door was no better.

From that day on, Ah Ying never again mentioned escape. She was obedient, submissive, and silent. Her owners were pleased with her changed attitude and were sure their intervention had saved Ah Ying from a horrible fate as an ungrateful and rebellious slave. Gradually, as the family grew tired of fetching their own meals, Ah Ying was allowed to resume her trips into Chinatown under the watchful eye of the matron.

CHAPTER 4

Gung Hay Fat Choy
Chinese New Year 1884

Ah Ying felt the growing excitement in the air as the whole Chinese quarter prepared for Chinese New Year. She and Sue Lee were running errands for their owners but secretly hoped to take part in the festivities.

Triangular yellow banners covered with Chinese dragons[18] fluttered from every flagstaff in honor of the beginning of the Chinese New Year celebration. Businesses and homes were brightly lit with scores of candles and colored lanterns above every door.

All of Chinatown was wide-awake at midnight on Saturday to welcome the Year of the Monkey with firecrackers and exploding bombs. The air was thick with smoke and the smell of sulfur. The whole city joined in the festivities as prominent White citizens mixed with the Chinese, all under the watchful eye of the San Francisco police. Sidewalk stands did a booming business selling sugar cane, Chinese dried clams, and an infinite variety of confections.

[19]

"Hurry, Sue Lee! We can see the Dragon Dance coming down Dupont!" exclaimed Ah Ying as the girls walked along Jackson Street into the heart of the festivities.

"We should get the meals and return home before we are missed," worried Sue Lee.

"We have time for a quick peek. Look there is the Dragon! Let's run before we miss the celebration."

A barrage of firecrackers exploded as the yellow and red Dragon danced by weaving its way along Dupont Gai keeping time to the sounds of the drums and gongs.

"Gung Hay Fat Choy!" called out the vendors to the girls.

Ah Ying and Sue Lee knew all the vendors and store owners along Dupont Gai. These men were like their family in Gum Saan.

"Here, have some sugar cane! And here is some sweet ginger and dried coconut. Today you can celebrate with your friends."

The girls smiled and took the treats from their friend Ah Chan, who worked in the Hang Far Low restaurant where their owners bought their meals.

"Thank you Uncle Chan. Gung Hay Fat Choy!" exclaimed both girls in unison.

The sweets were delicious and rare treats for the girls. Both girls were now fifteen years old by Chinese counting, and the men had seen the girls grow up along these streets. When they first arrived, the little *mui tsai* were scarcely taller than the stacks of food they dragged back to their owners on Jackson Street twice a day. Now they were young women, though still small in stature. Their initially timid smiles had long ago been replaced with a friendly wave to their ever-watchful "Uncles" along Dupont Gai.

The brightly colored yellow and red dragon danced and weaved its way down Dupont Gai. To the delight of the children and adults lining the street, its huge head with blinking eyes bobbed up and down and shook side to side, accompanied by the "pop, pop, pop" and smoke of nonstop firecracker explosions.

Once the dragon passed by, a Chinese band replaced it. Dozens of Chinese school children danced with their brightly colored ribbons and fans as glittering floats covered with flowers and golden tinsel followed in their festive wake.

As Ah Ying was about to turn to leave, she felt a warm glow on her face and turned back to look at the parade. Across the street she saw the face of a tall Chinese man looking in her direction. Their eyes met. Neither of them looked away as the sounds of the parade seemed to fade. For a moment it was only the two of them. Then the crowd closed in, and he was gone.

Turning back to her friend, Ah Ying asked, "Did you see that Chinese man looking at me?"

"What are you talking about? I just saw a dragon and children!"

"No, I saw him, and he was watching me. I wonder who he is."

"Don't be silly, Ah Ying. But if you insist, we can call him your Dragon Boy!"

With that the girls turned and ran back to complete their errands before their owners found out about their excursion to the see the Chinese New Year's Parade. The glow on Ah Ying's face did not go away for some time. She may have still been a *mui tsai*, but she was quickly growing up to be a young woman in Dai Fow.
[20]

CHAPTER 5

Ah Ying Meets Gee Sung

Ah Ying remembered the day she met her Gee Sung. It was a sunny spring day in April 1885. This was indeed a special day for it was the day of the Good Lady Festival. Every seven years the Chinese women and girls were allowed to walk alone in Chinatown with all the rights and privileges of a Chinese man. Ah Ying was dressed in her finest Chinese robe and her hair was braided into a long ponytail, the sign that she was an unmarried woman. She and Sue Lee were sent out to purchase food for the home at the Lung Chung store. Ah Ying loved the freedom of leaving the apartment on Jackson Street. The air was cool, but the sun on her face was warm and inviting. The girls walked down Dupont Gai towards Sacramento Street where Ah Ying turned right instead of left.

"Where are we going? This is the wrong way," protested Sue Lee as they trudged up Nob Hill.

At Waverly Place Ah Ying whispered, "Come. Let's go see the men getting their hair cut! For fifteen cents we can get a haircut and a shave!" she laughed.

The Chinese called this Ho Boon Gai, meaning 15-cent Street. It was lined with barbershops where the Chinese men came to have their queues washed and braided and their forehead shaved.

"We can't go in there! You just want to stare at the men. We have to go to the market, buy the food, and go right home before the evil matron misses us."

"Oh, you worry too much. Come, on. We have time for a quick look!" Ah Ying laughed, already halfway down the street.

Sue Lee followed her friend reluctantly with a concerned look. Ah Ying was always getting her into mischief. The girls stopped in front of the first barbershop and stared through the window. Chinese men were sitting on stools with their faces over steaming porcelain bowls filled with hot water. The barbers were washing the long black hair of the undone queues. Others were shaving the customer's foreheads.

They spotted a tall Chinese man in the shop staring back at them through the shop window. His long queue was being braided with strands of silk ribbon after the wash. He almost smiled at the girls but seemed more curious than amused.

"Come! Let's get out of here!" hissed Sue Lee as she tugged on Ah Ying's robe.

"Not yet," replied Ah Ying. "I recognize the tall one."

The tall Chinese man stood, paid the barber his fifteen cents and headed for the door. Ah Ying stood transfixed as he strode out the door and looked at the girls with a now clearly amused smile.

[21]

"Do you like to spy on us? Aren't you afraid that the highbinders will find you here spying on the Chinese?"

"I am not afraid of you!" said Ah Ying a little louder than she had intended.

"I can see that," said the man softly.

Her friend was now clearly shaking with fear, but Ah Ying stood her ground, unable to take her eyes off the tall Chinese man. He was so close she could reach out and touch his robe.

"My name is Gee Sung. What is your name? Or should I just call you brave little one?"

"I am Ah Ying, and I am not a child! I am sixteen years old and can take care of myself!"

"Why do you stare at us through the glass like we are on display?"

"Because we spend every day taking care of fat crying babies and cooking and cleaning for our mean Chinese owners!"

The expression on Gee Sung's face softened as he gazed down at the young girls. He towered over them but recalled what it was like to be young and unafraid.

"Don't worry. You can come to see me getting a wash anytime."

With those words he turned up the street and started off towards the center of Chinatown.

Before he had made it to the end of the block he heard a soft voice that made him smile.

"When are you coming back?"

"I will be back next Sunday, same time," said Gee Sung as he turned and saw Ah Ying still standing her ground.

The girls ran down the alley back towards Sacramento Street giggling and hoping they had time to complete their shopping before their owners sent out someone to hunt them down.

CHAPTER 6

Urgent Plea for Help

Ah Ying continued her secret meetings with Gee Sung outside the barbershop on Waverly Place. Like all Chinese men he had three names. His boyhood name was Hung Poy, and his married name would be Hung Lai Wah. For now, he was Gee Sung, which was his business name. Gee Sung was tall and very serious and was nineteen years older than Ah Ying.

"Do you remember the Chinese New Year festival last year? I saw you across Dupont Gai as the dragon passed by," recalled Ah Ying.

"Yes, I thought you were so young and pretty, but then you vanished. I searched the faces on the streets for days afterwards but could not find you," explained Gee Sung.

"It is lucky for you that I came to see the men getting haircuts on Ho Boon Gai," smiled Ah Ying.

"Sometimes you are little too bold for your own good, Ah Ying. But I am glad you found me."

"Gee Sung, I have told you about my family in Bok Sar village and my Baba who sold me at the Dragon Boat Festival. But you are so quiet. You never talk about your life, Gee Sung. Tell me something!" implored Ah Ying sounding a little hurt.

"Well, I work at the cigar factory on Sacramento Street. It is a good job and I will open my own cigar store someday with the money I have saved," offered Gee Sung tentatively.

"Yes, but when did you come to Gum Saan?"

Gee Sung looked away and recalled his hard life and the

bitter cold of the mountains and offered simply, "I came as a young boy to build the great railroad through the Sierra Nevada Mountains."

Ah Ying was hoping for more but was happy that Gee Sung was opening up a little. She decided not to probe any further for now. Instead Ah Ying reached into her tunic and pulled out a neatly wrapped piece of paper with three chicken feathers attached to it.

"Please take this *Gai Mo Soon*[22] message to the Jesus House on Sacramento Street. It is not far from your cigar factory."

Seeing the three chicken feathers Gee Sung understood this was an urgent message.

"What is this, Ah Ying?"

"I can't stand my miserable life. My owners are so cruel. I want to be rescued, so I can live at the Jesus House until I can be with you, Gee Sung."

Her expression was so serious that Gee Sung simply took the letter, placed it safely in his tunic pocket and replied, "I will help you, Ah Ying."

"Thank you my Gee Sung. But do not let anyone see the letter. If my owners find out my plan, they will torture me or sell me to a brothel!"

"Don't worry, Ah Ying. If I had enough money, I would buy your freedom so that we could be together. I will guard your letter and your secret with my life."

With that simple exchange Ah Ying's plan for escape was set in motion. Now all she could do was to wait and to pray to the gods for deliverance from her life as a *mui tsai*.

CHAPTER 7

Ah Ying's Rescue

It was Thursday morning September 9, 1886. Ah Ying was scrubbing the parlor floor of the boarding house at 611 Jackson Street[23]. Personally, she preferred the solitude of cleaning the floors to the wailing babies she

had to carry around on her back and feed for most of the day. Suddenly, Ah Ying heard a crashing from the front door. She looked up just in time to see the door fly open in a blur of black coats and beards as three men stormed into the house. She would learn their names later. For now, she knew the day she had been praying for had finally come.

Chief Patrick Crowley, accompanied Mr. Nathaniel Hunter, the secretary of the Society for the Prevention of Cruelty to Children, and Rev. Daniel Vrooman burst into the house.

Laura Wilson, the middle-aged owner of the boarding house, rushed into the parlor.

"What's going on here?" She demanded.

"Get out of our way, before we arrest you again!" shouted Chief Crowley immediately recognizing the despicable woman from the foundling home. She was infamous for selling White babies to Chinese merchants.

Grabbing Ah Ying, they pushed the lady aside. It all happened so fast that Ah Ying hardly had time to blink. She dropped the bucket she was carrying and the soapy water ran across the clean parlor floor. The men spirited her out the door and away from the boarding home where she had been kept as a slave girl for six years.

Her short journey to freedom would take her less than one mile to the Mission Home at 933 Sacramento Street. For Ah Ying this would be a trip to another life.

Ah Ying did not care where these White men were taking her as long as it was far away from her cruel owners. She thought the two men looked odd. The younger man was the leader and the older man they called Reverend was the tallest person she had ever seen. With his white beard and long black coat he towered over the Chinese they passed on Jackson Street. She also spotted the policeman nearby watching them closely.

Suddenly, she was startled when the old man spoke to her in Chinese, "Get in the wagon!"

She looked to her left and saw the wagon they had hidden in Cooper Alley off Jackson Street. It was hitched to a white horse, which was waiting patiently. The old man took Ah Ying's hand and helped her into the wagon. She climbed up onto the seat in the back, while he sat next to her. The young man sat in front and took up the reins. With a creak the old wagon wheels rolled forward through the hordes of Chinese men. As they left the alley, Ah Ying looked back at the wretched boarding house that had been her prison for six years and hoped she would never see it again. She whispered a prayer of thanks to the gods that had delivered her and to Gee Sung for delivering her letter.

The horse and wagon traveled briskly along the streets of Chinatown that she knew so well. She liked the "clip clop" sound of the horse's hooves on the cobblestone street. They traveled west on Jackson, passing DuPont and Ross Alley and then turned left on Stockton. Her heart leapt, as she knew they were heading towards the Jesus House – and freedom. Passing Washington Street and then Clay, they arrived at Sacramento Street, where she saw the three-story brick building that housed the Presbyterian Mission Home[24] positioned half way up Nob Hill. The 25-room building had once been a fashionable mansion before it became a boarding house. Now, it was covered in a peeling coat of dull grey paint, but to Ah Ying it was a palace.

[25]

As the old man helped her out of the wagon, Ah Ying broke free and ran up the ten steps to the door. Margaret Culbertson threw open the door and whisked little Ah Ying and her rescuers inside. She gave a quick glance down the street checking for any highbinders that might have followed the trio from Jackson Street.

Once inside the parlor, Miss Culbertson took Ah Ying by the hand and led her into a sitting room. "What is your name, little one?" she asked through her interpreter Chun Fah, whom she called "Spring Blossom".

Ah Ying looked up at the White matron. She had a kind face, but Ah Ying thought they she would not reveal her real name in case she needed to escape from the Home any time soon.

Warily she offered, "They called me Sun Choie, but I do not like that name. My real name is Tom Gew Ying. You can call me Ah Gew."

Culbertson closed the door so that it was just the two of them in the room. Turning to her new charge she said, "Alright Ah Gew, let's see how you were treated."

She looked at her young face and thought she could not be any older than twelve years. As she looked over the girl, she spotted the telltale signs of abuse that all the girls bore. [26]

"What is that bruise on your leg?"

"They hit me with a stick when I did not work fast enough," replied Ah Gew matter-of-factly.

Margaret Culbertson knew there would be more but was surprised by Ah Gew's boldness.

"Here look at this!" exclaimed Ah Gew as she lifted her gown for Miss Culbertson to inspect her back.

Maggie Culbertson was used to the inhumane treatment of these innocent Chinese girls, but even so, she winced when she saw the large ugly burn on Ah Gew's back.

"How did you get this?" she asked softly.

"My owner burned me with a hot iron because I tried to run away."

Miss Culbertson lowered Ah Gew's gown and pulled her close.

"You are safe here Ah Gew. No one will ever hurt you again."

Ah Gew fought back the tears welling up in her eyes. She had not felt that anyone cared for her in a very long time. She looked over at Spring Blossom, who took her hand and led her upstairs to join the other girls in the Home. Her new life was about to begin.

Downstairs Maggie Culbertson sat down at her desk and

opened the Register of Inmates. She flipped through the pages and pages that described the lives and stories of her girls. She thought about Ah Gew's all-too-familiar story as she picked up her pen and on page 100 entered the 185th Chinese girl rescued by the Presbyterian Mission Home.

Sept 19/86 | Sum Choie alias Ah Gue 185

A young girl of perhaps 12 years was brot to the "Home" this morning by Mr. N. Hunter Sec for P.C.C. assisted by Rev. D. Vrooman, from 611 Jackson St. Ah Gue says the people who owned her were cruel, she has a large scar on her back, which she says was made by their burning her with a hot iron, and a bruise on her leg, which she received from a [illegible] with a stick. Sum Choie wishes to take the name of Ah Gue.

[27]

CHAPTER 8

Life at the Presbyterian Mission Home

The Presbyterian Church founded the Occidental Mission Home for Girls in 1874 with the mission to intervene on behalf of vulnerable Chinese women and children smuggled into America and sold into a life of domestic slavery or prostitution. In the first ten years 129 women and children were rescued and given shelter within the walls of the Mission Home. By 1877 the need for additional space for their growing family prompted the move from 8-1/2 Prospect Place to the old mansion turned boarding house at 933 Sacramento Street. In 1878 Margaret Culbertson became the matron of the Occidental Mission Home for Girls, where she found a family of ten girls, who playfully referred to themselves as "the original ten." Maggie called them the foundation stones from which the Home grew to 26 by the end of the year. The family was constantly changing as new members arrived, and others departed to start new lives. By 1883, of the original ten, only Ah T'sun[28], Chin Mui, the blind girl, and Ah Mooie[29] remained at the home. Margaret Culbertson dedicated the rest of her life to protecting these young Asian women and children, her Mission Home family.

Ah Gew's arrival in September 1886 marked the 185th woman rescued since the Occidental Mission Home for Girls had opened its doors. Ah Gew was among seventeen women and children, who came to the home seeking shelter that year. In 1886 the Mission Home took care of fifty inmates, although the size of the family fluctuated as they came and went at different times. The Home was bustling when Ah Gew arrived with 39 girls and children living in the three-story brick building at 933 Sacramento Street. Somehow Maggie and her staff always found a way to make room for one more.

The daily routine for the girls at the Mission Home was non-stop from sunrise to bedtime. Every minute was filled with activities, schoolwork, household chores, and religious studies. The girls were not given an idle moment and had no time to think about anything other than the tasks at hand.

The day began with 7:00 a.m. prayers and morning worship, which included bible study in English, a hymn sung in English, and a recitation of the Lord's Prayer in English and Cantonese.

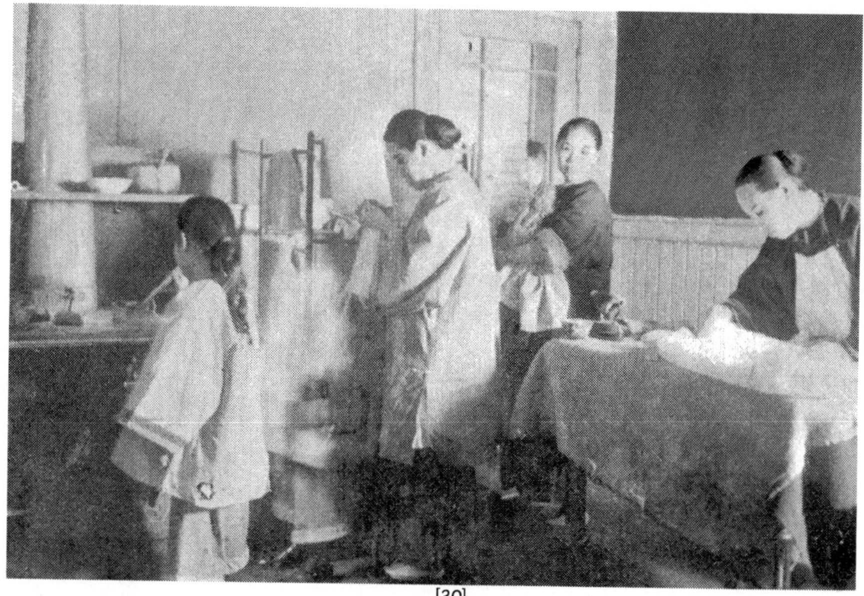

[30]

This was followed by breakfast in the big dining room downstairs. All of the girls did chores for an hour after breakfast. They worked in pairs and were assigned to a task each day; cooking the Chinese and American meals, housekeeping, or caring for the babies in residence. Taking care of the babies was a favorite assignment for the girls. Even Ah Gew, who had had more than her share of fat wailing babies, enjoyed the company of these happy Chinese babies.

[31]

Every weekday morning after chores, all the girls attended the Daily Home School with classes in English, Cantonese, and mathematics. In the afternoon the girls worked on sewing and knitting projects, followed by hymns in Cantonese.

Dinner was at 7:00 p.m. followed by a worship services held in the schoolroom, with more bible study, hymns and prayers. The day closed rapidly with lights out and bedtime. On Sunday morning, they all attended the Chinese Presbyterian Church on Stockton Street. Sunday evenings the girls and staff gathered for bible study and hymns in Cantonese led by Mrs. Tam Ching.

Ultimately, a goal of the missionaries was to prepare the women and girls of the Home for a productive and pious Christian life after they departed. They were taught the practical skills of cooking, sewing, and housekeeping and were immersed in the religious training that would allow them to establish a Christian household of their own.

Throughout the year, there were special occasions at the Mission Home including five baptisms the year Ah Gew arrived as young Chinese girls were received into the church. Nine weddings occurred at the Home in 1886 but in truth the demand for wives was far in excess of the supply. Prospective suitors from all over the country sent letters requesting permission to take one of Margaret's girls as a wife. The vetting process was thorough, as prospective suitors were extensively interviewed to screen out the unsuitable, who did not exhibit the good Christian values of the Presbyterian Church. The first question that Miss Culbertson asked was whether the Chinese suitor had another wife in China or here in America. Those who answered in the affirmative were immediately ushered to the door.

The fight to keep the girls from falling back into the clutches of the Chinese brothel owners was never ending. Their physical protection when they left the Home was obvious, but the fight also extended to the courts. In 1886 Margaret Culbertson and her interpreter little Chun Fah made nine trips to Superior Court to fight unscrupulous Chinese, who had obtained a writ of habeas corpus seeking to "rescue" girls from the Mission Home. In each case Miss Culbertson was victorious in maintaining custody. Margaret was ferocious in her determination to protect her girls.

For Ah Gew, the full day of the Mission Home life was a breeze. The work was easy, and there was no one beating her with a stick until she was black and blue. During home school, her nimble mind soaked up the lessons like a sponge.

Ah Gew felt like her whole world was born anew. And for the first time in her life she had friends! These other girls understood her and treated her with kindness. If only her mother could see her now. Her worthless father, who had tricked her and sold her, was another matter. Some of the girls in the Home had gone back to China, but she doubted she would ever see her parents again.

But not everything at the Mission Home was perfect for Ah Gew. The missionary women taught her English and sewing, which she loved, but this Jesus stuff was another matter entirely. She refused to convert to Christianity and was punished for her headstrong stubbornness.

CHAPTER 9

The Christian Stairway

Ah Gew had been at the home for several months, settling into the routine of chores, lessons, and religious studies. One day, while stacking dishes, her sleeve slipped down to her elbow as she stretched to reach the highest kitchen shelf. She paused, surprised by the sight of her own pale, even skin. The bruises on her arms and legs had disappeared, and the memories of her old life as a slave were beginning to fade as well. She knew the ugly burn on her back would always be there to keep her company; a reminder of her cruel and worthless past. But she was not ashamed of her scars. Rather, they were a symbol of the shared suffering that bound her new family together.

Suddenly, Ah Gew was startled by the matron's voice, "After your chores, you must put on the new Chinese gown you have been sewing and meet me in the parlor. Wear your jade earrings!"

The other girls in the room looked up at Miss Culbertson, but she was already onto the next room making the same announcement.

"What is a Chinese gown?" asked Ah Gew.

"She means to dress in your new *saam* with the *ou* (tunic) and *foo* (trousers) you have been sewing in class," explained Chun Fah.

"I thought she meant to dress in a formal *aofu*. I don't have such a fine garment to wear," sighed Ah Gew.

"No just put on the pretty *saam* from the sewing class."

"I wonder what is going on," puzzled Ah Yoke.

"She probably has visitors and wants us to perform for them," offered Sing Kum.

"She probably wants you to sing your hymn for the visitors, Chun Fah! You have the voice of an angel," said Ah Gew.

They all knew it was true. Chun Fah had a beautiful voice and often sang with accompaniment from Ah Yoke on the piano. The two of them made beautiful music performing Christian Hymns for the Mission Home guests. But Ah Gew liked it best when Chun Fah softly sang Chinese songs from their childhood as the girls went to sleep each night.

After their chores were completed, the girls met in the parlor. As instructed, each wearing her new Chinese robe and matching shoes. They had been working for months on the light-colored gowns with pretty dark stripes. The four girls from the next room, Ung Wah, Ah Ling, Wo Ah Moy, and Ah Seene, arrived in their new dark gowns and sandalwood shoes. All of the girls wore identical jade earrings, a gift of the Presbyterian Mission.

"Girls, you look so pretty! Now let's go out onto the back-porch stairs," instructed Miss Culbertson, as she came bustling into the room.

The girls headed through the kitchen, out the back door, and down the wooden staircase. The cool San Francisco air felt good on Ah Gew's face. The girls were rarely allowed to go outside for fear they might be kidnapped by the highbinders that were always lurking about. They looked around for an explanation for their unexpected excursion but saw nothing out of the ordinary.

Just then, a tall man with a tripod and wooden box came around the corner.

"Mr. Houseworth! You are right on time!" exclaimed Miss Culbertson.

"Yes, let's get the girls seated on the stairs. Hurry up now. I want two girls on every other step!"

The girls sat down as instructed and looked at the man expectantly.

"No! No! No! Not like that! I want two dark girls on the top and then two light girls below. Just keep alternating like that dark and light, dark and light! Now do it!

I have other appointments this morning," commanded Houseworth in exasperation.

The girls looked at each other unsure of what to do.

Ah Gew looked up and smiled, "Ah Ling and Ah Moy you sit on the top step! Ah Yoke and Sing Kum you sit below them. Ah Seene and Ung Wah on the next step. And Chun Fah you sit next to me on the bottom step!"

The girls quickly rearranged themselves as Ah Gew looked up and laughed, "We look like a multicolored Chinese dragon!"

"Alright, ladies, now fold your hands in your lap and smile!" instructed Houseworth, who had set up his camera and tripod on the sidewalk.

He ducked his head under the black cloth with his right hand holding up the flash.

"When I count to three, hold very, very still. Ready now one, two, and....three!"

There was a bright flash and puff of smoke as the eight girls held themselves motionless.

"Ok, girls! That's it! Thank you."

He turned to Miss Culbertson, "With any luck this photograph will be in the San Francisco Chronicle later this week. What should we call the article?"

"We will call this The Christian Stairway," she beamed.

[32]

The girls stood up and milled about on the sidewalk. They were hoping for an excuse to take a stroll down Sacramento Street, which they called *Tong Yan Gai*, the Street of the Chinese.

"Come, girls. Let's go back inside. We have lessons and sewing class. No time to waste."

With a groan the girls turned and headed back up the stairs into the kitchen.

Lingering just a moment, Ah Gew looked down the cobblestone street at Chinatown wondering when she would find a chance to visit her Gee Sung.

CHAPTER 10

Plotting to See Gee Sung

Ah Gew could hardly contain herself during the next week. The Mission Home matrons did not tolerate idle daydreaming when there were chores and lessons to be completed. They were quick to use the switch, which seemed to find Ah Gew more often than not. But Ah Gew had a plan and would not be deterred.

"Ah Gew, get to work!" scolded Miss Cable

The girls were in midst of their evening religious studies class, which was never to Ah Gew's liking. She knew better than to openly defy the mission ladies, but she hated being told what to believe.

"Yes, Ms. Cable" replied Ah Gew obediently.

For now, all she could do was to secretly plan her reunion with Gee Sung.

The class droned on endlessly into the evening. Finally, they ended with the Lord's Prayer, and the girls all went upstairs to bed.

As she was leaving, Ah Gew saw her opportunity. She was sitting next to Sing Yee the young Chinese woman she had met on the boat from Kwangtung. Sing Yee came to the Home to attend the evening bible study classes. They had talked briefly, and she was sympathetic to Ah Gew's story. Ah Gew had even worked up the courage to mention Gee Sung and told her how much she missed him.

As the other girls were getting up to leave, Ah Gew slipped Sing Yee a note.

"Please take this to Gee Sung. He works at the cigar factory on Sacramento Street just two blocks from here. Please, please help me!" implored Ah Gew.

[33]

Sing Yee looked into the girls pleading face and remembered what it was like to be so young. She slipped the note into her coat pocket without saying a word and walked away towards the parlor. Just as she was leaving the room, Sing Yee turned around and flashed a brief smile that made Ah Gew's heart soar!

Once tucked away safely in her bed, Ah Gew pulled the covers over her head, and whispered, "Sue Lee, are you awake?"

Her friend Sue Lee had also been rescued by Mr. Hunter and was now Ah Gew's roommate.

"Yes, but just barely," Sue Lee moaned sleepily.

"Tomorrow is Sunday. We have to go back to the barber shop after church to see Gee Sung."

"No! Are you crazy?" replied Sue Lee, now wide-awake. "We cannot meet anyone! If the matrons find out they will never stop punishing us! Don't even think about it."

"We have to go! I sent him a note promising we would meet him. He will be waiting for us! If we aren't there, what will he think? Please, you have to help me," pleaded Ah Gew. "Besides, I can't stop thinking about him."

"You only said a few words to him the first time you met, and you were yelling at him most of the time!"

"I was not yelling. I just did not want him to think I was afraid!"

◆ ◆ ◆

[34]

The next morning all the girls gathered downstairs for breakfast. They were a large family and they barely fit around the wooden table. The older girls took care of the younger children and assisted the mothers in feeding their babies. After breakfast the girls sang the morning hymn as usual, then repeated the 23rd Psalm.

Ah Gew was waiting in tense anticipation for the right moment to launch her plan. As they were clearing the table of the dozens of plates, cups, and chopsticks, Miss Culbertson passed by. Ah Gew sprang into action.

"Miss Culbertson, I have been making a list of supplies we need for the home. Sue Lee and I can go to the store this morning after church services to buy the goods. We are very strong and can carry everything you need in our baskets."

Miss Culbertson inspected the list that Ah Gew held out and then looked at the young girl.

"Alright, but also buy some dried fruit from the vendor on Commercial Street. He gives us good prices to help the girls. You will go with a chaperone."

Perhaps Ah Gew is finally growing up and showing that she is more than a stubborn daydreamer, thought Maggie Culbertson.

Ah Gew beamed, "Yes, Miss Culbertson. You can count on us! We can help you buy supplies every week! We will go with Sing Yee from the bible class."

Ah Gew grabbed Sue Lee by her sleeve and pulled her towards the parlor.

"Come. Let's go. We need to move fast or we will miss Gee Sung!"

Sue Lee, shook her head wondering how far her friend would go and how much trouble they were going to find.

CHAPTER 11

Attending Church

Each Sunday morning, all of the girls and the women of the Home attended services at the Chinese Presbyterian Church just around the corner on Stockton Street. Even this short journey put the girls at risk from the highbinders, who lurked in every dark alley. Their increasing boldness in kidnapping the Chinese girls and selling them back to their slave owners was an ever-present threat. For their protection, police and good Christian Chinese men always accompanied the forty girls and missionary women.

In truth, this Sunday walk to the Presbyterian Church by the Chinese maidens had become one of most anticipated events for the Chinese bachelors in *Tong Yan Gai*.[35] While the girls shuffled along gaily in their wooden shoes and latest Chinese fashions, hundreds of men lined the streets calling out to their favorite maiden. The girls chatted and laughed ignoring the attentions of the throngs of ponytailed Chinese mashers each dressed in the finest high fashion. Miss Culbertson had asked Chief Crowley to drive the crowds away so the entire Chinatown squad was on hand for crowd control. Six to eight policemen charged the Celestial crowds, swearing at the flying queues and giving a swift kick or a blow with a club to any Chinese that did not immediately disperse.

Despite the threat of abduction, the girls loved their freedom. Sunday morning was a brief respite from the stifling daily chores and studies at the Home. Each girl put on her very best *saam* and jewelry and helped the younger children to prepare for church. The family assembled downstairs in the parlor. They were a colorful lot each dressed in traditional Chinese costume. Miss Culbertson liked to show off her Chinese family and gave them strict instructions to dress Chinese!

I. W. TABER.

The girls and children hopped down the steps of the Mission Home. The three-story brick building had been home for so long that that they knew every crack in each step. All the children and the older girls lined up walking two-by-two down Sacramento Street laughing and chattering as they passed the shops along the way. They turned left on Stockton Street walking downhill the one block to the huge stone church at 911 Stockton Street. Ah Gew thought it was the most magnificent building she had ever seen.

"Girls, line up here on the steps," instructed Miss Emma Cable. "The children stand in front on the sidewalk and the older girls in the back!"

Ah Gew spotted Mr. Taber setting up his tripod and camera on the sidewalk. The girls had met Isaiah Taber at the Home where he visited to make his pictures. They liked Mr. Taber's friendly smile and giggled about his large furry mustache.

"You look splendid today," encouraged Mr. Taber as he adjusted his camera and backed up a few feet to accommodate the growing throng of Chinese parishioners who wanted to be in the photograph.

"Now on the count of three hold very still. One...two...and three!"

Just before the brilliant flash, there was a crash in the back row and everyone turned to see the commotion! One of the girls had fainted and was on the ground.

Rushing up the steps Miss Cable came upon Ah Yute. "Are you alright my dear Ah Yute?"

Ah Yute looked up sheepishly, "Yes Miss Cable, I was just dizzy and everything became dark and started spinning around my head."

"Well try sitting up slowly. Bring her some water quickly!" instructed Miss Cable.

Chun Fah brought a glass of water, which Ah Yute sipped slowly.

"I feel better now. I am so sorry I ruined your photo Miss Cable."

"Don't you worry about that, Ah Yute. We can always take another," consoled a concerned Miss Cable.

Ah Yute stood up slowly and looked at her family gathered around.

"Alright! Let's try that photograph again, Mr. Taber, instructed Miss Cable.

With that the girls lined up, Mr. Taber counted to three, and the perfect Chinese family portrait was taken for the second time that Sunday morning.

"That one was perfect," exclaimed Mr. Taber. "I will bring

you a print for your Home next week. Thank you, girls."

[36]

As Mr. Taber packed up his equipment, the girls and women of the Mission Home turned and walked up the stairs into the Chinese Presbyterian Church where Mrs. Condit, the wife of Reverend Ira Condit, greeted each girl personally.

Ah Gew spotted Sing Yee ahead walking up the aisle. Squeezing between the other girls Ah Gew tugged on Sing Yee's sleeve.

"Can you take us to the market after church, so we can buy supplies for the Home? Miss Culbertson said Sue Lee and I could go shopping if you are our chaperone."

"Another favor I see," replied Sing Yee with a smile. "OK, you can sit with me in church, and we can leave right after the morning service."

Ah Gew motioned for Sue Lee to join her, and the two girls sat in the pew next to their friend Sing Yee. Ah Gew looked closely at the young Chinese woman and realized she was not much older than she was.

But she will seen be married and will start a family, thought Ah Gew. *I wonder what it would be like to have a husband and my own home...*

Suddenly, Sing Yee interrupted her daydreaming, "I don't suppose you are planning any extra stops during your shopping trip today."

Ah Gew felt her face flush, but said nothing as she looked straight ahead. Sing Yee smiled at Ah Gew but said nothing more.

As always, Reverend Condit delivered his sermon flawlessly. After the congregation sang the final hymn for the day, "Bringing in the Sheaves" they finished by reciting the Lord's Prayer in unison. Even the little children knew all the words and recited them perfectly.

As they filed out of the church, Ah Gew spotted Miss Culbertson and pulled Sue Lee and Sing Yee in the opposite direction afraid that Maggie Culbertson would change her mind about their shopping trip into Chinatown.

"Come on! Let's head out the side door. It will be faster and we can get a head start on our walk down Sacramento Street to the market," implored Ah Gew as she pulled them along between the pews.

As they came upon Waverly Place, Ah Gew looked at Sing Yee, "We need to make a special stop here to meet someone."

Sing Yee frowned, "You should not go in there alone."

"I won't be alone. You and Sue Lee will be right behind me," offered Ah Gew.

"Ah Gew! You are impossible!" said Sing Yee. "Alright go ahead but stay where I can keep an eye on you. We do not want any trouble with highbinders while I am the chaperone."

Suddenly, Ah Gew stopped short. "Wait! I have to do something!"

She reached into her pocket and pulled out a yellow ribbon and started to braid the ribbon into her hair.

"What are you doing, Ah Gew?" asked Sue Lee.

"Nothing. I just want to look my best today," smiled Ah Gew.

"He probably won't even be there."

"It's not for him. I just feel like looking nice today."

Sue Lee smiled at her best friend but said nothing.

As the girls turned onto Waverly Place, they approached the barbershop.

Ah Gew looked expectantly for Gee Sung, but her heart sunk when she did not see him among the Chinese men in the shop.

"I guess I was just being silly, Sue Lee. How could I think a man would notice me?" whispered Ah Gew looking at her feet.

"It's alright, Ah Gew. Gee Sung is a fool to miss out on the prettiest and bravest girl in Chinatown!" Sue Lee consoled her friend as she noticed the small tear trickle down Ah Gew's young face. Sing Yee put her arm around Ah Gew.

Ah Gew was about to thank her friends when she felt a tap on her shoulder. She turned to find Gee Sung standing right behind her. He was so tall that he looked like a giant.

"You came!" exclaimed an excited Ah Gew.

"I came early so that I would not miss you Ah Ying," explained Gee Sung.

Ah Ying beamed with a smile that lit up the entire alley, "You got my note!

"These are my friends, Sue Lee, and you have met Sing Yee. And this is Gee Sung."

"Are you Ah Ying or Ah Gew today?" asked Sing Yee with a smile.

"Ah Ying is my real name. I just told Miss Culbertson to call me Ah Gew in case I had to run away from the Mission Home."

Sue Lee beamed, "Finally, I can call you by your real name, Ah Ying!"

"Well, Ah Ying, you are full of surprises," remarked Sing Yee. "Sue Lee and I will wait over by the store for five minutes while you talk to Gee Sung. Only five minutes, and then we must go to the market!"

The five minutes flew by as Ah Ying and Gee Sung talked quietly and planned their next meeting. It was an encounter that Ah Ying would treasure and retell over and over to her children and grandchildren in the years to come.

CHAPTER 12

Ah Yute's Illness

Ah Yute's fainting on the church steps was the first sign of her illness. Her story was all too familiar. Ah Yute's mother, a poor widowed Chinese woman, sold her when she was ten years old. After being resold several times Ah Yute was bought by the evil pawnbroker Chen Gooie Leng for $300. He wished to make her his half wife and half servant. She refused and was beaten for her disobedience.

In September 1882, fifteen-year-old Ah Yute sought refuge at the Mission Home. The evil Chinese pawnbroker used every imaginable maneuver to regain his property. He eventually resorted to threats of the law, obtaining a writ of habeas corpus demanding return of the girl. Maggie Culbertson initially refused to produce the girl in court causing a firestorm of vitriolic abuse from Chen Gooie Leng's drunken attorney. After several delays and the involvement of the Chinese Counsel General, the pawnbroker abandoned his case and Judge Halsley allowed Ah Yute to return to the Mission Home and awarded guardianship to Miss Culbertson.

Over the next four years Ah Yute made good progress in learning to read, write and speak English. At family worship, she regularly joined in reading the lesson for the day.

But Ah Yute, a frail and timid person by nature, had become weaker in the past four months. The initially sporadic cough had become constant and started to produce bloody phlegm - a sure sign that consumption had set a course to claim its victim. Her weight loss, fever, and night sweats made Ah Yute even frailer.

Ah Yute's best friend in the Home, Ah Yane, stayed at her side nursing and comforting her. Sitting by her bedside, she heard Ah Yute's weak voice.

"I am very sorry I have made Miss Culbertson, Miss Green and the girls so much trouble. I think I am going to die and I feel sorry for I fear God will not take me to heaven."

"You need not worry, for if you ask Him to forgive all your sins, he will do it," replied Ah Yane, trying hard to conceal the concern in her voice. "Just ask God if it is his will to take you away, ask him to receive you into heaven above."

Ah Yute opened her eyes and smiled at her best friend. "If it is God's will to take me, I want to go now. I don't want to stay on earth any longer, where I have pain and sickness."

The girls were very happy to hear this. They gathered around Ah Yute and sang the hymns that she liked best "Have You Any Room for Jesus" and "Savior, More than Life to Me."

When the Bible class was just over, Ah Gew called Miss Culbertson to come up stairs. When Miss Culbertson came up, she said, "Ah Yute is now going home to heaven."

In a few moments Ah Yute closed her eyes and looked as if she were sleeping. She was dead. Chinese people are very much afraid of the dead, but the girls were not afraid of their dear Ah Yute.

On May 9th Ah Yute died from consumption surrounded by the light and love of her friends. Hers was the first death at the Presbyterian Mission Home.

CHAPTER 13

A Chinese Picnic

Several months later, unable to sleep with all the excitement in the air, the girls of the Mission Home were stirring about long before sunrise. The usually quiet pre-dawn hour at the Home was interrupted by whispers and giggles from the still darkened bedrooms.

"Sue Lee, are you awake?" Ah Gew whispered from under her blanket.

"Of course! I haven't been able to sleep for hours!"

"Do you think it is time to get up? We don't want to be late for the ferryboat. If we miss the ferry, we won't be able to have our picnic!" Ah Gew lamented.

"Don't worry, it is still dark and the ferry doesn't run this early."

It was Wednesday July 20, 1887, and today was the day for the annual Mission Home picnic. The girls had been bursting with anticipation for weeks as they waited for the big day to arrive. The trip this year was across the bay to Piedmont Springs. Just up the hill from Oakland, Piedmont Springs really wasn't that far away. But for the girls, who were used to being sequestered within the four walls of the Mission Home, it might as well have been on another world.

"Come on, Sue Lee. Let's get up and start preparing breakfast for the family."

Sue Lee groaned but sat up in bed. She knew that she might as well get up, because there would be no stopping her friend once her mind was made up. Removing the warm blankets, she gave a little shiver as the cold San Francisco air welcomed her to the day.

"OK, but be quiet. Miss Culbertson is probably still sleeping!"

The two girls tiptoed downstairs and began preparing breakfast for the family. By the time the other girls and children arrived at 7 a.m. the meal was ready and waiting. Ah Gew and Sue Lee stood by smiling as their surprised family came down the long wooden stairs into the kitchen.

"Ah Gew, Sue Lee! You must have gotten up hours ago," exclaimed Maggie Culbertson.

"We wanted to get started early so we don't miss the ferryboat to Oakland!"

Maggie Culbertson nodded and smiled knowing how excited all the girls were for this very special day. Every year was the same. Yet every year was special with new girls and children to join in the outing.

"Alright girls, take your seats and enjoy the bountiful meal your sisters have prepared for you this morning."

The older girls helped the children find their places, and then they all gathered around the table and bowed their heads as Miss Culbertson said grace.

"Our heavenly Father, please bless this food and this special day as we enjoy the fellowship of our sisters in Christ's name Amen."

Ah Gew and Sue Lee beamed as their family enjoyed the special breakfast they had prepared. The girls chattered excitedly anticipating the day that had seemed for so long like it would never arrive.

"Have you ever been on a ferryboat, Chun Fah?"

"Of course, I have. In fact, all the girls are from the Pearl River Delta in Kwangtung. But it was a long time ago when I was very young."

"Those sampans were much smaller than the ferryboat we will take across the bay to Oakland," Maggie Culbertson explained with a smile. "And don't forget the cable car rides!"

All the girls had seen the cable cars. But none of the girls had set foot on one, except for Chun Fah, who often accompanied Miss Culbertson to court, and Ah Gew who had ridden the cable car with Billy to escape the highbinders.

After breakfast, the girls recited the 23rd Psalm and then scrambled upstairs to prepare for the day's adventure.

The ride down Sacramento Street to the Ferry Building was an adventure. All thirty girls, the little children, Miss Culbertson and Miss Green managed to squeeze onto a single cable car. The girls were dressed in their finest Chinese *saam* with the *ou* and *foo*. The girls had bundled the children in layers of clothing to keep them warm in the cool San Francisco summer weather. As the cable car rumbled down towards the wharf, the merchants and tourists waved and shouted out at the girls.

"Hold on tight!"

"You are going the wrong way! Church is the other direction!" they all laughed.

All of Chinatown seemed to be enjoying the spectacle of the Mission Home Chinese girls on their annual outing. Ah Gew spotted Uncle Chan as they passed Dupont Gai.

"Look, Sue Lee, there is our Uncle Chan! "*Nei hou*, Uncle Chan! We are going on the ferryboat to Oakland!"

Ah Chan smiled and waved as the cable car rumbled past Dupont and continued on down towards the wharf.

As the cable car slowed to a stop, Ah Gew spotted the grey Ferry Building tower with its gigantic clock.

"Look, Sue Lee! I remember seeing that building when I was a little girl! After we arrived at the docks, Wong Shee put me on a wagon that passed by here on the way to Chinatown. I had never seen such a tall building."

Ah Gew looked at the masts of sailing ships at the Pacific Mail Docks. It seemed like a lifetime since she landed at the wharf with that mean old woman Wong Shee. So much had happened since then. Now she was free and nearly grown up. Someday soon she would marry her Gee Sung and start a family here in Dai Fow.

"Come now, girls. We must hurry so we don't miss the ferry

to Oakland," shouted Maggie Culbertson as she stepped down off the cable car in her long grey dress. Her hair was tied up neatly beneath a bonnet.

Eager to start their adventure the girls jumped down from the cable car. Ah Gew and Sue Lee helped two children off and then held their little hands tightly as they followed Miss Culbertson towards the ferry building. They wound their way past the wagons, carts, horses and streetcars. It was a world of chaos for the girls who were used to the sheltered environment of the Mission Home. It was a little taste of freedom, and it was marvelous.

As they boarded the ferry, Ah Gew pulled Sue Lee to the railing.

The salt air and the smell of the sea were intoxicating.

"Isn't this wonderful?"

Before Sue Lee could answer, they were startled by the blast of the ferry's bellowing horn. There was a gentle lurch as the ferry pulled away from the dock.

"If I had my three Chinese coins, we could toss them into the water for good luck. But I have none," lamented Ah Gew recalling her mother's instructions from years ago.

Sue Lee stooped down and picked up three small pebbles from the deck. Handing them to her friend she beamed, "Here, let's pretend these are Chinese coins!"

Ah Gew smiled as the girls took turns tossing their makeshift coins into the ocean.

"There, that should protect the family."

A group of sea gulls trailed behind the ferry as it made its way across the bay. The ferry building and Dai Fow grew smaller and smaller as the ferry churned its way through the blue waters.

In Oakland the family exited the ferry at the docks. They were immediately met by an overhead cable car, which had been sent specially to transport them up the hill to Piedmont. The girls and children crowded onto the small car filling it to the brim. They were indeed a sight for the citizens of Oakland.

Each girl was dressed in her finest Chinese costume, and they sung their favorite Gospel hymns as they practiced for their afternoon performance at the Piedmont Hotel.

"Come on now girls. Raise your voices in praise of the Lord Jesus. Let the good folks of Piedmont know that the Presbyterian Mission Home is coming to rejoice on this glorious day," encouraged Miss Green.

Passing curious onlookers and horse-drawn wagons, the overloaded little cable car made its way up the one-mile street to Piedmont Springs.

"Look at that pretty Yellow House up on the hill!" exclaimed Sue Lee. "It looks like a palace it is so fine. Maybe the emperor of Piedmont lives there!"

It was indeed a fine mansion painted bright yellow. It was the home of Isaac and Sarah Requa and was a landmark, which everyone in the East Bay knew as the Highlands.

Reaching the top of the hill the streetcar slowed to a crawl as it approached the clubhouse and gardens of the Piedmont Springs grounds. The clubhouse had a red roof and was surrounded by an enclosed porch with ornate wooden arches.

[37]

On the porch, Ah Gew spotted well-dressed gentlemen in long black coats and tall funny black hats. The women wore long dresses and hats of every imaginable shape and color, and young girls spun parasols around and around over their heads.

"Come girls. We are going to have our picnic in the Japanese Tea Garden," Maggie Culbertson said smiling.

"It looks a little like the pagodas back home," Chun Fah murmured as they admired the Tea Garden building, surrounded by a Japanese rock garden and pools of bubbling water.

"We must be near the mineral springs, judging by the bubbles in those pools of water," observed Miss. Cable. "Let's take a look inside the Tea Garden for a spot to have our picnic."

The older girls unloaded the large picnic baskets, while Ah Gew and Sue Lee spread blankets on the ground under the shade of a magnificent oak tree. The children needed no further instructions as they all gathered around the baskets.

After everyone was served, Ah Gew and Sue Lee laid back on the blanket. Munching absently on their sandwiches, they gazed across the landscape at the bay in the distance.

"Isn't this perfect?" Ah Gew sighed.

"Yes, I wish we could stay here forever and make this our new Mission Home!"

"The Tea Garden Pagoda could be our new church and Reverend Condit could come to preach every Sunday. We could live at the Piedmont Hotel and bathe at the mineral springs. It is perfect!" exclaimed Ah Gew.

"We would be free from the highbinders and those silly Chinese mashers, who are so in love with themselves."

Miss Culbertson interrupted their daydreaming, "We are expected at the Piedmont Hotel in fifteen minutes. There is already a crowd gathering to hear your performance."

The Piedmont Springs Hotel was a new two-story wooden building with ornate gingerbread trim and a fresh coat of white paint. The girls assembled in the hotel lobby lining up in rows three deep. They were a choir of forty girls and a handful of children. Chun Fah was prepared to accompany them on an old upright piano. With a signal from Ms. Green, the girls began their performance singing all of their favorite Christian hymns. In memory of their dear sister Ah Yute, they sang her favorite hymns "Have You Any Room for Jesus" and "Savior, More than Life to Me." Spontaneously, the older girls shifted leaving an empty space in the middle of the choir in honor of their dear departed sister.

The crowd of White spectators grew until there was no more room in the lobby. The latecomers overflowed out onto the porch as everyone strained to see the source of the angelic music that flowed from the hotel. The sight of the forty Chinese maidens in their native costumes was by itself enough to cause a commotion. The sweet sound of their young voices was more than the men could bear. At the conclusion of the performance, the entire audience erupted into uproarious and appreciative applause with calls for an encore!

The young girls, who were not used to this type of attention, smiled meekly, giggled, and looked at the floor.

"I told you this was the perfect place for us to live," Ah Gew proclaimed proudly.

Later that afternoon as they filed back onto the ferry, Maggie Culbertson smiled to herself. Ah Gew was right. This really had been a most perfect day.

A CHINESE PICNIC.

The Presbyterian Mission Home on a Tour.

The girls of the Presbyterian Chinese Mission Home held their annual picnic yesterday at Piedmont Springs. The expenses of the trip were kindly borne by philanthropic friends of the Mission. A special car at Oakland conveyed the party to the springs, where a bountiful lunch was partaken of. The girls entertained the guests at the Piedmont Hotel by their singing. The Matron of the home reports a pleasant day, and says that the girls, who of necessity spend most of their time within the walls of the Mission, wished to take up their abode at the springs.

[38]

CHAPTER 14

Christmas Celebration – Celestials Made Glad

Christmas is a special time for the Chinese in Dai Fow. 1887 marked the 25th anniversary of the Presbyterian Mission in San Francisco, which was started in 1852 by Dr. William Speer, a missionary returning from China, as its first pastor. Reverend Ira M. Condit was the second and current pastor in charge of the Mission. Mrs. Ira Condit was instrumental in convincing the Women Board of Foreign Missions on the Pacific Coast to serve the Chinese women and girls being trafficked and sold in San Francisco as prostitutes and *mui sai*. In the early years only, a few Chinese men attended Christmas celebrations. This year the church was packed with hundreds of Chinese men and women and children.

Waiting in a room behind the communion table, Ah Gew and the other girls of the Presbyterian Mission Home were dressed in their finest Chinese robes. The girls were nervous but they had practiced their part of the evening's program.

Ah Gew searched the faces hoping to spot Gee Sung. It was colorful a gathering. Chinese men of all ages stood on one side of the church. On the other side were the women with babies in arm and their toddlers clinging to their skirts. The Chinese children looked like a field of multi-colored poppies in their native costumes. A gaily-decorated Christmas tree at the far end of the hall was covered with colored trinkets and pretty waxed candles.

Reverend Ira Condit began the program with a prayer delivered in Cantonese followed by "Merry Bells" sung by the younger girls of the Home. Bennie Hon Yee recited "The Silver Plate," and the children sang "Jolly Old Saint Nicholas.

Ah Gew glanced at Ah Seen and Chun Fah as the three girls stood and walked to the front of the church. They recited the Occidental School Anthem perfectly. As they finished, Ah Gew let out a sigh of relief. The applause was polite and brief except for someone in the back of the church who clapped a little too long. Ah Gew looked up and saw her Gee Sung applauding and smiling at her! She felt her face flush but couldn't help smiling.

"Is that him?" asked Ah Seen. All the girls knew of Ah Gew's illicit Sunday meetings with Gee Sung. Secrets were hard to keep in the Home. But they were all sworn to secrecy and always helped her make the list of items for the Sunday shopping trip with Sing Yee.

"Shush!" replied Ah Gew. Unable to contain her happiness, she murmured, "Yes that is my Gee Sung."

Ah Gew's joyful smile was like a beacon – one that was not missed by Maggie Culbertson, who was sitting in the front pew. She looked first at the radiant Ah Gew and then followed her gaze to the tall Chinese man in the back, who seemed more than a little interested in her charge. Miss Culbertson's mental note to get to the bottom of this flirtation could only mean trouble for the two lovers.

The evening's program continued with songs, prayers, and performances by children and girls of all ages. Ah Gew's favorite was the song "The Little Manger" sung by the babies of the Home. For a full two hours the children acted their little parts and the adults ate or stood and listened, smiling and applauding roundly.

In a patriotic spectacle twenty-eight American-born sons and daughters waved the national colors and sang "Columbia, the Gem of the Ocean," which succeeded in bringing rounds of applauses from both Americans and Chinese.

At the conclusion of the program there was a commotion in the back of the church as a Chinese Santa Claus entered in all his glory bringing presents and joy to all the children and adults of the Chinese Presbyterian Church.

"Glory to God in the highest, and on earth peace and goodwill toward men."

CHAPTER 15

Ah Gew's Friendship with Chin Shee
January 1888

Ah Gew searched for her friend Sing Yee amongst the women streaming into the Home for the reception. The occasion was a reception for the missionaries about to depart for Canton, China. All of the Presbyterian Church Board Members, and many of the Chinese women from the community were crowding into the downstairs parlors. Several newspaper reporters were milling about looking for a story.

The parlors of the home were artistically decorated with bouquets of white roses. The program was rendered by 35 girls, ranging in age from ten to twenty years, in their finest Chinese native costumes. The girls sang Gospel hymns in English and several girls recited stories and poems.

Among the ladies present, were Mrs. P.D. Browne, president of the Occidental Board; Miss Emma Cable, the Chinese home missionary; and a delegation from the Daughters of the Good Shepherd.

After the reception, Ah Gew approached Sing Yee and pulled her aside eager to hear more about her life with her new husband.

"Sing Yee, I mean Chin Shee[39], please come and tell me about your wedding!"

Sing Yee turned and smiled at her young friend. "I will always be Sing Yee to you, but yes, Chin Shee is my new married name."

The two had grown close during their weekly trips into Chinatown. Their shared secret of Ah Gew's meetings and letters, cemented the bond between the two women.

"We were married by the Chinese custom one month ago on December 23rd. This is the first time I have been allowed to leave our home. My husband is Gin Lun Chee. He is an herbalist and partner of the Chee Sang Tong Company at 710 Dupont Gai."

"What is he like, Sing Yee? How did you meet him? I want to hear all about him."

"My parents met him years ago and approved of him. Remember on the boat I told you he sent my parents the bride price? Well, after all this time, I finally met Lun Chee! He is wonderful, Ah Gew. He is kind, well educated, and speaks perfect English. You must meet him soon."

"But tell me how you met him and all about the wedding ceremony and the feast!" begged Ah Gew.

"Chee Sang Tong is right next door to Louie Sung Low, or the Spanish building[40] where I live. I went to his herb shop for medicine for my mother, and he helped me to pick the perfect remedy for her cold. He was so nice to me and later stopped by to check on my mother. I think he really had an eye on me, but I didn't mind. He is very handsome and so intelligent."

"The wedding ceremony, please tell me, Sing Yee," reminded Ah Gew.

"Oh, yes. A good fortune woman combed my hair four times with a special comb and said the four blessing at our home. His father did the same for him at their home above the store."

"What are the four blessings, please tell me, Sing Yee!"

"Well, I remember the special words clearly because I wrote them down later in my journal. I was sitting by the window and looking out at the moon. With each hair combing, she said a blessing."

'Continuous from beginning to end
May you be together all of your lives'

'May you have closeness and harmony
in your marriage for a hundred years,
till a ripe old age'
'May you fill your home
with children and grandchildren'
'May you enjoy a long life together,
until your hair and even eyebrows are white'

"I drank a sweet soup with white and pink rice balls symbolizing our sweet marriage together. My dear mother gave me a farewell gift. It was a treasure box with jewelry and *lai see*[41]."

"Then my parents took me to meet my husband at his home above the Chee Sang Tong Company. He took me into his home, and we were married by the Chinese custom in front of the family altar. We said blessings to Heaven and Earth, the family ancestors, and *Jo Gwun* the Kitchen God. Lun Chee and I bowed three times to each other, and we were married. We then served tea to his family with red dates, peanuts, and lotus seeds."

"The wedding feast for the women was attended by all the women in our families and several friends as well. There must have been twenty courses. I wish you could have been there, Ah Gew. The men had a much larger feast at the Hang Far Low Restaurant across the street on Dupont."

Wide-eyed at her friend's story, Ah Gew replied, "Oh, I do wish I could have escaped the Home long enough come to your wedding, Sing Yee! What is it like being married? Are you in love?"

"Ah Gew, you are such a romantic! But yes, we are very happy together!"

"I hope someday I can be with my Gee Sung," replied Ah Gew softly.

"Don't worry, Ah Gew. We will find a way for you two to be together. Just be patient, my young friend. I will be at your wedding. I promise."

The two young girls looked at each other and then smiled and burst out laughing for no reason except that they were happy and young.

CHAPTER 16

Ah Gew's Depression

But soon the hope of fulfilling Sing Yee's promise began to feel more and more remote. Maggie Culbertson's sighting of the tall Chinese man at Ah Gew's Christmas recital had raised her suspicions that something was amiss. The women of the Mission Home eventually got word of their illicit meetings and forbid Ah Gew from seeing Gee Sung. He was not the proper Christian Chinese man that they sought for their girls. The stern looking Gee Sung did not meet their requirements of an acceptable suitor. Worst of all, the matrons confined Ah Gew to her room except for meals. The Mission Home, which had been her salvation, was now just another prison.

It was 1888, and for the first time in her eighteen years Ah Gew was truly miserable. As a *mui tsai*, she had learned to never hope for anything. Now the Mission matrons had taken away the only thing that she had dared to hope for - her Gee Sung. Life without him was unbearable. In all of her tormented years as a *mui tsai* she had never given her owners the satisfaction of seeing her cry. But now, she wept inconsolably with a deep hollow pain in her chest that consumed her.

It was noon on *Tin Joong Jit*, the day of the Five Poisons, on the 5th day of the 5th month of the lunar calendar. This is the day the Chinese mark for evil. It was also the day she had been kidnapped eight years ago. Looking through the bathroom cupboard she found the container of *Pow Fah Gow* bark[42] used to mix for hair treatment. Placing the bark in the hot water she had prepared in the kitchen she stirred the ingredients until the foamy water was an ugly dark brown color.

Bringing the cup to her lips, she whispered, “Good bye, my Gee Sung.”

The bitter tea made her gag, but she sipped and then gulped the poisonous brew until the cup was empty. Ah Gew held her breath as she waited. At first, nothing happened. Disappointed Ah Gew began to mix another cup, when she suddenly began to wretch and vomit. She felt a horrible stabbing pain in her stomach. Gasping for air between bouts of retching, her head became light as the room spun around and around. The brightly lit room became dim, and then she was surrounded by darkness. Her last thought was of her mother reaching to her with three Chinese coins in her outstretched hand.

Ah Gew opened her eyes and looked at her surroundings. Surely this must be Tiān, the Chinese heaven. I am free at last. No more pain and loneliness.......and no more life without Gee Sung. When her room came into focus, her heart sank as she realized she was still in the Mission Home. Then she saw Sue Lee’s concerned and tear-streaked face.

“My Ah Ying, why did you want to leave me? I was so worried and sad!” whispered Sue Lee forgetting to use her friend's Mission Home alias.

“I am sorry, Sue Lee,” whispered Ah Ying weakly. “My loneliness without Gee Sung was too much for me to bear.”

“Here, drink this broth. It will help you to regain your strength.”

Ah Ying sipped the salty broth silently and then coughed as the salt burned her raw throat.

“Ah Ying, you always have me and the other girls to care for you. You must not despair. Please *promise* me you will never do this again. I cannot live without you! You have been my only friend since we were young girls. Please promise me!” begged a clearly distraught Sue Lee.

Ah Ying saw the pain in her friend’s eyes and felt ashamed of her selfishness.

“I am so sorry. I missed Gee Sung so much that I only

thought of myself. I promise, Sue Lee." The pain in Ah Ying's heart was still there, but she knew she could not leave her only true friend alone.

The two girls sat quietly holding hands, but Ah Ying's thoughts were a million miles away. She was now certain that her days at the Home were numbered. If the Gods did not want to take her, then she would escape this prison. As before, escape was now the only path to a life with her Gee Sung.

"And from now on my name is Ah Ying. No more hiding," she declared.

CHAPTER 17

The Great Escape 1889

The Mission Home matrons soon learned of Ah Ying's attempt to end her life. They initially watched Ah Ying like a hawk, unsure of what she would try next. Gradually, the weeks and months passed with Ah Ying biding her time and behaving like a perfectly obedient inmate. She was slowly granted a few more freedoms.

[43]

On Saturday May 4, 1889 Ah Ying was allowed to run errands for the Home.

Finding Sue Lee in the parlor, Ah Ying whispered to her best friend, "Did you have Sing Yee deliver my letter to Gee Sung?"

"Yes, of course. What was so important about this letter?"

Ah Ying whispered in her friend's ear, "I am going to find Gee Sung! Do not tell anyone!"

Sue Lee's eyes grew large with fear as she saw the determination in Ah Ying's face, "Be careful. Go quickly!"

With that simple goodbye, the friends parted for the last time. Ah Ying opened the front door and slipped down the ten steps to the street. Not looking back, she began to run down Sacramento Street. Imagining her life of freedom with Gee Sung, she flew past the shops and bagnios[44]. When she got to the cigar factory, she found Gee Sung waiting for her!

Flying into his waiting arms, the two embraced.

"My Gee Sung!" sobbed Ah Ying. "I thought I would never see you again!"

"We must hurry, Ah Ying, before they discover you are missing and send the police to take you back to the Mission Home! Come this way. I have our own home waiting for us," explained Gee Sung as he took Ah Ying's arm.

Ah Ying needed no encouragement. She ran alongside Gee Sung down Sacramento Street. At Dupont Gai they turned left and hurried past the stores and restaurants she knew so well.

"Néih hóu, Uncle Chan!" she called out as they passed the Chinese restaurant.

"Néih hóu, Ah Ying! Where are you going so fast my little friend?"

"To my new home and my new life, Uncle!" shouted Ah Ying as they whisked up Dupont Gai. [45]After they passed Clay Street, Gee Sung slowed to a walk and then stopped in the middle of the block at 821 Dupont Gai[46]. They entered the boarding house on the west side of the street and took the

stairs to the second floor. Gee Sung opened the door to their new apartment and led Ah Ying inside.

"This is our new home, Ah Ying. I didn't have much time after your last letter said you were going to runaway from the Home. I found this apartment and have tried to get it ready for your arrival," explained Gee Sung expectantly. "I hope you like..."

"It is perfect, Gee Sung!"

Exploring the apartment, she found a bedroom and a living room with a small kitchen, all neatly furnished and remarkably clean. She now really *was* in heaven. She had not felt such freedom since that day nine years ago with her Baba along the river in Bok Sar village.

Ah Ying began to cry in relief, "Thank you, Gee Sung."

Gee Sung pulled her close and wrapped her tiny body in his arms. Ecstatic, the two imagined a happy future together.

"Tomorrow we will go to the Hall of Justice to obtain a marriage license. But tonight, I have asked your friend, Chin Shee, and her husband the herbalist, Gin Lun Chee, to help us perform the Chinese marriage ceremony. "

Later that evening, Chin Shee entered the apartment with her husband carrying trays of food and Chinese delicacies.

"I promised that I would be at your wedding, Ah Ying!" exclaimed a smiling Chin Shee.

"How did you know?" Ah Ying began.

"I was visiting the Home this morning and Sue Lee whispered to me that you left to find Gee Sung."

"Oh, my friend, I am so happy you are here today!" beamed Ah Ying.

Chin Shee lit some candles and placed them by the altar Gee Sung had prepared. She then took Ah Ying's hand and led her into the bedroom, while Gin Lun Chee and Gee Sung stayed in the living room.

"Well, I am your good fortune woman, Ah Ying. I am not a grandmother, but I do have happy children, so I will perform the hair combing ceremony."

She took Ah Ying to the window and stood behind her. Pulling out a beautiful comb from her tunic, she slowly combed Ah Ying's hair, reciting the four blessing with each stroke.

'Continuous from beginning to end
May you be together all of your lives'
'May you have closeness and harmony in your
marriage for a hundred years, till a ripe old age'
'May you fill your home
with children and grandchildren'
'May you enjoy a long life together,
until your hair and even eyebrows are white'

Ah Ying could not help but to think of her parents, who should have been at her wedding. So much had happened in her young life since her mother had given her those three coins. She felt a warm glow on her face and heard her mother's faraway wishes, *Be happy, my little Ah Ying.*

Chin Shee took her friend's hand and led her back to the living room. Gee Sung and Gin Lun Chee were waiting for them in front of the altar.

Gee Sung took Ah Ying's hands and the two said blessings to Heaven and Earth, the family ancestors, and Tsao-Chun. They bowed three times to each other. With that, they were married.

Chin Shee and Lun Chee brought out the small wedding feast they had hurriedly prepared. The four friends ate and laughed late into the night, their faces lit with warm candlelight and newly-wed love.

◆ ◆ ◆

Monday morning Ah Ying awoke to find that Gee Sung had already risen. From their bed she heard the sounds of Chinatown preparing for the day. The clip clop of horses pulling their loaded wagons up the cobblestone street was mixed with the sounds of vendors putting out their daily produce. Looking around the small apartment for her husband, she spotted him staring out the window. The morning sunlight on his face highlighted a faraway look.

"Where are you, my Gee Sung?" she asked softly.

Startled, Gee Sung turned and gazed at his young wife.

"I am sorry, Ah Ying. I was just remembering my boyhood and family in Dai Long Village. I have four brothers. It has been many decades since Jick Wah and I left the village to come to Gum Saan. In all those years I have not seen the faces of my parents or three other brothers. I am certain that my parents are no longer living."

"I hope I can meet your brother Jick Wah someday."

"Yes, and you will recognize him, because he only has one eye. He lost the other eye in a blasting accident, when we were building the railroad across the mountains in California. They called him the 'one-eyed Chinaman.' I think it was a bad joke. We called our foreman, Strobridge, the 'one-eyed bossy-man,' because he lost an eye in different explosion."

Changing the subject abruptly, Gee Sung announced, "Today we will go to the Hall of Justice on Kearny Street to get the marriage license. It is only two blocks away, across from *Fah Yuen Gok*, Portsmouth Square."

After a breakfast of tea and dousha bao, sweet white buns filled with red bean paste, and tea, Ah Ying and Gee Sung started their short journey to the Hall of Justice. The rickety wooden steps of the apartment house led them out onto the brightly lit Dupont Gai already bustling with early morning activity. The street was clogged with horse-drawn wagons and merchants unloading the fruits, vegetables, and dry goods. The darkly clad Chinese men were busy setting up their stores and sidewalk stalls for the day's business. Ah Ying knew most of the men by name, and she smiled at them as she proudly walked next to her Gee Sung through Chinatown.

[47]It was a short one block up Dupont Gai to Washington Street. They cut through Portsmouth Square with its grassy lawns and tree-lined walkways. Exiting the park Gee Sung stopped at the steps of the Hall of Justice a large stone building at 750 Kearny Street, directly across from Portsmouth Square.

Taking Ah Ying's hand, he led her into the building. They took the stairs up to the 2nd floor to the Office of the County Clerk.

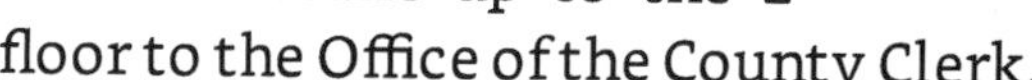

"Are you ready, Ah Ying?" asked Gee Sung looking down at his wife as they stood in front of the dark wood and glass door.

"Yes, my *geuhng fu* [48]. I have waited for so very long to be your wife! Now we will be married by the White laws as well as by our Chinese custom. I am so very ready," she smiled.

Gee Sung turned the knob and pulled the door open revealing a small office with a few old chairs and a counter. A white-haired woman wearing spectacles watched them suspiciously from behind the counter.

"What do you want?" she asked looking them up and down.

"We want to get a marriage license," explained Gee Sung.

"Chinese don't come here for a license. They just do that thing with their heathen ceremony."

"Well, we want to be married by the American laws," insisted Gee Sung.

"Alright, but it will cost you money for the license!"

"I have the money!" sniffed Gee Sung indignantly.

The clerk took his money and shoved the application across the counter muttering, "You will have to fill this out first."

Sensing the clerk's unease, Ah Ying suggested, "Can you please help us? We have waited for so long. We only wish to be married and happy together."

The clerk's stern face softened as she looked down at young Ah Ying's pleading expression.

"Yes, of course. What is the bride's full name? How old are you?"

"I am Tom Gew Ying. My family name is Tom. I am nineteen years old," explained Ah Ying shyly.

"And what is the groom's full name and age?"

"I am Gee Sung. No, my married name is now Hung Lai Wah! I am 38 years old," exclaimed Gee Sung proudly.

The clerk filled out the form in neat and practiced writing.

"Now, you must both sign right here," she commanded pointing to the bottom and handing the pen to Ah Ying.

With a trembling hand, Ah Ying carefully made her mark on the application. Gee Sung, now Lai Wah, took up the pen next and proudly signed his name with large bold letters: *Hung Lai Wah*. Both let out a sigh of relief as they completed the form.

"Take a seat over there and wait while I process your application and prepare the marriage license."

The clerk returned twenty minutes later and handed Lai Wah the very official-looking marriage license issued by the State of California, County of San Francisco on May 6, 1889. Ah Ying and Lai Wah beamed as they examined the document.

"*Doh jeh*. Thank you!" exclaimed Ah Ying to the now smiling clerk.

The happy couple exited the office and triumphantly strolled back to their apartment on Dupont Gai with their treasured marriage license tucked safely in Lai Wah's pocket.

As they walked along without a care in the world, they did

not notice the eyes peering out at them from the shadows of Brenham Place.

That evening after dinner Lai Wah and Ah Ying discussed plans for their American wedding. Ah Ying suggested having Reverend Condit perform the ceremony but immediately realized that she was a fugitive. They would be looking for her, and she could not safely show her face around the Mission Home or the Presbyterian Church. She thought of her friend, Sue Lee, and hoped that she had not been interrogated too severely by the Mission matrons once Ah Ying's disappearance was noted. No matter, Sue Lee would never ever give up her best friend.

"Perhaps we can go back to the Hall of Justice tomorrow and have the Justice of the Peace perform the marriage ceremony," suggested Lai Wah. "Judge Hebbard is the new Justice and a regular customer at my new cigar store," he noted proudly.

"We can invite Chin Shee and Lun Chee to be witnesses," suggested Ah Ying. "Then they will have taken part in both our Chinese and American wedding ceremonies."

With the plans for the wedding settled, Ah Ying and Lai Wah settled in for their third night as newlyweds.

Shortly after midnight, Ah Ying awoke with a terrible pain in her stomach. She lay in bed quietly hoping the pain would go away, but it grew worse. She was soon doubled over and moaning.

"Ah Ying, what is the matter?"

"My stomach hurts! It must be my cooking!" Ah Ying joked, although she was clearly in distress. "Lai Wah, please go and have Lun Chee give me some medicine for my pain."

Lai Wah quickly got dressed and hurried out the door to their friends' nearby apartment in the Spanish Building.

He looked back at his wife, promising, "I will be right back,

Ah Ying. Don't worry! Lun Chee will help us."

[49]Ah Ying heard her husband's footsteps running down the wooden stairs and then onto the cement sidewalk along Dupont Gai. The sound grew fainter as he quickly made his way down the street to the Spanish Building on the next block.

Ah Ying's pain subsided, and she immediately felt sheepish for making Gee Sung go out at this hour of the night.

Fearless Ah Ying is such a baby! she thought.

Just as she was considering how to admit her recovery to Lai Wah, she heard the doorknob turn.

"Gee Sung? Is that you? Why are you back so soon?"

There was silence as the doorknob stopped turning. Ah Ying sat frozen in bed, unable to move or breathe. Her heart was racing. She stared at the doorknob lit by the flickering light from a single candle. Its stillness screamed at her.

Suddenly, the door flew open followed by two Chinese men brandishing long knives and .45 caliber revolvers.

"Quick! Grab her before she tries to run!"

The men came at Ah Ying. The ugly one with a long scar on his face placed a towel over her eyes and nose.

"Aaagh!" cried out Ah Ying. Her eyes were burning, and she could not see. She swung at them wildly. "My husband, Gee Sung, is coming right back!"

The two highbinders ignored her threats, laughing, "This little one is a fighter! Well, try to fight this!"

Ah Ying froze when she felt the cold barrel of the revolver at the back of her head.

"Do as we say, or you will die right here on your honeymoon bed!" the highbinder sneered.

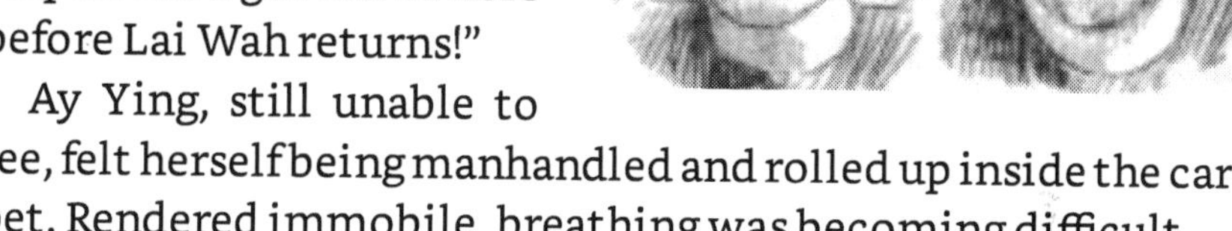

The short Chinese man with stringy hair rolled out a carpet on the floor. The other grabbed Ah Ying and threw her onto the carpet.

"Quick! Roll her up in the carpet! Let's get out of here before Lai Wah returns!"

Ay Ying, still unable to see, felt herself being manhandled and rolled up inside the carpet. Rendered immobile, breathing was becoming difficult.

"Let me go!" she tried to scream.

But her muffled voice was barely audible from inside the carpet.

Stay calm, Ah Ying, she thought.

She felt herself being lifted up in the carpet. Her precious flower vase crashed to the floor. The door squeaked open, and she heard footsteps and grunting as the men carried her down the creaky wooden stairs to the street.

"Throw her in the back."

Ah Ying felt a jarring impact as she and the carpet were unceremoniously dropped.

"Giddy up!"

Ah Ying heard the slap of the reins and felt the carriage start to roll along the cobblestones lining Dupont Gai. The clip clop of the horse's hooves and the rolling of the carriage wheels echoed in the dark and wet Dai Fow night.

The carriage picked up speed. Ah Ying heard the big bell at the Old St Mary's Church. It grew fainter as they passed California Street. They were headed south on Dupont! After a few more minutes the carriage slowed and turned. Ah Ying felt the carpet roll to the left. They must be turning right! She had no idea where they were, but they must be outside of Chinatown.

The carriage stopped. Ah Ying heard the horse breathing hard and the men jump down from the carriage.

"Grab the carpet and get her inside before someone spots us."

"Stop worrying! It's the middle of the night. Everyone is asleep!"

"You had better start worrying! If Gee Sung finds out we kidnapped his new wife, the Bing Kong Tong he pays for protection will come for us, and it will be another blood bath!"

With a loud grunt they lifted the carpet from the back of the carriage and dropped it on the sidewalk.

"Pick up your end, stupid!"

"Shut up! This little girl is heavy!"

Ah Ying heard the squeak of an opening door as they carried her inside. With a rude thump, they dumped the carpet and Ah Ying onto the floor. She felt herself being rolled along the floor as they unwrapped their captive. With the final turn Ah Ying rolled out onto the wooden floor and squinted at her captors lit by the yellowish light from a dim kerosene lantern.

"You devils! When my Gee Sung finds you, you will pay for this!

"Your Gee Sung does not scare us!" sneered the scar-faced highbinder.

He shoved her into the back room and slammed the door shut.

"Stay in there and be quiet if you want to ever see Gee Sung again! If you try to escape, we will cut you up with our hatchets and send you back to him in little boxes!"

Ah Ying silently looked around the room. As her eyes adjusted to the darkness, she could make out washtubs and row of ironing boards.

This is a laundry. There must be another way out of here.

Ah Ying remembered hearing about the mah jong and other gambling games that took place in the back of every Chinese laundry.

They must have a back way out to escape the police.

She searched the walls for another door and found one along the back wall. Ah Ying turned the handle and pulled on the door with all her strength but it would not give.

It must be boarded up from the outside.

Tall stacks of crates blocked the wall on the left. To her right was a solid wall of bricks. Looking back to her left at the stacks of crates she reasoned that there would not be another door in this small room. With a sigh of exhaustion, she sank down to the floor with her head bowed.

Please, Gee Sung! You must find me!

CHAPTER 18

Chased by Highbinders

With a start Ah Ying opened her eyes as she felt a rat scurrying over her legs.

"Aiyah!' she screamed kicking the rat away. "How could I fall asleep? I have to get out of here!'

Looking to her left, Ah Ying spotted morning sunlight coming in from the wall behind the crates.

There must be a window back there!

She quietly climbed up onto the crates and peered over the top crate. Sure enough, there was a small window covered with dirt and cobwebs! Suddenly, she heard noises from the front room as the two highbinders arose from their slumber.

Quickly climbing down, Ah Ying reached the floor and started pushing the crates against the wall to hide the window. There was still too much light coming in! They would find her escape route! Looking around she found an old canvas tarp, which she frantically dragged up the crates and flung across the window. Now the room was in total darkness. As she carefully climbed back down to the floor, her hands were shaking with fear and exhaustion. She waited in the dark, listening to her heart pounding.

Through a slit under the door, Ah Ying saw the shadows of the men walking. She heard their muffled voices arguing, loudly about the Hop Sings.

She suddenly understood. *I am in the middle of a tong feud! These are Hop Sing men, and they are afraid of what the Bing Kongs will do in retaliation.'*

The door swung open. The short stringy haired highbinder stumbled in carrying a tray, while scar face watched from the doorway.

"Eat this and don't complain, or next time we feed you to the rats!"

As he slid the tray across the floor, a bowl of rice porridge tumbled off the tray and spilled its contents onto the wooden floorboards.

"Ah, that's too bad! Now, Gee Sung's *baak haak chai* will have to go hungry!" laughed scar face.

Ah Ying reached down, picked up the bowl, and silently ate the remaining rice porridge, all the while glaring at the highbinders. She knew she would need her strength to escape. Gee Sung would be looking for her by now, but he would never find her here. It was up to her to find a way out.

Stringy-hair laughed as he turned back to the door, "She is not so tough this morning! Gee Sung's girl is as meek as a baby lamb!"

They slammed and bolted the door leaving Ah Ying in darkness.

She waited in the darkness for several hours, listening to the two highbinders in the front room. Around mid-day, she heard one of the men leave to get food.

Good, that leaves just one of those idiots to deal with, thought Ah Ying.

Thirty minutes later she heard soft snoring coming from the front room.

This is my chance. I have to act now before the other highbinder returns!

She silently climbed up the crates. Ah Ying reached the top, and pulled back the tarp, revealing the filthy window.

Now, how can I open this window? Gwoon Yum[50]*, goddess of Mercy, please give me the strength of ten men!*

She pushed on the window gently. Nothing happened. She pushed harder. Still nothing moved. Finally, she found a small metal latch, flipped it, and pushed with all of her strength. The window moved an inch!

Thank you Gwoon Yum...

A blast of cool air flowed into the room as she pushed the window all the way open. The opening was tiny. It was far too small for a grown man to pass through, but it was perfect for little Ah Ying. She stuck her head through, followed by her shoulders and wiggled her body out the window until she was halfway in and halfway out. Looking down Ah Ying spotted the ground ten feet below.

Well, don't stop now. Let's get out of here!

With one final push of her legs, Ah Ying tumbled out of the window and landed with a thud on the hard dirt in the alley. She rolled over and sat up, smelling the slime that was bubbling out from the laundry.

I have to get out of here! Let's go Ah Ying before scar face returns and finds stringy hair sleeping!

Even in the heat of the moment, Ah Ying had to smile and laugh to herself as she imagined the two highbinders realizing that they had been duped by a young girl!

Ah Ying stood and ran to the back of the laundry property. Jumping up on a crate, she easily scaled the fence. Just as she hit the ground Ah Ying heard yelling coming from inside the building and then footsteps as the highbinders gave chase.

She looked right and then left desperately trying to get her bearings.

Which way? No time! Just run, Ah Ying!

Just then she heard the familiar *Clang! Clang!* of a cable car. She took off running, down the alley towards the sound. The dark shapes of the buildings on each side were a blur as she raced by. Her heart was pounding. She reached the street just as the Powell Cable Car passed by. She knew this car! It ran on Powell Street just up the hill from the Mission Home on Sacramento Street!

Ah Ying turned right and ran along Powell Street trying to avoid the stares of the White people. This was not Chinatown. Men in suits and bowler hats strolled with White women in long dresses. Little Ah Ying was so out of place that the first policeman would probably arrest her!

She heard shouts far behind her just as the next cable car rumbled past her on its slow trek up the hill. Not caring what anyone thought, Ah Ying raced ahead and caught up with the cable car. She looked up and saw a hand reaching down to her! It was a young boy with curly yellow hair. He looked at her and then back down Powell Street. Not thinking, Ah Ying took his hand and jumped up on the sideboard as the cable car picked up speed! Looking back, she spotted the highbinders far behind.

"Quick, squeeze in here so they don't see you!" the boy urged her.

Trying desperately to hide Ah Ying squeezed between the men next to the young boy, not looking at anyone. She said a prayer of thanks and tried to shrink down into the corner of the car.

"*Doh jeh*, I mean thanks," mumbled Ah Ying still uncertain what to think of this White boy.

"No problem, I do this all the time!" he replied with a mischievous smile. "Why are they chasing you?"

"I was kidnapped last night from my husband's room by those men. They are Hop Sing highbinders," she added calmly.

The boy's eyes grew wide with excitement. "Highbinders! Did they have guns and hatchets?"

"Yes. They threatened to cut me up into pieces, if I tried to escape."

Ah Ying looked at the boy more closely as the cable car rumbled up Powell Street. He was several years younger than she was. His freckled face, curly sandy hair, and blue eyes were unlike any person she had ever seen up close.

"My name is Billy! You're the most exciting thing to happen

to me all week!" he added sticking out his hand.

Ah Ying looked at his hand and then back at his smiling face. She took Billy's hand and held it gently in hers as he pumped his arm up and down.

"I am Ah Ying. This is the second time I have been kidnapped and the second time I have escaped!" added Ah Ying proudly. "The first time I was only nine years old!"

Billy had never met such a girl. Chinese or not, this girl had gumption! Wait until he told his friends about her!

The cable car rumbled and clanged past horse-drawn wagons, carriages, and the sidewalks packed with San Franciscans, a world apart from the people of Chinatown. Ah Ying spotted a grassy park on the right with funny little trees.

"Look there's Union Square! My Ma works in that hotel over there!" exclaimed Billy proudly pointing to a magnificent brick building with tall arched windows. "She cleans room for rich people, who have too much money. At least that's what she tells me."

Ah Ying gazed in awe at the high-rise, for she had never seen such a fine building.

"Do you live there?"

"Oh no, we live in Irish Hill on Portrero Point. It's a far ways from here, near the Union Iron Works where my Pa has a job," Billy explained. "I just come down here to visit my Ma. Sometimes we have lunch in the park on one of those benches. Where do you live?"

"I live in *Tong Yan Gai*, I mean Chinatown, on Dupont Gai. I used to live at the Mission Home on Sacramento Street until I ran off to get married to Gee Sung. He is my husband."

The cable car passed the next street and then headed up a steep hill.

"Quick, we have to get off the cable car!" exclaimed Billy looking at the conductor coming towards them.

Ah Ying followed Billy's gaze and spotted the man in the funny dark hat looking right at her as he worked his way to the back of the car.

"What does he want?"

"He wants money for the fare. We don't have any. Let's go!" With that Billy jumped off the slow-moving car as it crept up the hill.

Not wanting to be left alone, Ah Ying leapt off right after her new friend and landed roughly on the cobble stone street. She ran to catch up with Billy just as the conductor spotted them.

"Hey, you two, don't let me catch you riding again for free! Next time I will skin you alive, if I catch you!" the conductor chuckled to himself knowing that Billy had bested him again.

"Billy, I don't know where we are. Which way is Chinatown?" asked Ah Ying clearly worried about finding her way back to Gee Sung.

"Well, I never have been in there. My Pa forbids it. He says they eat boys for lunch and dinner. So, I don't want to get caught in there by your highbinders!"

"We eat lots of good food, but not very many little boys," replied Ah Ying with a smile.

"I don't think we are far, but you should hide here," advised Billy pointing to a cellar door below a flower shop window. "I will get my Ma after she is done working, and she will help you to get home. I promise! If you stay out here someone will spot you, and those highbinders that were chasing you will find you and lock you up again!"

Ah Ying saw the wisdom of Billy's plan as he opened the cellar door and ushered her down the steps.

"Now wait here, and I will be back with my Ma in a bit. Don't make a sound and don't wander off and get yourself lost!"

With that Billy shut the cellar door, and Ah Ying once again found herself huddled in the dark, listening to the cable cars and wagons that worked their way up the steep street.

I hope I can trust Billy. But what choice do I have? Better sit tight, Ah Ying.

She heard Billy's footsteps receding as he ran back down Powell Street towards Union Square and his Ma's hotel.

CHAPTER 19

Return to the Mission Home

Ah Ying awoke with a start. Light was streaming in from the open cellar door, and someone was shaking her.

"I think it's her!"

Squinting at the bright daylight, Ah Ying now could make out two men in funny black bowler hats, and black coats with shiny golden buttons. The short one stopped shaking her.

"Are you Ah Gew?"

"Yes, please take me back to my Gee Sung. Our home is on Dupont Gai," she pleaded relieved that she had been found by policemen and not highbinders.

"Well, your husband is looking for you but so are other people."

"Let's take her to the Bing Kong Tong and collect the $120 reward!" offered the tall policeman. "Her husband wants her that badly, she must be something special."

"Look Smith, I am in charge here, and I will tell you what we will do with her!" snapped Officer Williams. Covering his face with his hand he turned his head, and whispered, "She is going back to the Mission Home, and they can decide what to do with her!"

The two police officers escorted Ah Ying out of the cellar to their waiting police wagon. After helping Ah Ying into the back, Officer Smith then sat down next to her watching her closely.

"Keep an eye on her Smith! This one is slippery! She evaded

the Hop Sing highbinders, and now those boys are the laughing stock of Chinatown. They were outsmarted by this dainty Chinese maiden!"

With a slap of the reins the two horses pulled the police wagon up the very steep Nob Hill. Ah Ying looked back and spotted Billy and his Ma standing helplessly in the middle of Powell Street as they drove off. Billy was shouting and waving at her, but she couldn't understand his words.

At Sacramento Street the wagon turned right and headed downhill. Ah Ying immediately realized where they were taking her: back to the prison of the Mission Home!

Ah Ying hid her face, hoping they would pass by the Home and continue on to Dupont Gai and her Gee Sung. But instead the police wagon slowed and stopped in front of 933 Sacramento Street.

"No! I can't go back here! I spent months trying to escape! You must take me to my husband on Dupont Gai! Please don't do this!" pleaded Ah Ying, as the officers climbed down from the wagon.

Officer Williams offered Ah Ying his hand, but she only glared at him.

"Have it your way, young lady!"

Williams reached up putting his burly arm around Ah Ying's waist as he picked her up and carried her up the steps like a sack of potatoes. Ah Ying kicked and protested the whole way to the front door.

After a solid knock on the front door, Margaret Culbertson appeared. After sizing up the trio with a look of astonishment, she regained her composure.

"Bring her inside."

She stepped aside, and Officer Williams still carrying Ah Ying entered the parlor followed by Officer Smith.

"Thank you, officers. You are good friends of the Mission Home."

Officer Williams put Ah Ying down, and the two policemen turned to leave. Through the open-door Ah Ying spotted the horses waiting for them on the street. For an instant she was tempted to run past them and jump in the wagon and flee to her Gee Sung. In the next moment, the large wooden door closed sealing her young fate.

"Well, Ah Gew. Where have you been these past three days? We were very worried about you! You shouldn't have run away like that!" scolded Miss Culbertson.

Ah Ying looked away, "My name is Ah Ying, and this is no longer my home. I am married to Gee Sung. We have our own home on Dupont Gai!"

"We will see about that. For now, you are an inmate of the Mission Home." Seeing Ah Gew's defiance she added, "You will stay in your room!"

With all the commotion a group had gathered in the parlor. The young children shyly peeked out at Ah Ying from behind the older girls. Looking around the parlor Miss Culbertson spotted Chun Fah and nodded to her to take Ah Ying away.

Chun Fah stepped forward. Before she could take Ah Ying's hand, Sue Lee squeezed between the girls and hustled her friend out of the parlor.

She whispered, "Don't worry, Ah Ying. We will find a way."

She smiled at her friend and took her hand as the girls ascended the flight of stairs to their second-floor bedroom.

Ah Ying recalled the first time she had gone up these same stairs three years ago as a young *mui tsai*. She thought of how her life had changed and how it all seemed the same.

"Will I ever be free?" she wondered.

As they entered the bedroom, Ah Ying found Sing Kum, Ung Wah, Wo Ah Moy and Ah Seene waiting for her. They greeted her with smiles as they gathered around, eager to hear about her romantic adventure.

All the girls were talking at once.

"Tell us what happened. Don't leave anything out!"

"We have all been talking about you for the past three days!"

"Are you going to try to escape again?"

"Where is Gee Sung? Did you marry him?"

Ah Ying was overwhelmed by all the attention and was a bit embarrassed when she realized she had not thought about her friends in the home since she escaped three days ago.

Sitting on the bed surrounded by her friends, she then proceeded to tell them the details of her escape from the Home. She described her elopement and marriage to her Gee Sung, the midnight kidnapping by highbinders, her escape from the laundry, meeting Billy on the cable car on Powell Street, and the two policemen who found her hiding in the cellar. The girls were spellbound by Ah Ying's romantic tale.

"Gee Sung is my husband. I must go home to him," she finished.

The girls sighed in unison.

"Don't worry, Ah Gew. We will help you to find Gee Sung," offered Ah Seene.

"You should call me 'Ah Ying'. That is my real name."

Ah Ying then got up from the bed and went to the window. She looked longingly at the scene on Sacramento Street below. Her taste of freedom these past four days had been intoxicating, and she knew she could not stay here. Her heart and her mind were a million miles away from the Home.

Suddenly, she saw someone waving at her from across the street. It was Billy! He had followed the police wagon from her hiding spot on Powell Street! Billy mouthed words and gestured down Sacramento Street. Unable to understand his meaning, she waved back enthusiastically. The girls all crowded around the window to see with their faces pressed against the windowpanes. They all began to wave!

Billy laughed at the sight of the six Chinese girls peering down and waving at him from behind the window! What would his friends say about this? He then took off running down Sacramento Street towards Dupont as fast as his legs would carry him.

I hope I can outrun any hungry Chinese! he thought.

Late that night, after all the family was asleep, Maggie Culbertson sat down at her desk, opened the ledger and found Ah Gew's first entry on page 100 September 1886. She recalled when she had come to the Mission Home three years before as a scared but defiant little *mui tsai*. So much had happened at the Home and with Ah Gew since then. She picked up her pen and added to Ah Gew's story.

Apr 18. Ah Gue ran away from the Home.. and after a few days absence was brot back by two police officers. They found her in a large boarding house where a number of Chinese [illegible] are employed

[51]

◆ ◆ ◆

Ah Ying looked up in terror as Scarface raised his gun to her head,

"Your Gee Sung cannot save you now!" He snarled and pulled the trigger.

Ah Ying screamed, "No, wait!"

She woke up in a cold sweat trembling as Sue Lee and Chun Fah shook her violently.

"Ah Ying, wake up! What's wrong? You were screaming!"

"They are going to kill me! I have to get away! No matter how fast I run I always end up back at the laundry tied up with their ugly faces leering down at me!" It's horrible sobbed Ah Ying.

"It was only a dream, Ah Ying. You are safe here with your family!"

Ah Ying looked at the concerned expressions of her two friends and sighed, "Those highbinders will never leave me in peace. I have to go to my Gee Sung. He will protect me."

"Then you must have Gee Sung apply for a writ of habeas corpus," explained Chun Fah.

"What is that?"

"It is an order saying that Miss Culbertson must go before the court to prove she is not keeping you here against your will. If she cannot convince the judge, she must release you. I know all about these writs, because I go with her to the court as her interpreter. All of the slave owners use writs to try to force Miss Culbertson to give the girls back. She is always in court fighting to keep the girls here at the Home. Usually she wins in court, but not always," explained Chun Fah.

"Where do I get this writ?"

"Gee Sung must go to a lawyer to apply for the writ of habeas corpus. It will cost money."

"We must get a message to Gee Sung about this writ," Ah Ying said with a glimmer of hope.

Chun Fah took out a pen and paper and began writing the message with instructions to Gee Sung about applying for the writ of habeas corpus.

"Alright, you sign here, so he knows this is from you and not a trick."

Ah Ying took the pen and made her mark on the letter, saying, "Thank you, Chun Fah. I am glad you know about the courts."

By now all of the girls in the room were awake and had gathered around Ah Ying's bed. They inspected the letter approvingly as Chun Fah added, "We must all be sworn to secrecy and never say a word about this plan to anyone else!"

The girls nodded their agreement in silence as Ah Ying neatly folded the letter and placed it in her pocket.

"Now, how do I get this to my Gee Sung?" she wondered.

The next morning was Thursday May 9th. Ah Ying was allowed to leave her room to help with chores and attend the Morning Prayer. Miss Culbertson hoped that a little spiritual guidance might bring Ah Gew back into the flock. Just in case, she assigned one of the little children, Gee Shin, to follow Ah Gew around and make certain she did not stray.

Ah Ying was cleaning the parlor floor and dusting the shelves when there was a soft knock at the front door. At first she wasn't sure she had heard anything, but then she noticed Gee Shin staring up at the large oak door. The two of them looked at each other unsure of what to do. The Home's assigned door monitor was absent.

There was another knock, a little louder this time. "Rap, rap, rap!"

Ah Ying decided to act. She unlocked the door, grasped the brass knob, turned it, slowly pulled the door open, and peered around the edge of the door. She was afraid she would come face to face with her highbinder tormentors, but was amazed when she saw the visitor was Billy from the cable car!

"Hello, Ah Ying!" beamed Billy with the same mischievous smile. "I bet you're surprised to see me!"

"Hello, Billy! How did...," began Ah Ying.

"I followed the police wagon after they took you away from your hiding place!" Billy interrupted. "It wasn't hard. Their old horses move pretty slowly up that steep hill, and I can run really fast when I need to!"

"Yes, we saw you yesterday from our bedroom window, but you ran off down Sacramento Street."

"Well, I went into Chinatown to look for Gee Sung. I figured I could outrun any hungry Chinese plus I had my trusty slingshot with me for protection," offered Billy pulling out his weapon of choice to show Ah Ying. "I went to the building you told me on Dupont and looked for a tall Chinese man. I wanted to tell him where to find you. But I am sorry, Ah Ying. I couldn't find Gee Sung for you."

Ah Ying looked at Billy's sad expression and smiled at her friend, "Don't worry about that Billy. You can still help me." She reached into her pocket and pulled out the letter to Gee Sung that Chun Fah had written, urging, "Please, Billy, take this letter to Gee Sung where he works. He owns a cigar store on the corner of Commercial and Kearny Streets. Do you know where that is?"

"Don't worry I'll find it!"

As she heard someone entering the parlor, Ah Ying whispered urgently, "Quick, Billy! You have to leave now!"

Billy tucked the letter into his front pocket, jumped down the ten steps in two strides, and took off running down Sacramento Street intent upon completing his mission. Before he reached the corner he turned around and gave a quick wave.

Ah Ying hurriedly closed the door and found little Gee Shin staring up at her wide-eyed.

She pulled her little friend close and whispered, "This needs to our secret! OK?"

Gee Shin nodded giving his favorite big sister a hug before scampering off in search of someone to play with.

CHAPTER 20

Writ of Habeas Corpus – Judge Murphy's Court

When Ah Ying first disappeared, Lai Wah appealed to the Bing Kong Tong, which offered a reward of $120 through the Chronicle for her recovery. Previously, the Bing Kongs had demanded protection money from him when he opened his cigar store on Commercial Street. Resisting the Tongs was unwise, so Gee Sung paid them every month. At least now, maybe they would help him rescue his wife. The rumor in Chinatown was that the Hop Sings were behind the kidnapping, but there was no proof. Not yet anyway. If a Tong War was brewing, he and Ah Ying were going to be right in the middle of it all.

After Billy found Gee Sung and delivered Ah Ying's letter, Lai Wah immediately went to Thomas Riordan, the White attorney, who often represented the Chinese. On Thursday afternoon May 9th Lai Wah made application for a writ of habeas corpus on behalf of Ah Ying alleging that she was being restrained of her liberty in the Presbyterian Mission House at 933 Sacramento Street by Dr. Loomis, the reverend in charge of the Home.

Chinatown was buzzing with stories about Ah Ying's adventure. The San Francisco Chronicle picked up the story and sent a reporter to interview Ah Ying at the Mission Home. The story ran on Thursday, May 9th, and soon the whole city knew about the daring exploits of this young Chinese girl.

The lawyer Riordan contacted the San Francisco Call when he and Lai Wah filed the writ of habeas corpus in the city's Superior Court. A brief article in Friday, May 10th edition of The Call described Hung Lai Wah as "a villainous looking Chinese." As the drama unfolded in the local news columns, the good White citizens of San Francisco were soon following the story of Ah Ying and Gee Sung. The first court hearing was scheduled for that Saturday, May 11th, before Judge Daniel Murphy

[52]

After a Chinese Girl.

Hung Le Wah, a villianous looking Chinese, made application for a wri: of habeas corpus yesterday in behalf of Ah Ying, who, he alleges, is restrained of her liberty in the Presbyterian Mission House, No. 933 Sacramento street, by Dr. Loomis. The matter will be heard at 9:30 this morning by Judge Murphy in Department 12 of the Superior Court.

On the appointed day, Lai Wah walked the one block from his apartment on DuPont to the Hall of Justice at 750 Kearny Street, which the Chinese called *Ngah Moon Gai* (Court House Door Street). Just last week he and Ah Ying had been so happy and excited while taking this walk to the courthouse to obtain their marriage license. Today, Lai Wah was at the head of a throng of Chinese, who were all intent upon seeing Ah Ying returned to her husband.

"Don't worry, Gee Sung. We will get Ah Ying back. All the Chinese are with you today!"

Lai Wah was lost in his thoughts but now looked up and spotted Chin Shee and Lun Chee. And there was Ah Ying's friend, Ah Chan, from the restaurant. The crowd of Chinese following Lai Wah had grown to over three-dozen as more friends and curious onlookers joined in the march to the Hall of Justice. Over the years little Ah Ying had made many friends in Dai Fow, all of whom were intent upon gaining her freedom from the Mission Home.

◆ ◆ ◆

Lai Wah strode up the steps of the Hall of Justice three at a time. At over a head taller than any other Chinese man or woman, he cut an impressive figure as he strode with purpose, his entourage trailing behind him. The commotion from the noisy and excited throng echoed loudly in the huge entry hall of the courthouse.

"Shush!" scolded the guard. "This is a courthouse not a market! You can't come in here making that racket! Be quiet or go back to Chinatown where you belong!"

Lai Wah glared at the guard but then turned around, to address the crowd, "Alright, be quiet, so we can see the judge and free my Ah Ying."

The Chinese calmed down, and their talking subsided to a low rumble as they looked around the grand building. Most had never been inside the Hall of Justice even though it was right in their backyard.

Lai Wah's lawyer, Thomas Riordan, approached and noted, "Your hearing has been delayed until late this afternoon. There is a trial of some murderous highbinders that bumped our appointment. Your hearing will now be the last case of the day, but you better stay nearby in case they finish early. You never can tell about these things!"

Lai Wah's heart sank - another delay until he could see Ah Ying. It was more than he could take.

"We better go outside," he sighed, "There is no place in here for all of us to wait."

They all strolled across the street and sat in the new park benches in Portsmouth Square. Lai Wah watched the men playing mah jong to pass the time. After several hours, Chin Shee, and Lun Chee appeared with baskets full of food from the restaurant. The lunch disappeared quickly, as no one had left in spite of the long wait.

"Are you ready to testify?" asked Ah Chan between bites of *cha siu bow*. "There will be a court interpreter, so you can speak in Cantonese. Just speak slowly and tell the truth."

"What will they ask me?"

Riordan advised, "They will question you about your relationship with Ah Ying and about your job. The judge will want to be certain you are not a slave owner trying to get his property back."

"Ah Ying is my wife, and I am her husband!" snorted Lai Wah indignantly.

"Yes, of course. But don't be surprised if their lawyer tries to lie to convince the Judge that you are an evil Chinese brothel owner."

"I will be ready to defend my Ah Ying's honor!"

"Don't get angry and try not to look so mean," cautioned Mr. Riordan.

Lai Wah scowled but remained silent thinking about what was in store.

Hours passed, and the late afternoon air was growing cooler as the sun began to pass behind the buildings. Just as Lai Wah thought he could not wait any longer, Mr. Riordan came running across the street from the courthouse.

"Come quickly! Your hearing is next!"

Lai Wah jumped to his feet and began to run across the park towards the steps of the Hall of Justice.

Finally, I will get my Ah Ying back! he thought.

"Slow down!" Riordan called after him, "You don't need to run. You're going to start a stampede with all your friends!"

Looking back, Lai Wah realized that dozens of Chinese were running with him towards the courthouse. He abruptly stopped, took a deep breath, and walked next to Mr. Riordan up the steps.

They found their way to Judge Murphy's chambers in Department 12 of the Superior Court. Opening the huge wooden doors to the courtroom, Lai Wah felt as if he had entered another world. A towering oak desk at the far end dominated the white walled chamber, and wooden benches stretched out like rows of kneeling supplicants. Riordan ushered Lai Wah to a table on the other side of a curved rail, which was rendered a rich, dark color by the thousands of hands that had passed over it in their quest for justice... or mercy.

Lai Wah sat nervously at the table, but relaxed slightly when he noticed his friends behind him, dutifully taking their places on the rows of benches. Just then, from the doors beyond their smiling faces, a new group filed into the courtroom in an odd looking procession. First was a matronly White woman wearing a long blue dress, with her graying hair pulled back into a bun. Next, a small White man dressed in a long black coat with a funny, tall black hat.

And then, Lai Wah's heart stopped as he spotted his little Ah Ying bringing up the rear. She was dressed in the light colored *saam* with the *ou* (tunic) and *foo* (trousers) she had made in the sewing class at the Mission Home. She looked stunning but frightened. Lai Wah could not take his eyes off her. He wanted to call out, but felt Riordan's hand restraining him. Instead, he watched in silence as Ah Ying walked slowly past the benches and spotted her friends. He saw her searching in vain to spot him in the large room.

As Lai Wah watched them reach the table across the aisle from his own, Maggie Culbertson sat down and Ah Ying's eyes met his. His heart soared as he saw her for the first time in what had felt like months. She smiled and gave a little wave to him as she took the seat on the left side of the table next to the lawyer. Lai Wah beamed inwardly, ecstatic.

A sharp voice rang out, "All rise. The Superior Court of San Francisco County, State of California is now in session, the Honorable Daniel J. Murphy, presiding."

Mr. Riordan stood and grabbed Lai Wah's sleeve, pulling him up out of his seat. Maggie Culbertson and her lawyer rose and helped Ah Ying up gently. The Chinese in the back looked around the room, unsure of what to do, and slowly joined in standing up.

There was a creak from behind the imposing desk as the ornately carved oak doors swung open. Judge Murphy, dressed in a long black robe, strode straight to the tall oak desk and struck his gavel to begin the court session.

After the introduction of the case, the judge told Ah Ying to approach the bench. Attorney Ruef, who handled all of the Mission Home's legal affairs, escorted Ah Ying to the stand. Judge Murphy through an interpreter swore in Ah Ying.

"Raise your right hand. You do solemnly state that the testimony you may give in the case now pending before this court shall be the truth, the whole truth, and nothing but the truth, so help you God."

Ah Ying nodded.

"You have to say 'I do' out loud, instructed the Judge."

Looking at the interpreter, Ah Ying replied, "I do," and nodded for good measure.

"State your name and age for the Court," Riordan prompted.

"I am Tom Gew Ying. I am nineteen years old."

Judge Murphy interjected, "You don't look your age. You can't possibly be that old. You don't even look sixteen!"

Ah Ying blushed rosily and replied, "Yes, your honor. I was born in China in 1871. I have been in Gum Saan for nine years. I am nineteen years old!"

"Well, we will need some proof of your age later young lady," noted Judge Murphy with a smile, clearly smitten by the dainty Chinese maiden.

"Tell us your relationship with Hung Lai Wah," Riordan continued.

"Gee Sung is my husband."

"Who is Gee Sung?"

"Gee Sung is Hung Lai Wah. They are the same. Hung Lai Wah is his married name. His childhood name is Hung Poy. I have known him as Gee Sung for many years."

"Where are you now residing?"

"I am at the Mission Home on Sacramento Street with Miss Culbertson."

"How long have you lived at the Presbyterian Mission Home?"

"I have lived there for three years now, since I was rescued as a *mui tsai*, a child slave. They rescued me from cruel owners on Jackson Street and took me to the Mission Home to live. Last week I ran away from the Home to be with Gee Sung."

"Do you now wish to return to the Mission Home to live?"

"No! I want to go to my Gee Sung. He is my husband. I truly love him. We have an apartment on Dupont Gai."

"Haven't they been good to you at the Mission Home?" pressed Judge Murphy. "Why do you wish to leave the safety of the Home?"

Thoughtfully, Ah Ying offered, "Miss Culbertson has been good to me. The girls at the Mission Home have been my family. But the matrons forbid me from seeing Gee Sung, and they whipped me when I disobeyed them. I have been sad for so long now. A year ago, I tried to kill myself." Looking at the floor with tears streaming down her face, she declared, "I will not go back to the Mission Home."

"Young lady try to compose yourself. I think that is enough for now," comforted the Judge looking first at Ah Ying and then giving a disapproving look in the direction of attorney Rueff. "Call your next witness!"

Miss Culbertson took the stand and was sworn in.

[53]

"Tell us your relationship with Ah Ying," Rueff instructed.

"I am the director of the Presbyterian Mission Home at 933 Sacramento Street. I am responsible for the safety of the forty plus Chinese women and girls, who live with us at the Home. Ah Gew, whom you know as Ah Ying came to us in September of 1886. She was rescued from a merchant family, who horribly abused her as a child slave. She looked to be only twelve years old at the time. We have cared for her and educated her for three years now. She is part of our family."

"Why do you wish to keep her at the Mission Home?"

"Ah Ying is clearly less than eighteen years of age, and she cannot be treated as an adult. She will not be safe, if released into the custody of that Chinese man, who claims to be her husband," she exclaimed pointing her finger at Lai Wah. "All of the Chinese slave owners use these writs of habeas corpus to take the girls back to a life of servitude or worse! I will not tolerate their evil intentions for any of our girls and certainly not for Ah Gew!"

Turning to Mr. Thomas Riordan, Judge Murphy instructed, "Call your witness to the stand."

Mr. Riordan led Lai Wah to the witness stand.

"Raise your right hand. You do solemnly state that the testimony you may give in the case now pending before this court shall be the truth, the whole truth, and nothing but the truth, so help you God."

"Of course, I do," snorted Lai Wah.

Mr. Riordan gave Lai Wah a warning look.

"State your name for the record," he continued.

"I am Hung Lai Wah also known as Gee Sung. I am 39 years old."

"What is your relationship with Ah Ying?"

"She is my wife. We were married by the Chinese custom last Saturday. On Monday we went to this courthouse to obtain a marriage license, so we could be married legally by the White laws."

"Why did you not get married in a church or courthouse yet?"

"Because, early Tuesday morning, Ah Ying was kidnapped by Hop Sing highbinders and taken away in the middle of the night. The cowardly scum took away my wife at gunpoint," Lai Wah glared directly at the Hop Sing highbinders in the back of the chamber. "I looked all over for her, and even had the Bing Kong Tong take out a reward of $120 for her return. After she escaped and was found by the police, they took her back to the Mission Home against her will!"

"What became of the marriage license?"

"Now that Ah Ying is again imprisoned in the Mission Home, we have no use for it. I have the license locked away in a chest," answered Lai Wah sadly.

"If she is returned to you, are you able to take care of and provide for Ah Ying as your wife?"

"Of course, I can take care of her," scowled the sleek and saffron Lai Wah, clearly irritated by the question. "I am a cigar maker and a merchant. I own my own cigar store on Commercial Street. If anyone tries to harm my Ah Ying, they will answer to me," Lai Wah added in a menacing tone again looking directly at the highbinders.

Attorney Rueff rose to cross-examine Lai Wah.

"Isn't it true that you are a slave owner and work at the bordello in Ross Alley? Ah Ying is your slave isn't she?"

"I am no more a slave owner than are you!" Lai Wah growled at the White attorney rising out of his seat with clenched fists. "I am a merchant. I own my cigar store. Ah Ying is my wife," continued Lai Wah trying hard to control his anger.

Defusing the tension, Judge Murphy quickly interrupted, "We will need to see proof of your occupation and social standing and also of Ah Ying's age when we reconvene next Wednesday May 15th. Until then, I will take this case under advisement and consider the facts presented here today at this preliminary hearing. Court is adjourned!"

As the courtroom began to empty, Lai Wah sat in his chair

stunned. "I thought the Judge would give me Ah Ying to take home today. Why did we come here and waste my time?"

"Today was just a preliminary hearing," replied Riordan, encouragingly. "The real hearing starts next Wednesday. Don't lose hope, Lai Wah. We will do everything possible to free Ah Ying. Besides, I think that Judge Murphy likes her. and that is good for you. Just try to control yourself and stay calm."

Lai Wah sat at the table wondering how he would last until next Wednesday, knowing that his Ah Ying was being held captive in that Jesus House on the Hill. He had come to get his wife today, but he was going home alone. He slowly rose and was the last person to leave the courtroom that afternoon.

Outside the Hall of Justice, a San Francisco Chronicle reporter stopped Riordan, looking for a story. By the time the Sunday May 12th morning edition of the Chronicle hit the streets, all of San Francisco knew the story of Ah Ying and Gee Sung.

HIGHBINDERS' WORK.

A CHINESE WOMAN'S CAPTURE AND ESCAPE.

Taken From Her Husband's Room and Hidden in a Laundry—Her Thrilling Experience.

The Ping Kong Hong Society of Chinatown will save $120 by the recovery yesterday of Ah Yeng, the coy, and, in a simple Chinese way, pretty wife of Gee Sung, who was stolen from her husband's room at 821 Dupont street early Tuesday morning. The almond-eyed beauty is now 20 years of age and was educated in the Presbyterian mission on Sacramento street. She was not a willing convert, however, and about a year ago attempted suicide because the ladies of the mission would not let her keep company with Gee Sung, whom she had known for a long time.

Last week she was allowed more than usual liberty and took advantage of it to leave the mission and seek Gee Sung. The latter promptly made her his wife and furnished two rooms at 821 Dupont street.

Tuesday morning, about an hour after midnight, Ah Yeng wanted something and sent Gee Sung out for it. While he was gone two highbinders broke into her room, and, after blinding her with pepper, muffled her in a blanket, bore her down stairs to a carriage and took her to a Chinese laundry. She was kept under close watch, but on Tuesday afternoon managed to climb the back fence and get away. Her captors discovered her and gave chase, but she eluded them and sought refuge in a basement on Powell street, where she was found by Policemen Smith and Williams, who, with Gee Sung, were hunting for her. She was taken to the Chinese mission and is still there, waiting for Gee Sung to take her away.

When Ah Yeng first disappeared Gee Sung appealed to the Ping Kong Hong Society, which offered a reward of $120 through the CHRONICLE for her recovery.

[54] [55]

MRS. SUNG'S AGE.

SHE SAYS SHE IS OLD ENOUGH TO MARRY.

Judge Lawler Thinks Not, and Will Investigate—Highbinders in Court.

Judge Lawler's department of the Superior Court was crowded with Chinese yesterday when the writ of habeas corpus sworn out by Hing Si Wah was heard. Hing, who is a beauty in a petite oleaginous way, is the maiden who eloped from the Presbyterian Mission with Gee Sung, a cigar-maker, last week, but who, after a honeymoon of three days, was kidnaped in the night, and taken to a Chinese laundry, from which she escaped in a most thrilling and melodramatic manner, in which highbinders, big guns and carving knives played an important part. When rescued she was returned to the mission much against her will. Gee Sung, her husband, engaged a lawyer and secured the writ, which was the last case called by Judge Lawler.

Mrs. Sung told the Judge that she wanted her husband, and that she would not go back to the mission. She said she was 19 years of age, had known Gee for a great many years, and was truly in love with him, although as he sat in the courtroom, Gee did not present the figure of a fitting cavalier for the pretty young wife. The Court told Mrs. Lung that she did not look her age, and the little lady blushed rosily, but appeared to prove that she was.

Gee, sleek and saffron-brown, scowled as he took the chair and told the Court that he was a cigar-maker fully capable ot taking care of his wife.

Mrs. Culbertson of the mission said the girl was less than eighteen, and that she would not be in safe hands if turned over to her husband.

In order to obtain more evidence concerning Gee's social standing and Mrs. Gee's age, the case went over until next Wednesday.

San Francisco Chronicle
Thursday May 9, 1889

HIGHBINDER'S WORK.

A CHINESE WOMAN'S CAPTURE AND ESCAPE

Taken From Her Husband's Room And Hidden in a Laundry Her Thrilling Experience

The Ping Kong Hong Society of Chinatown will save 120 by the re covery yesterday of Ah Ying, the coy, and in a simple Chinese way, pretty wife of Gee Sung, who was stolen from her husband's room at 821 Dupont street early Tuesday morn ing. The almondeyed beauty is now 20 years of age and was educated in the Presbyterian mission home on Sacra mento street. She was not a willing convert, however, and about a year ago attempted suicide, because the ladies of the mission would not let her keep company with Gee Sung, who she had known for a long time.

Last week she was allowed more than the usual liberty and took advantage of it to leave the mis sion and seek Gee Sung. The lat ter promptly made her his wife and furnished two rooms at 821 Dupont street.

Tuesday morning, about an hour after midnight, Ah Ying wanted some thing and sent Gee Sung out for it. While he was gone, two highbinders broke into her room, and after blind ing her with pepper, muffled her in a blanket, bore her down stairs to a carriage and took her to a Chinese laundry. She was kept under close watch, but on Tuesday afternoon man aged to climb the back fence and get away. Her captors discovered her and gave chase, but she eluded them and sought refuge in a basement on Pow ell street, where she was found by Policemen Smith and Williams, who, with Gee Sung, were hunting for her. She was taken to the Chinese mission and is still there, waiting for Gee Sung to take her away.

When Ah Ying first disappeared Gee Sung appealed to the Ping Kong Hong Society, which offered a reward of 120 through the CHRONICLE for her recovery.

San Francisco Chronicle
Sunday May 12, 1899

MRS SUNG'S AGE

SHE SAYS SHE IS OLD ENOUGH TO MARRY

Judge Murphy Thinks Not, and Will Investigate - Highbinders in Court

Judge Murphy's department of the Superior Court was crowded with Chin ese yesterday when the writ of ha beas corpus was sworn out by Hing Si Wah was heard. Hing, who is a beauty in a petite oleaginous way is the maiden, who eloped from the Presbyterian Mission with Gee Sung, a cigarmaker, last week, but who, after a honeymoon of three days, was kidnapped in the night, and taken to a Chinese laundry, from which she escaped in a most thrilling and melodramatic manner, in which high binders, big guns and carving knives played an important part. When res cued she was returned to the mission much against her will. Gee Sung, her husband, engaged a lawyer and secured the writ, which was the last case called by Judge Murphy.

Mrs. Sung told the Judge that she wanted her husband, and that she would not go back to the mission. She said she was 19 years of age, had known Gee for a great many years, and was truly in love with him, although as he sat in the courtroom, Gee did not present the figure of a fitting cavalier for the pretty young wife. The Court told Mrs. Lung that she did not look her age, and the little lady blushed rosily, but appeared to prove that she was.

Gee, sleek and saffronbrown, scowled as he took the chair and told the Court that he was a cigarmaker fully capable of taking care of his wife.

Mrs. Culbertson of the mission said the girl was less then eight een, and that she would not be in safe hands if turned over to her husband.

In order to obtain more evidence concerning Gee's social standing and Mrs. Gee's age, the case went over until next Wednesday.

Lai Wah spent a sleepless night imagining his wife being held captive at the Jesus House on the hill by that White woman. His Ah Ying called to him from her room's barred window, but he could not help her. For the first time in his life Lai Wah was powerless. He could blast tunnels through solid granite mountains, but he could not free his wife.

What kind of a husband am I? Lai Wah lamented miserably.

Finally, exhaustion overcame him, and he dozed fitfully for

a couple of hours.

The early morning light filtered through the buildings lining Dupont Gai, signaling the beginning of another day for the Chinese in *Tong Yan Gai*. Lai Wah sat up in the bed and swung his bare feet down onto the rough wooden floor. He was exhausted, but still anxious to start preparing for the next court hearing. Skipping breakfast, he hurriedly dressed and left the apartment in a rush, heading for the law offices on Clay Street.

Arriving at Riordan's office quickly, he pounded on the door. When there was no answer, he grew impatient, and pounded again, more forcefully. Finally, a sleepy Mr. Riordan opened the door a crack.

"Do you know what time....”?

"It is time to get my Ah Ying back," Lai Wah barked excitedly.

"OK. Come in. Just give me a minute to get dressed."

The office was small and simply furnished. Thomas Riordan was the principle attorney representing the Chinese in the 1880's and 1890's and was retained by the Chinese Six Companies, the Chinese Consulate, and the Chinese Merchant's Exchange for high profile cases. Throughout Chinatown and across the circuit courts of California Mr. Riordan was a well-known defender of Chinese interests.

Lai Wah waited impatiently. A single oil lamp hung over a huge oak desk, which was piled high with stacks of papers. One wall was lined with bookshelves crammed with books that had unintelligible names. The opposite wall was graced with a single framed diploma and a cabinet with square cubbyholes containing an assortment of odds and ends. A black coal-burning stove stood in the corner. The stove was unlit, and the room was cold, but Lai Wah didn't notice.

After ten minutes, the door opened, and Thomas Riordan reappeared dressed in his black suit and tie. His long black beard and mustache offset the gold wire rimmed glasses perched high on his nose. “Alright, Lai Wah. Let's get down to business!”

Lai Wah sighed, "Finally! Where do we start?"

"At the next court hearing on Wednesday we have two goals. First, we have to convince Judge Murphy that you are an upstanding merchant in Chinatown, and that you can support your new wife. Their lawyer will continue to argue you are a brothel owner, who wants to enslave Ah Ying and return her to a life of shame. Second, we have to present evidence that Ah Ying is legally an adult; that she is at least eighteen years old."

"We have already told the Judge these things! What else does he want?" demanded an exasperated Lai Wah.

"Your word is not enough. We need witnesses to prove these facts. Today we will make a list of your merchant friends in Chinatown, who will testify on your behalf. Proving Ah Ying's age will be more difficult."

"I have hundreds of merchant friends here in Chinatown, and they will all testify for me. That courtroom is not large enough to fit all of Chinatown in there!"

"OK. Let's make a list and visit these friends of yours in the next few days to choose the best character witnesses to speak on your behalf."

Anxious to get started, Lai Wah started rattling off names and businesses:

"Ah Ying's friend Gin Lun Chee is an herbalist and owner of the Chee Sang Tong Company at 710 Dupont Gai. My good friend Su Duc is a cigar maker, who works at 635 Commercial Street. His business is just down the block from my new cigar store. Chin Kit is a merchant at the Quong Sue Lung & Company on Dupont Gai. My old friend Wing Lee owns a Chinese laundry. Wing is blind but very sharp. He misses nothing. And the Chinese Consul General Liang Ting Tsang lives in my building!"

"That's a good start, but we will need many more and will need to visit and interview these people to establish their testimony on your behalf."

The two men continued working throughout the morning generating a long list of merchants and friends. Lai Wah was certain that Judge Murphy would be convinced that he was an honest man, who could provide for Ah Ying.

"Now, we still have the problem of proving Ah Ying's age," observed Riordan. Her word may not be enough to convince Judge Murphy, although he does seem to favor her," observed Mr. Riordan. "Without proof of her age, all of your witnesses are of no use!"

"I can vouch for her age! She is nineteen years old! She is twenty years old by Chinese counting!"

"I am sorry, Lai Wah. Your word is of no use to us in court. Think! Who else can prove Ah Ying's age?"

Lai Wah sat glumly pondering their dilemma. How could they prove what was obvious to him? Ah Ying did not look her age, but he knew she was nineteen years old. At least that is what she had told him.

Suddenly, he looked up with a light in his eye exclaiming, "I know! Her friend Chin Shee came with her from China on the same ship! She has known her for nine years since they were young. Let's go to ask her right now!"

Lai Wah jumped up out of his chair and started heading for the door of Riordan's office.

"Slow down! That is a good plan but we can talk to Chin Shee and her husband Lun Chee at the same time. We don't have to rush out the door yet," Riordan advised trying to calm Lai Wah.

Lai Wah reluctantly sat back down and waited for Riordan to finalize his list of witnesses.

After a few minutes of fidgeting in his chair, Lai Wah jumped up once more and shouted, "Enough! Let's go and get Ah Ying! I can't wait for you any longer, Riordan!"

Riordan looked up at his client and realized that restraining him was like trying to hold back a wild horse.

"OK! You win! Let's go into Chinatown and start lining up your witnesses. We can start with your cigar maker friend Su Duc on Commercial Street. That way I can visit your cigar store so I can question you about it at the hearing on Wednesday."

Riordan stood, put on his jacket and hat and headed out the door onto Clay Street, surrounded by the din and Sunday morning bustle of *Tong Yan Gai*. Lai Wah was a step behind as the two men headed towards Commercial Street in search of the witnesses that would secure his future with Ah Ying.

CHAPTER 21

Chinatown Overflows Judge Murphy's Court

On Wednesday afternoon May 15, 1889 Judge Murphy's courtroom was packed with nearly 100 Chinese, men and women, clamoring for justice for Ah Ying and Lai Wah. The din of their excited discussions and the smell of Chinese food filled the courtroom. Trying to bring some order to the room before Judge Murphy arrived, Bailiff Smith, barked, "Stop that jabbering, you heathens! And who brought food in here? Remove yourself immediately, or I will have you all arrested and thrown in jail!"

The room quieted down momentarily, and someone reluctantly carried a steamer full of food toward the exit. Quick hands reached into the steamer as he passed, plucking out a few choice dim sum to last through the proceedings.

Lai Wah and Riordan were seated on the right side of the table as before, and Margaret Culbertson was seated with Ah Ying and their attorney on the left. Ah Ying tried to get Gee Sung's attention, but he stared straight ahead as he nervously rehearsed the testimony that Riordan had prepared for him.

A new face was also in the room. White haired Jerome Millard was the official court interpreter. Lai Wah looked at Millard and immediately recognized him from his days on the railroad twenty years before. Millard was older, but this White man's face was unmistakable. He had been one of the few friends of the Chinese railroad workers and spoke Chinese fluently. Millard had even supported their strike and argued on their behalf, all to no avail.

"What is he doing here in this courtroom?" Lai Wah wondered.

"All rise. The Superior Court of San Francisco County, State of California is now in session, the Honorable Daniel J. Murphy, presiding."

Judge Murphy's vice boomed out, "In the case of writ of habeas corpus brought by Hung Lai Wah on behalf of Ah Ying against the Presbyterian Mission Home at 933 Sacramento Street the court will now hear witnesses for the prosecution. Mr. Riordan, call your first witness."

"We call Hung Lai Wah to the stand as our first witness."

Lai Wah stood, took the stand, and was sworn in, this time knowing to place his left hand on the bible while raising his right hand. Taking the seat in front of the court, Lai Wah scowled nervously at the room full of reporters and spectators.

"Stop frowning Lai Wah. You look menacing!" hissed Riordan to his client.

Lai Wah attempted a smile, but only managed a pained grimace.

"Tell the court your business," instructed Riordan.

Millard started to translate Riordan's English into Chinese, but Lai Wah interrupted, hissing indignantly in Chinese, "I understood the question!"

"OK, then just answer and I will translate into English for the Court," replied Millard a bit taken aback by Lai Wah's bravado.

"I am a cigar maker and have been one for over eighteen years. I have my own cigar store at 635 Commercial Street."

"Then you are not a brothel owner?" Riordan offered.

"Of course not!" replied Lai Wah, starting to rise up from his seat.

Riordan motioned for Lai Wah to sit back down as he continued, "Tell us how you know Ah Ying."

"Ah Ying is my wife! I have known her for many years. I knew her before she went to live at the Mission Home on Sacramento Street. We were married by the Chinese custom and have a marriage license from the County Clerk."

"Why is she not with you now?"

"She was kidnapped from our home by highbinders! She escaped and was found by police, who took her back to the Mission Home. They should have brought her back to me!"

"Riordan, we know this story," scolded Judge Murphy. "As dramatic as it is, we are here today to prove Lai Wah's social status in this community not to retell the highbinder drama."

Then we call Gin Lun Chee as our next witness." As Lun Chee took Lai Wah's place, Riordan began, "Mr. Lun Chee, tell the court your business and your relationship with Hung Lai Wah."

"I am an herbalist and partner in the Chee Sang Tong Company at 710 Dupont Gai. I have known Gee Sung, I mean Lai Wah for several years. He and his wife, Ah Ying, are good friends," he added smiling at Ah Ying.

"And is Lai Wah a cigar maker or a brothel owner?"

"Lai Wah is a cigar maker. He recently opened his own cigar store on Commercial Street. You can see it yourself. It is not far from here!"

"OK, Mr. Riordan, do you have any other witnesses," interrupted Judge Murphy.

"Riordan smiled and looked at the long list of Chinese merchants he had lined up to testify for Lai Wah.

The rest of the afternoon was a blur of Chinese witnesses taking the stand one after the other all in support of Lai Wah and Ah Ying. From each, Riordan elicited a name and occupation.

"I am Quan Chick. My shoe factory is at 628 Commercial Street. I have known Lai Wah for many years. He is a good man, who can support his wife."

"My name is Ow Chong. I am a shoe dealer at 211 Clay Street"

"Wong Far. I have a shoe factory at 413 Commercial Street...."

"I am Wong Li the butcher. I own my butcher shop at 757 Sacramento Street."

"I am Cheong Sim a general merchandise dealer at 707 Dupont Street."

"I am Quan Chuck, a chicken dealer, at 30 Washington Alley."

"I am Chim Sim Jeong. I am a butcher at 729 Dupont Street."

"Pung Choy; storekeeper 802 Dupont Street

"Cheng Wy; a dealer in fine Chinese goods at 1019 Dupont Street."

"I am Fong Chin, and I own the shoe factory 122 Waverly Place."

By the end of the hour thirty Chinese merchants had testified, each one asserting that Lai Wah was a good man who could support his wife through his work as a merchant and cigar maker.

The Chinese in the gallery got into the action, cheering with the testimony of each new witness.

Judge Murphy banged his gavel shouting, "Order in the court! My courtroom is not a circus! Be quiet now, or I will clear this room and have you all held in contempt!"

He turned to Riordan, remarking, "All right, that is enough merchants! Call your next witness to establish Miss Ah Ying's age.

"We call Ah Ying as our next witness."

Ah Ying stood and was escorted to the stand by Mr. Millard, the interpreter.

"Tell the court how old you are and how you know Lai Wah," instructed Riordan.

"I am nineteen years old; actually, I am twenty years old by Chinese counting! I have known Gee Sung for many years, since I was a *mui tsai* on Jackson Street. He helped to have me rescued and taken to the Mission Home."

"Why do you wish to leave the Mission Home, if they rescued you and have given you a place to live? Surely, you must appreciate the life of freedom they have given you."

"Miss Culbertson has been good to me. But now I wish to go to my Gee Sung. I truly love him. He is my husband. You must let me go to him," pleaded Ah Ying.

"I will not stay at the Mission Home. For my disobedience, they whipped me. I will run away again, if you send me back there!" Ah Ying continued defiantly looking at the court while avoiding Margaret Culbertson's gaze. She then looked demurely at Judge Murphy, who smiled at Ah Ying's boldness.

Catching himself, Judge Murphy added, "How can you prove Ah Ying's age? She looks to be no older than fifteen years old."

"We call Chin Shee as our next witness."

Mr. Millard escorted Chin Shee to the stand, and she took her seat, visibly nervous.

Riordan prompted her gently, "Chin Shee, please tell the court how you know Ah Ying."

"I have known Ah Ying since we came to Gum Saan together on the steamer in 1880. She had been sold by her parents to Wong Shee and was being taken to Gum Saan as a child slave. We became friends, and she told me her story."

"And how old did she say she was at that time? Remember, you are under oath to tell the truth, Chin Shee."

"She told me she at the time that she was nine years old."

"Do you swear that is the truth?"

"Yes, I swear she told me that she was nine years old."

"So how old would that make her today?"

"She is now nineteen years old!" proclaimed Chin Shee. The Chinese in the gallery erupted in applause.

"Bailiff, clear the courtroom!" Judge Murphy yelled over the din. "I warned you all to be silent!"

As the cheering onlookers herded slowly from the room, he continued, "I will consider the evidence presented today and will announce my decision on Saturday morning. Court is adjourned!"

The San Francisco Chronicle reporter was the first to leave

the courtroom, running to his office to beat the deadline for the next day's paper. San Franciscans were waiting expectantly for the next installment of the tale of Ah Ying and Gee Sung, and they would not be disappointed.

GEE SUNG'S WIFE.

Evidence at the Hearing of the Habeas Corpus Case.

The second hearing in the Ah Yeng habeas corpus case attracted nearly one hundred Chinamen to Judge Murphy's court yesterday afternoon. Witnesses were examined as to the reputation of Gee Sung, the coolie who induced the girl to leave the Presbyterian Mission and marry him, and testimonials were submitted from leading Chinese merchants attesting his ability to care for his wife.

Ah Yeng, the little Chinese wife, was put on the stand and said that she was 19 years of age, and did not want to go back to the mission, where they had whipped her. She wanted to go to her Gee Sung, and would not stay at the mission if sent there.

Judge Murphy took the case under advisement until Saturday, when he will announce his decision.

[56]

San Francisco Chronicle
Thursday May 16, 1889

GEE SUNG'S WIFE
Evidence at the Hearing of the Habeas Corpus Case

The second hearing in the Ah Ying habeas corpus case attracted nearly one hundred Chinamen to Judge Murphy's court yesterday afternoon. Witnesses were examined as to the reputation of Gee Sung, the coolie who induced the girl to leave the Presbyterian Mission and marry him, and testimonials were submitted from leading Chinese merchants attesting his ability to care for his wife.

Ah Ying, the little Chinese wife was put on the stand and said that she was 19 years of age, and did not want to go back to the mission, where they had whipped her. She wanted to go to her Gee Sung, and would not stay at the mission if sent there.

Judge Murphy took the case under advisement until Saturday, when he will announce his decision.

CHAPTER 22

Judge Daniel Murphy's Decision

Judge Daniel J. Murphy was born in Lowell Massachusetts in 1834. At the age of nineteen, he left his home for California, and by 36 he was elected District Attorney for San Francisco. He served for three terms with a most distinguished career. In 1884 he was elected Judge of the Superior Court in San Francisco. By the time he presided over Ah Ying and Gee Sung's case, he was bald, heavily mustached and of ample girth. "Hizzoner," as the press frequently referred to him, tolerated no nonsense by attorneys or spectators.

[57]

As one article described, "He was an unassuming man, a gentleman and a scholar; bold as a lion in behalf of what he recognizes as the right; but calm and self-possessed in his manner of defense, and he evinces a high degree of sympathy for the suffering and oppressed." Judge Murphy built his home at 159 Liberty in Noe Valley in 1878 in the Italianate style. His liberal tendency included support of the women's suffrage movement as evidenced by an invitation to the house to meet Miss Susan B. Anthony, Rev Anna Shaw and other figures in the movement.

Early Saturday May 18th the court was once again packed with Chinese. Lai Wah came with friends from his apartment on Dupont Gai in Chinatown and Maggie Culbertson brought Ah Ying on the cable car from the Presbyterian Mission Home. Eager to hear the Judge's decision both groups had arrived early.

Miss Ah Ying was dressed in a flowing blue and yellow robe with her hair pomade. Lai Wah, also wore his finest robe, and towered above the other Chinese in the room. He showed a placid countenance that belied the turmoil he was feeling. Ah Ying looked across the room at her husband with a small smile. He did not respond, but her mere glance made his heart soar.

"All rise. The Superior Court of San Francisco County, State of California is now in session, the Honorable Daniel J. Murphy, presiding."

By now all the Chinese knew the routine as the entire courtroom rose in unison to greet the judge as he took his seat on the bench.

"Be seated," instructed the bailiff.

"In the matter of the writ of habeas corpus sworn out on behalf of Ah Ying vs. the Presbyterian Mission Home, I have considered the evidence presented in this court."

Lai Wah and Ah Ying listened intently as Judge Murphy continued, "The court is sympathetic to the concerns of Miss Culbertson, whose sole purpose is to protect her charge from harm at the hands of unscrupulous Chinese."

Lai Wah and Ah Ying sank down in their seats as the Judge's words destroyed their hopes for a life together. Lai Wah placed his hands over his face, his rage and disappointment boiling rapidly to the surface. He felt Riordan's hand on his shoulder.

"Let him finish, Lai Wah. Don't react yet."

The Judge continued, "However, in this case the plaintiff's attorney has established to my satisfaction that Ah Ying is in no danger from this man, Lai Wah. In fact, he has shown great passion in attempting to keep his wife out of harm's way. They have both sworn that they love each other and wish to be together."

With these words, Ah Ying and Gee Sung both rushed to each other and stood beaming, holding hands as Judge Murphy continued, "We have established that Lai Wah is a merchant, who is more than capable of providing for Ah Ying. The testimony of Chin Shee has satisfied the court that Ah Ying is ninteen years old and can therefore go wherever she chooses. With these facts clearly and firmly established the Superior Court rules in favor of Ah Ying and Lai Wah. You two are free to go, and I suggest that Mr. Millard escort you next door to be married by Justice of the Peace Hebbard!"

The entire courtroom erupted in cheers and laughter as Ah Ying and Lai Wah embraced. Judge Murphy smiled broadly, grateful for any case in which a just decision was one that could elicit such happiness.

In the next moment Ah Ying and Gee Sung were running hand-in-hand through the corridors with their friends trooping after them. Interpreter Jerome Millard guided them into Justice Hebbard's court.

"Do you have the marriage license?" Hebbard asked.

Lai Wah's face fell, "No. It is locked in a trunk in our apartment on Dupont Gai. I did not think we would ever need it again!"

The room fell silent at the unexpected complication.

"Well, we will need to see the license before you can be married,"

From the back of the room a woman's voice, offered. "I can get you a certified copy."

The entire room of Chinese turned around. Ah Ying and Gee Sung smiled as they immediately recognized the clerk who had helped them obtain their marriage license.

Running out of the room, she quickly returned with the certified copy of their license in hand. "Here you are, Judge."

[58]

The Chinese crowded around Judge Hebbard as he examined the license. At the bottom Ah Ying's mark and Lai Wah's

boldly printed signature stood out prominently.

"Good! Then let's proceed."

"By the power invested in me by the State of California, I now pronounce you Mr. and Mrs. Hung Lai Wah!" proclaimed a beaming Judge Hebbard to the cheers and congratulations of over forty of their friends.

At 821 Dupont Gai the couple now, "newly-married" for the second time, entertained their friends in the afternoon and evening as sandalwood and blue fire were burned in profusion. The guests and reporters enjoyed an elaborate assortment of Chinese dainties served by their charming hostess, Ah Ying.

Hearing a soft knocking at the front door, Ah Ying got up to see who the latecomer could be. Opening the door, she was greeted by Billy's smiling face.

"Billy! Come in! You are my guest of honor!"

"Hi, Ah Ying! I saw you in the courtroom and followed the parade to your home."

"I am so glad you did, Billy. Come in and meet our friends and have some delicious Chinese treats!"

Ah Ying then proceeded to tell her guests how she met Billy chasing the cable car up Powell Street, and how he delivered her secret message to Gee Sung.

"Without Billy, I would not have escaped the highbinders and found my Gee Sung!"

The Chinese crowded around Billy patting him the back. It was hard to tell who was happier, little Billy or his admirers. "Way to go, Billy! You are an honorary Chinese from this day forward," proclaimed Uncle Chan.

Late in the evening, after the last well-wishers had departed, an exhausted but radiant Ah Ying snuggled closer to her husband. She looked closely at Gee Sung's face lit by the glow of candle light and whispered, "Gee Sung, my love, will we always be this happy?"

Gee Sung's heart was full as he held his young bride close and replied, "My Ah Ying, you have made my life complete. I will love you until the day I die."

"Someday we must tell this story to our grandchildren," Ah Ying sighed, and she closed her eyes as she fell asleep in the arms of her Gee Sung.

That evening Margaret Culbertson sat down at her desk in the Mission Home and reflected on the sudden turn of events that had occurred that day. She remembered little Ah Gew, who had arrived at the Home's doorsteps as a frightened but defiant *mui tsai* three years ago. Ah Gew was a headstrong dreamer, who knew her own mind. Maggie Culbertson would miss her, but she smiled to herself when she pictured how happy the two lovers looked in front of the judge that afternoon.

"Be happy Ah Gew and stay safe in the love of Jesus," she prayed.

She then turned to page 100 in the Register of Inmates and made her final entry in the story of Ah Gew.

Apr 18th 89 | Took Ah Gew to court. She testified to the court that she was 19 yrs old, and was given permission to go where she pleased - and was then married at the City Hall by Justice Hibbard

[59]

The next day, May 19, 1889, the Sunday Chronicle ran the final installment of the story of Ah Ying and Lai Wah on page 16. The whole city had been waiting with baited breath, and hoping for a happy ending to their saga. They were not disappointed.

LI WO'S. GIRL.

AFTER MUCH TROUBLE HE MAKES HER A BRIDE.

Judge Murphy Releases Her, and They Proceed to Get Married—Reception in Chinatown.

Miss Ah Yeng, in a flowing robe of blue and yellow, and her hair well greased, was one of the early birds to catch the eye and attention of Judge Murphy yesterday morning. Miss Yeng is the little Chinese maid who made a record for herself a couple of weeks ago by eloping from the Presbyterian Mission with Hong Li Wo, alias Lee Sung, a Chinese shoemaker. Hong Li secured a marriage license and locked it up in his trunk, subsequently telling Judge Murphy that he and Ah Yeng had no use for it.

Succeeding this peculiar observance of the law, Ah Yeng was stolen from her home by highbinders, had a number of remarkable adventures, and finally landed in the mission again. She did not like the place, however, and with Hong's assistance secured a writ of habeas corpus.

The writ was considered by Judge Murphy for a couple of weeks, and yesterday, upon Hong establishing his ability to care for his bride, and the latter proving that she was old enough to care for Hong, he released them.

Both Hong and Ah Yeng needed an interpreter when they were on the stand, but they understood English as spoken by Judge Murphy yesterday well enough to be at each other's side before he had ceased speaking, and in a moment were tripping through the corridors with their friends trooping after them.

Interpreter Millard guided them into Justice Hebbard's court, and after a certified copy of the license had been secured, Ah Yeng was made Mrs. Hong Li Wo, and Mr. Hong Li Wo was receiving the congratulations of two score of his fellow-countrymen.

At 821 Dupont street the "newly married couple" were at home to their friends in the afternoon and evening, and sandalwood and blue fire were burned in profusion. An elaborate collation of Chinese dainties was served, and Mrs. Li Wo made a charming hostess.

[60]

San Francisco Chronicle
Sunday May 19, 1889

LI WO'S GIRL AFTER MUCH TROUBLE HE MAKES HER A BRIDE

Judge Murphy Releases Her, and They Proceed to Get Married - Reception in Chinatown

---

Miss Ah Ying, in a flowing robe of blue and yellow, and her hair well greased, was one of the early birds to catch the eye and attention of Judge Murphy yesterday morning. Miss Ying is the little Chinese maid, who made a record for herself a couple of weeks ago by eloping from the Pres byterian Mission with Hong Li Wo, alias Lee Sung, a Chinese shoemaker. Hong Li secured a marriage license and locked it up in his trunk, sub sequently telling Judge Murphy that he and Ah Ying had no use for it. Succeeding this peculiar observance of the law, Ah Ying was stolen from her home by highbinders, had a number of remarkable adventures, and finally landed in the mission again, and with Hong's assistance secured a writ of habeas corpus.

The writ was considered by Judge Murphy for a couple of weeks and yes terday, upon Hong establishing his ability to care for his bride, and the latter proving that she was old enough to care for Hong, he released them.

Both Hong and Ah Ying needed an interpreter when they were on the stand, but they understood English as spoken by Judge Murphy yesterday well enough to be at each other's side before he had ceased speaking, and in a moment were tripping though the corridors with their friends trooping after them. Interpreter Millard guided them into Justice Heb bard's court, and after a certified copy of the license had been se cured, Ah Ying was made Mrs. Hong Li Wo and Mr. Hong Li Wo was receiving the congratulations of two scores of his fellow countrymen.

At 821 Dupont street the newly married couple were at home to their friends in the afternoon and evening and sandalwood and blue fire were burned in profusion. An elaborate collation of Chinese dainties was served, and Mrs. Li Wo made a charm ing hostess.

CHAPTER 23

Family Portrait

"Wake up!"

Ah Ying felt someone gently shaking her. She opened her eyes slowly squinting in the early morning sunlight.

"Gee Sung, is that you?"

"No! Grandma, it's me! Wake up!"

Ah Ying looked down at her four-year-old grandson and smiled as the fog cleared and her story faded into the past. This one did remind her of Gee Sung. He was bold and full of mischief.

"I am sorry, Gwunde. I must have dozed off."

"Grandma, don't stop your story now! What happened to the highbinders? Did they come back? What happened to Gee Sung?" asked Gwunde still trying to rouse Grandma from her slumber.

"Gwunde, let's take a break. I will tell you more of my story after I find your mother and say hello to your brothers and sisters."

"OK, grandma, but it could take all morning to find us all! There is Elsie, and Ella, Bill, Albert, Isabel, Leslie, Stanley and me!" exclaimed Gwunde counting off each sibling on his little fingers. "That's eight of us!"

"Your poor mother!" sighed Grandma. "She must be exhausted! She is so young"

"But Gwunde we must use your Chinese names and not just your American names.

"I can tell you our Chinese names," offered Mei Gil proudly. "Mei King, Mei Sin, Wy Fay, Wy Sing, I am Mei Gil, and of course Gwunde, Wy Bew, and Wy Ying is little Stanley."

"Very good, Mei Gil! You are a very clever girl!"

The screen door opened and Mother, carrying baby Stanley in her arms, came out onto the porch.

"*Neih hou,* my Ah Kay! Gwunde and Mei Gil have been keeping me company. They tell me I have eight grandchildren. Is that true?" asked Grandma with a smile.

"Aiyah! Some days there are too many children to keep track of!" laughed Ah Kay.

"Well, have them all come out onto the porch so your brother Kim can take a family portrait," instructed Grandma.

"Mei Gil and Gwunde, run inside and fetch your brothers and sisters for the photograph!"

Running up the steps in search of his siblings Gwunde stormed into the house with the screen door slamming behind him. Mei Gil followed slowly and called out to her brothers and sisters.

"Come out onto the porch so Uncle Kim can take our picture!"

In a few minutes the entire Hop Lee family had assembled on the porch steps lined up neatly with the little ones nestled up against mother.

"Too bad Hop Lee is not here to complete the family portrait," lamented Kim.

"He is always working at the laundry or poultry store or inspecting the hop farms," explained Ah Kay.

"OK! Now hold still and smile! One, two, and three!"

With a click the moment was preserved for all time. The children immediately all ran up to greet Grandma Hong who had been waiting patiently behind Kim.

[61]

"It has been too long since my last visit," lamented a smiling Ah Ying surrounded by the love of her eight grandchildren.

After lunch, Grandma called the children over to her chair. "Would you like me tell you the story of your mother's birth during those early days in *Tong Yan Gai*, before the turn of the century?"

"Yes, Grandma!" they cried out in unison.

"Was she kidnapped by highbinders?"

"No, Gwunde, but those were the dark days of the Tong Wars in *Tong Yan Gai*. And the evil White devils who wanted to drive the Chinese out of California. But we fought back, and here we are today!"

CHAPTER 24

Chinatown Tong Wars and a Baby's Birth March 1890

It was always busy in *Tong Yan Gai*, but today was especially chaotic. It was moving day for the Hungs. Their two-room apartment on Dupont Gai had been a wonderful first home for the newlyweds, but they were going to need more room very soon.

Ah Ying rose slowly from the bed, holding onto the chair Lai Wah had placed nearby to assist his young wife. Her movements were awkward as she stood and sat down quickly in the chair. She smiled to herself, feeling the roundness of her belly and imagining the new life rapidly growing inside of her. Her time was near and her ankles were swollen. She no longer looked like the little *mui tsai* who had fallen in love with her Gee Sung. It was March, 1890, and Ah Ying was nine months pregnant.

Gee Sung came through the door carrying empty crates. Seeing Ah Ying, he put them down and came quickly to her side.

"Ah Ying, be careful, my love. You just sit and watch or have breakfast. I will do all the work today."

"No, Gee Sung. I can help! I will carry the little boxes!"

"You will not!" roared Gee Sung, more loudly than he had intended. Then, more softly he added, "You are too precious. We must take care of you and the baby."

Suddenly, Ah Ying smiled, took Gee Sung's hand, and placed it on her belly, asking, "Do you feel that?"

Gee Sung smiled broadly as he felt the life inside of Ah Ying kicking his hand.

"Our baby is feisty like his mother," he exclaimed.

Indeed, Ah Ying was famous in *Tong Yan Gai* as the little girl who had outfoxed and outrun the Hop Sing highbinders. All of the merchants on Dupont Gai bragged about their little Ah Ying as if she were their own daughter. Now that she was expecting, they all looked after her and were waiting to meet their new grandchild.

At first, Ah Ying and Gee Sung were certain the Hop Sings would return and attempt to kidnap Ah Ying again. Lai Wah was ever vigilant, watching for any sign of danger. By Chinese custom, Ah Ying was not allowed to leave the apartment for one month after their wedding. In their case, it was more for her safety than custom. When she did finally go out, it was under the watchful eye of Lai Wah or one of her uncles on Dupont Gai. Realizing that he needed help, Lai Wah went to the Bing Kong Tong headquarters at 815 Jackson Street. He paid the Bing Kongs to post a notice warning that if Ah Ying were kidnapped or in any way harmed, the Bing Kong highbinders would retaliate in force, and blood would be spilled in the streets of *Tong Yan Gai*.

Fears of retaliation by the highbinders gradually subsided as life returned to normal. In truth, the highbinders quickly found other, more suitable enemies. The Tong wars were rampant in *Tong Yan Gai,* and it seemed that every night someone was murdered in the Chinatown alleys.

In May of 1889, shortly after the wedding, Lai Wah came running up the stairs to their apartment and burst through the front door. His distraught expression told Ah Ying that something terrible had happened.

"Gee Sung, what's wrong?"

At first unable to speak, he finally blurted out, "Chin Ah You is dead!"

"But how can he be dead? We just visited him yesterday!"

Chin Ah You lived just up the street at 615-1/2 Dupont Gai.

Yesterday, he looked worried but would not tell them what was wrong. He insisted that he had to leave *Tong Yan Gai* in a hurry. Apparently, he did not leave soon enough.

Gee Sung recounted, "I just walked by his apartment and saw it happen. He was coming down the stairs and was being followed by a highbinder. He pushed him down the stairs and then raised his axe and chopped Chin's head! Other highbinders joined in chopping him to pieces! It was horrible, Ah Ying! There was blood everywhere. They ran off, leaving Chin on the ground bleeding to death. I ran up to him, but there was nothing I could do to save him!"

The police never apprehended the tong assassin, who was later identified as Mah Yet Muk. In truth, they did not look very hard, and Chin Ah You's death became just another in a long string of unsolved Chinatown murders. Like many unfortunate Chinese, Chin paid his debt with his life.

The tong wars were fought in the alleys and rooftops of Chinatown. Oftentimes, the war was fought over a woman. Other times it was over money or a perceived slight by one tong member against a rival. Recently, the tong hatchet men had adopted another favorite weapon: the deadly Colt .45 revolver. Just last week, the feud between the Hop Sing Tong and Suey On Tong had led to blood shed that left three more dead from an assassin's bullets in the streets of Tong Yan Gai.

No one was free from danger. Ah Tuck, a Chinese tailor employed at 325 Battery Street, was shot one morning while going to work on Commercial Street. Tuck was unarmed and never dreamed of being involved in the bloodshed. His only transgression was that he belonged to a rival Tong of the assassin, Ah Lee. After he was shot, Ah Tuck ran down Commercial Street, pursued closely by Ah Lee, who fired a second shot. Lee hid from police in a bunkhouse on Oneida Place, but was discovered, arrested, and taken to the City Prison. There, he was charged with assault to murder.

San Franciscans were fascinated with the news stories about the underbelly of Chinatown. These accounts of kidnappings, highbinders, and murders sold papers like hotcakes. Certainly, no story captivated their collective imagination more than the trials of Little Pete, aka Fong Ching. He was the leader of the Sam Yup Tong and a man who lived a Jekyll and Hyde existence. As a merchant skilled in commerce, he owned the F.C. Peters & Co. shoe factory at 819 Washington Street and had amassed a fortune worth millions. As the leader of the Sam Yup Tong, Little Pete was a hatchet man involved in prostitution, gambling and opium peddling. He was famous in Chinatown, where he was regularly seen walking about in his chain mail armor and steel reinforced hat, surrounded by his three bodyguards. Legends held that Little Pete had personally killed fifty men of the rival See Yup Tong during the gang wars, and most Chinese thought he was invincible. Truly, the larger than life Little Pete was both feared and beloved in Chinatown.

Even amidst all of the chaos and violence in *Tong Yan Gai*, the birth of a new Chinese baby was always a cause for celebration throughout the community. Against all odds, the bachelor society of *Tong Yan Gai* was seeing more and more new babies as Chinese bachelors and former slave girls found each other and started families.

Ah Ying and Lai Wah walked the short 1-1/2 blocks from their apartment on Dupont Gai over to their new home at 711 Commercial Street.[62] As was his custom, Lai Wah kept his eye out for trouble, but this day was peaceful in *Tong Yan Gai*. As he helped Ah Ying walk down Dupont Gai, the sun shone brightly, warming their faces. Ah Ying walked slowly, holding onto Gee Sung's arm for support.

She smiled as they passed the restaurant on Dupont Gai, but was disappointed when she did not see Uncle Chan at his usual spot. But as she turned her attention back to the short uphill walk, Ah Ying spotted Uncle Chan running towards them.

"Hello, my little Ah Ying! I thought I spotted you from the restaurant."

"Hello, Uncle Chan," Ah Ying beamed. "Today we are moving to our new home on Commercial Street. You must come to visit once the baby is born. Alright?"

"Yes, yes, of course! I can see by the shape of your belly that you are having a boy," he exclaimed, patting Ah Ying's round belly. "Here is some food for your new home." Ah Chan handed several bamboo steamers to Lai Wah. "Send word when the baby is born so I can visit after a month."

"Thank you, Uncle Chan!"

They continued another block on Dupont Gai to Commercial Street, where they turned left. The short walk down Commercial Street took them by shoe factories, a dozen other businesses, boarding houses, and Lai Wah's new cigar store. They stopped in front of the three-story building on the south side of the street, just before Kearny.

"We will raise our family here, Ah Ying," proclaimed Lai Wah proudly.

Ah Ying gazed up at the building. As was typical in Chinatown, the bottom floor was occupied by a commercial business. The Kwong Lee Kee Company was a wholesale provision house owned by the Ng family and managed by Ng Hon Kim. A narrow, dark wooden door led up stairs to the apartments on the second and third floors. Just above the door, the numbers 711 welcomed her to their new home.

Ah Ying smiled, breathing heavily from the short walk. She took Gee Sung's hand and followed him up the long stairway to the second floor.

"Close your eyes, Ah Ying!"

Lai Wah opened the door to the flat as he picked up his bride and carried her over a pan of burning coals placed at the entrance to the apartment, a Chinese tradition to ensure that she would pass through labor successfully.

"Alright, you can open your eyes now."

Ah Ying opened her eyes and gasped, "Everything is perfect,

Gee Sung. Now put me down so I can see our new home."

A quick inspection of the apartment revealed a much larger space for their growing family. There were two bedrooms and a kitchen with room for a dining table. Hung from the curtains directly over their bed was a piece of paper cut to resemble a pair of scissors and an elegant tiger skin, all to keep away the evil spirits.

"Chin Shee and Lun Chee helped me to get the apartment ready for you!" proclaimed Lai Wah proudly.

Ah Ying admired the curtains on the windows and the yellow flowers on the table. Clearly, a woman's touch had finished off the furnishings.

"We must have them over to thank them for their kindness."

"Yes, of course. But first you must rest. Here sit on the bed," suggested Lai Wah, gently taking his wife by the hand and leading her into one of the bedrooms. "I will continue to bring our belongings over from Dupont Gai in those crates I brought home. Remember to think pure and good thoughts to protect the baby from evil."

Indeed, there were so many ancient taboos that had to be closely followed by every Chinese woman during pregnancy. She needs to read good poetry. She should never gossip, laugh loudly, sit on a corked mat, look at clashing colors or lose her temper. Her food must be properly cut or mashed, or her child will have a careless disposition. Light colored foods must be avoided so the baby will not be fair skinned. Any construction work or hammering must be avoided in the home of a pregnant woman to guard against miscarriage. And obviously, it was absolutely forbidden for a pregnant Chinese woman to attend a funeral.

Ah Ying smiled at her husband as she reviewed the long list of behaviors she must avoid, wondering how her life could ever return to normal.

"I will be careful my Gee Sung. Now go away while I prepare your lunch!"

Ah Ying rummaged around the kitchen, looking for the wok to prepare lunch for Gee Sung. The cabinets were a mess! Just like a man to throw everything inside the same cabinet and then slam the door shut!

She laughed, "I will have to organize it all later."

For now she had what she needed. She began to hum the songs that Chun Fah used to sing to the girls at the Mission Home every night. They were songs from their home in Toishan—songs that she would sing to her baby very soon. As she stirred the bean sprouts and pork in the sizzling wok, Ah Ying felt a cramping pain in her belly that doubled her over in pain. The pain lasted for several seconds.

And just as it eased, she began to feel better another wave of contractions hit like a thunderbolt causing her to call out, "Gee Sung! Hurry home. I think the baby is coming!"

But Lai Wah was blocks away, at their Dupont Gai flat, gathering the last of their belongings and placing each item into the wooden crates. He turned around, took one last look at the apartment, and sighed. This had been a good first home for him and Ah Ying. Picking up the crates, he walked out and shut the door behind him.

Back on Commercial Street, Ah Ying was now doubled up on the bed, moaning in pain as wave after wave of contractions enveloped her. She felt and heard a pop and then felt a trickle of fluid on the inside of her legs.

"I must be bleeding! Hurry, Gee Sung!"

With those thoughts Ah Ying sat up in bed as the latest wave passed over her easing up momentarily.

"Get up, Ah Ying! You can't just lay here like a helpless baby! You have to find someone to help."

She grabbed the bedpost and pulled herself upright as the next wave of contractions and pain slammed into her belly. Ignoring the pain, Ah Ying stumbled to the door and opened it, stepping out into the dim hallway. Reaching the door of the next apartment Ah Ying pounded forcefully.

"Open up! Please help me!"

Silence, no answer! She was just about to go to the next door when she heard shuffling from inside the apartment. The door creaked open just a crack and a women peaked out.

"What do you want?"

"My baby is coming right now! Please help me! I am alone."

Immediately, the woman led her into the apartment. She could tell that Ah Ying was having a contraction right then.

Peering up at the woman's face as the contraction passed, Ah Ying grunted, "Is that you, Ah Mooie?"

The woman paused and then let out a delighted gasp, "My sister, Ah Ying! What are you doing here?"

The two women embraced one another quickly before Ah Ying's next wave of contractions. Their years living at the Mission Home had created an unbreakable bond of sisterhood that only Margaret's girls could understand.

"We are moving in today, but I am afraid my baby is in a hurry to see the apartment."

"Tell me about the pain. Let me know when the next one comes," Ah Mooie instructed Ah Ying gently.

It was less than a minute when the next wave of pain overwhelmed her.

"I think I am bleeding. I felt the blood running down my leg. Please send someone to get Chin Shee. She is my friend and a midwife. She lives in the Spanish Building on Dupont Gai!"

"OK, I will send for your friend, but you are in luck my little one. I am also a Chinese midwife. And you are not bleeding. Your water broke. The baby needs to come out, and I think it will be very soon! Now come and sit in this armchair."

Ah Ying sat in the chair while Ah Mooie went into her kitchen and began boiling water. She returned with a cup of steaming herbal tea.

"Drink this tea. It will help with the labor pains, and don't worry. I sent my son Beng downstairs to tell his father Ng Hon Kim to fetch your friend Chin Shee."

Not waiting for Ah Ying's reply, Ah Mooie positioned her on the chair, pulling her forward and gently spreading her legs.

"We must give the baby room. Now push gently. That's good, Ah Ying. Now push harder!"

Chin Shee came barging into the room through the front door. "Ah Ying! Your baby is coming! Why didn't you call me sooner?"

Chin Shee placed her hand on Ah Ying's belly, feeling the baby's position. She moved between Ah Ying's legs, spreading them far apart.

"I can see the baby's head already! Now with the next contraction push really hard!"

Ah Ying felt the next wave coming on and grunted and pushed.

"Aiyah! It hurts! She screamed.

"Stop talking and push again!"

The baby's head was now in Chin Shee's hands. The slippery shoulders were coming out next.

"Push one more time, Ah Ying. The baby is almost out!"

With one final push, the baby was in Chin Shee's hands. She deftly tied off the cord and cleared the baby's mouth with her fingers.

Ah Ying was faint but listened intently for her baby's cry. The seconds passed in silence.

"What's wrong with my baby!"

Ah Mooie and Chin Shee were both quiet and working quickly. Chin Shee turned the baby over. The baby's face was blue! The cord had been wrapped around the neck. She cleared the baby's mouth again. No response. The baby was limp. Quickly turning the baby over again, she slapped the baby's bottom with her hand once, and then again.

Suddenly, the baby gasped and let out a joyous ear-splitting wail, "Waaah!" and then another, "Waaah!"

Ah Ying cried with relief as Chin Shee placed her baby into her waiting arms.

"You have a new daughter, Ah Ying."

Looking at her daughter's face, Ah Ying thought she had never seen such a perfect baby. Her tiny hands were so small.

Ah Ying counted the fingers in Chinese and then the toes. "Nhut, ngee, sahm, say...."

The baby began to suck its fingers.

"You must try to feed her Ah Ying," urged Chin Shee. "Your little one is hungry. Here let me show you how to feed her."

There was a pounding at the front door.

"Ah Ying! Are you in there? Are you alright?"

"You better let him in before he breaks the door down," Ah Ying laughed.

Lai Wah came rushing into the room. But his panicked expression melted into a joyous grin when he saw his baby girl.

"Ah Ying, she is perfect. But I should have been here with you!"

"Don't worry," Ah Ying replied. "Ah Mooie and Chin Shee did everything. I had two midwives! Here, hold your daughter, Gee Sung."

Ah Mooie took the baby from Ah Ying, wrapped her in a blanket, and handed her to a very nervous Gee Sung. Cradling the baby awkwardly, he sat next to Ah Ying as they marveled at *Tong Yan Gai*'s newest arrival: Ah Kay, born on March 4, 1890.

"Now you must rest, little sister Ah Ying," Ah Mooie instructed softly.

Ah Ying smiled but had no idea of what was in store for her.

"What do you mean I can't wash my hair, or bathe?" Ah Ying protested, outraged. "And I have to stay inside all day?!"

"Ah Ying, you must do these things to recover from the pregnancy," Chin Shee explained. "And you are confined for one whole month, not one day! We call this *choh yuet*, the sitting month. Our mothers did this, and I did it, and you will do this as well, if you know what is good for your body.

You must lie in bed and rejuvenate your *hei* and renew your body. There are many rules for you to remember, but I will help you. You must keep your body warm. Cover your body entirely from head to toe. Never stand by the window, and never ever drink cold drinks. And avoid cold foods like watermelon," Chin Shee continued with a frown remembering how hard it had been for her two years ago with her first born.

"This is like being in prison, Sing Yee!" Ah Ying groaned. "I can't do this!"

"You can do it, my friend. Stop being so stubborn!"

Ah Ying moaned, not knowing how she could survive a month of confinement.

"First I was a prisoner as a *mui tsai* on Jackson Street, then I was held captive in the Mission Home, and now this!"

"Stop it, Ah Ying!" Chin Shee admonished with some impatience. "It is only for one month, and there are some benefits you know."

Ah Ying, looked up, asking "What could possibly be good about this baby prison?"

"Well, I will help you take care of the baby. And the special foods are delicious.

For the first week, they bring you *gai zhou*, a mild cleansing chicken soup in rice wine with wood ear and shitake mushrooms. Next, the real treat arrives. You get *geung cho*, pig's feet and roasted ginger in sweet and sour black vinegar. It is a very pungent and flavorful stew. This is every new mother's favorite dish, and you can have as much as you like. Uncle Chan has been preparing it for weeks!"

Chin Shee held a bowl up for her friend to inspect.

"Here, try the chicken soup"

"Let's skip the soup and move on to the pigs feet and garlic stew!" Ah Ying laughed, finally managing a smile.

"No, Ah Ying, you must eat properly to recover. First the chicken soup with mushrooms. Try it. It is delicious and just what you need."

The soup was much more flavorful than she had imagined.

"Mmm, good! Thank you, Sing Yee. But where is Ah Kay? I never get to see my baby!"

"Don't worry. We are all taking good care of your baby daughter. We will bring her to you to feed. Otherwise, your only job is to rest and eat and follow my instructions!"

"Sing Yee, I have been selfish. Tell me about your baby. How old is she now?"

"Qui Fong is now two years old. Remember she was born on April 11, 1888, almost one year after I married Lun Chee in 1887." Chin Shee smiled and leaned over and whispered in her friend's ear, "I will tell you a secret. I am expecting another baby."

Ah Ying looked at her friends glowing face and burst out in a laugh, exclaiming, "Sing Yee! We will have our babies together! And I will bring you the chicken soup during your sitting month!"

"But, I haven't told Lun Chee yet. So, this must be our secret for now! I think this baby will be a son. I must be very careful this time. I can't lose another baby."

There was silence between the two women as they both felt the pressures of providing a son to be the heir to their families. Only then could each woman assume her place of honor in the family hierarchy. By Chinese custom, the new wife became part of her husband's family, which was dominated by the family matriarch, the mother-in-law. Until the new wife produced a son, she was little more than a family servant. But producing a son would change everything, giving the new mother a place of reverence in the family. Both women loved their daughters but were secretly praying for a son to bless their families and to relieve this pressure.

Ah Ying sighed, "At least I don't have a mother-in-law to answer to. Gee Sung's family is all in Dai Long village, in Toishan. He does have one brother, Jick Wah, in Gum Saan, but we rarely see him."

"My mother-in-law is kind," Chin Shee said. "But the family is all waiting for me to give Lun Chee a son. The two miscarriages made us both very sad, so I don't want to tell him about this baby until I am certain."

"Your secret is safe with me, Sing Yee. Here, try some soup so you can practice for your sitting month," added Ah Ying with a sly smile. "And try not washing your hair for thirty days!"

"Believe me! I know what it's like!"

CHAPTER 25

Chasing a Chinese Beauty 1891

Maggie Culbertson opened the door at the Occidental Mission Home on Sacramento Street and immediately recognized the trembling girl and her escort. She was used to greeting dirty and disheveled young slave girls at her door. This young girl was different. Her face was tear-streaked, but her pale, white alabaster skin was flawless. Her fine features and exotic beauty would clearly turn heads. Even here, in the Mission Home the other girls had whispered for days about the beautiful Chin Lan Toi after her wedding last month to Loui Mong, a Christian student from the Mission School.[63]

Chin Lan Hoi.

Turning to her escort, "Ah Kim, what is she doing back here? And where is her husband?"

"He is gone! I went with him to the docks to help him with his work interpreting for the Customs Office. The next thing I knew he jumped onboard the Oceanic bound for China as they were pulling up the gangway! He yelled at me to bring his wife here for your protection," Ng Hon Kim explained.

"What on earth is going on? Why is Ah Mong fleeing to China and leaving his new wife behind?"

Ah Kim was silent looking down at the parlor floor, unsure of how to proceed.

Finally, he softly replied, "He owed a lot of money to everyone. His boss, US Assistant DA Witter, was after him for fraudulent bail bonds he obtained to help land Chinese."

"Do you mean Chinese like his own wife?" Maggie interrupted beginning to see the picture of deception Ah Kim was painting.

"Yes, Ah Mong convinced White people like Mrs. Cook and Mr. Lake to sign for the bail bonds guaranteeing that the Chinese would show for their court hearings. The Chinese were given temporary landing status and then ...."

"And then they never showed up for the hearing and just disappeared, leaving poor Mrs. Cook and Mr. Lake stuck with a forfeited bail bond," an exasperated Maggie finished for her friend.

"Yes, but that is not the worst of it for his wife."

"What else could there possibly be? He deserted his wife, and the officers of the court are after him for thousands of dollars of forfeited bail bonds."

"Ah Lan is being sought by the Customs officers for illegal entry and by the slave owner, Yup Chun Foo. Ah Mong agreed to buy Chin Lan Toi from Yup for $2400 but never paid him a cent. Now he is fuming and wants his money or his property."

"Ah Mong told me he had settled that matter with that evil pimp, before Dr. Condit agreed to marry him and Chin Lan Toi here in the Mission Home last month!"

Ah Kim was silent, not wanting to state the obvious. His friend had lied to Ms. Culbertson.

Chin Lan Toi had arrived on the SS Gaelic on September 17, 1890. Leong Ah Sing had offered to bring her and the other girls to Gum Saan to "marry their rich Chinese merchant husbands." The Customs House officials were dubious of Chin Lan Toi's story that she was a native-born Chinese American and refused to let her land. She had watched the interpreter Loui

Mong smoothly tell them such a convincing story built entirely on lies.

"These are her parents Wong Suey and Yun Suey. They own the business at 716 Dupont Street where the girl was born in 1869. She is American-born. You must let her land immediately!" he implored

The Customs House officials twice denied her entry into Gum Saan. But the wily Mong got a lawyer, Attorney Mowry, who filed a writ of habeas corpus. They appealed to the United States Circuit Court and won her temporary release with a $1500 bail bond to insure her attendance at her court hearing.

Instead of taking her to the court hearing Leong Ah Sing immediately took Chin Lan Toi to the Queen's Room on Dupont to meet her new husband. In truth, the Queen's Room was a well-known slave auction where Chinese girls were bought and sold like commodities.

Leong Ah Sing commanded, "Take off your clothes! Hurry up! We don't have all day!"

Not waiting for Ah Lan, Leong stripped off her clothing and shoved the naked girl up onto the wooden block.

"Now try to look good for your husband and stop crying!"

Ah Lan felt her face burning as the lecherous stares of the men turned her way. She tried to cover herself. Tears streamed down her face and she began to sob uncontrollably.

Yup Chun Foo approached Ah Lan first. A highbinder's sword had years ago cleanly sliced off Yup's nose. Now, anyone who dared to stare at his disfigured face risked a similar fate in a dark Chinatown alley.

Yup circled around Ah Lan as she stood on the auction block sobbing. He saw much profit in her perfect face and young body. She would go for a good price. He had to claim her quickly, before she piqued the interest of the other slave owners. Quickly pressing the gold coins into her hands, Yup roughly pulled the girl off the block.

This one is a real prize, he thought with a lecherous smile.

"Follow me and stop sobbing! Put on your clothes!"

At Ah Yup's brothel on Sullivan Alley, Chin Lan Toi was miserable. She cried and sobbed inconsolably. The men complained about her constantly. Her pretty face was a mess and her sobbing was unrelenting.

Over the months of the hearings interpreter Loui Mong, like most men, had fallen head-over-heels in love with Ah Lan. As always, Mong had a scheme. The next week Mong came to the brothel to finish up business with Yup Chun Foo. Observing Ah Yup's exasperation with the sobbing Ah Lan, he saw his opportunity.

"I will pay you ten dollars every week to rent the girl as my slave," Mong offered Yup Chun Foo.

"Ten dollars is not enough! She is worth ten times that much!"

"Yes, but she is always crying! No man wants to put up with her constant sobbing."

Yup mumbled, "She is a pain and not very good in bed. All the men complain about her."

"I'll tell you what. I will rent her for one month. If I like her, I will pay you the full price, $2400 plus interest, to take her off your hands!"

"OK, but you better have the money in one month or I will have my highbinders give you a nose job just like mine," he sneered.

In the parlor of the Mission Home, Maggie pondered their next move. Her problem now was protecting the young girl from both the Customs agents and the ruthless Chinese slave owner.

"We can't keep her here. This is the first place they will look."

"I can take her back to 711 Commercial Street, to our store,

Kwong Lee Kee Company. We can hide her upstairs in our apartment."

"I am afraid that you and Ah Mooie are well-known as friends of the Home and one of the few Christian households in Chinatown. They will eventually think to search your apartment."

"Don't worry, Ms. Culbertson. We have many friends in the building, including one you know," Ah Kim smiled.

"Are you referring to little runaway Ah Gew?"

"Yes, how did you know she lives in our building?"

"We keep track of all of our girls, especially the ones that might need a little guidance. You never know, the Lord's hand works in mysterious ways. And by the way, how good is your letter writing? I have a plan," Maggie smiled.

At 711 Commercial Street, Ah Kim and his wife Ah Mooie led Chin Lan Toi upstairs and explained her plight to Ah Ying and Lai Wah. They immediately agreed to hide her from the Customs officers and the slave owner, Yup Chun Foo.

"Where is baby Ah Kay?" Ah Mooie asked her friend.

"She is sleeping finally," Ah Ying sighed. "Sometimes she is too fussy."

"If you ever need help or a little break, just let me know."

"Thank, Ah Mooie, but I think you have your hands full with your four children!"

"There is always room for one more. Besides, my oldest Beng is a big help. When Ah Kim is working, Beng thinks he is the little man of the house! But we should leave you now. I think Ah Kim has some letters to write," Ah Mooie finished mysteriously.

Ng Hon Kim's practiced penmanship was perfect for Maggie's scheme. Letters addressed to Special Agents Pattison and

Noyes described in detail where Chin Lan Toi was being held captive. The first letter said she was in a home for Chinese women on Church Alley. The agents and interpreter Huff immediately went to the house and searched every nook and cranny and corner of the premises but did not find Chin Lan Toi.

The next day another letter arrived claiming that the girl had been in a secret hole dug in the ground of the cellar and covered with a board, which was buried under more dirt. Further instructions stated Chin Lan Toi had been moved to a house on Sullivan alley where they could now find her. The agents rushed to the Sullivan alley house and interrogated all the residents. This time they searched the cellar, sounded the walls for false compartments, and looked for freshly dug holes, all with no results!

The subsequent letter said they had missed her again, because she had been hidden in a secret closet built into the walls. Well, this cat-and-mouse game continued for weeks keeping the frustrated agents running in circles throughout Chinatown.

Ah Kim paused before fulfilling Maggie's instructions for the next letter.

He had argued with Ms. Culbertson but to no avail.

"Surely, this letter will lead them right to us!"

"Yes, but once they search your apartment, they will never come back," Maggie explained. "Just trust me."

Ah Kim picked up his pen and created the next cryptic message. *Hong Ah Poi, 711 Commercial Street.*

The agents would not know that Hong Poi was Lai Wah's childhood name, but the letter would lead them straight away to their building. *I hope Ms. Culbertson knows what she is doing.*

The next day Beng was posted as a lookout. When he spotted Agents Pattison and Noyes coming down Commercial Street he ran inside to find his mother.

"They're coming!"

Running next door, Ah Mooie found Ah Ying in her apartment.

"Quick! Get Chin Lan Toi now!"

The three women ran up the stairs to the 3rd floor and then entered a secret stairway that led to the roof. Beng shut the secret door and covered the opening with boxes. The hidden passageway had been built for Chinese gamblers to escape the local police raids but had not been used for years. The three women huddled in a corner trying stay out of the wind whipping across the roof.

Downstairs Agents Pattison and Noyes tore apart Lai Wah's apartment, searching the rooms, closets, and even the drawers for some sign of the missing Chin Lan Toi.

"She's not in the drawer, you idiots!" Lai Wah growled. "If you damage anything I am sending the bill to your office for full payment!"

In truth, the agents had grown weary of this cat-and-mouse game. They suspected they were being played again and were tired of being made to look foolish in the newspapers. They did not really expect to find anything and left after thirty minutes of fruitless searching.

The letters continued. Next sending the agents to 613 Dupont Street where they engaged in yet another fruitless search. Eventually, their real focus became finding the author of these fraudulent letters. The handwriting was all the same with exacting and perfect penmanship. The author had wasted countless hours of their time, used up valuable city resources, and had made them look like fools! The agents fumed about being duped for some time but never did find the culprit.

It was late at night a month later when Ah Kim drove them to the docks expertly navigating the wagon through the dark cobblestone streets of Chinatown. The fog rolling in from the bay was settling on the city like a wet blanket, quickly muffling the clip clop of the horse's hooves. The excitement had passed, but Maggie Culbertson was ever cautious. Even on this final trip she continued to keep Ah Lan in careful disguise in order to avoid detection by prying eyes. Once at the Pacific Mail Docks Maggie said her final goodbye to Chin Lan Toi.

As Ah Lan prepared to board the SS City of Rio de Janeiro bound for China, Maggie pulled her close and whispered, "Stay safe in the love of our dear Jesus, Ah Lan. And don't be too hard on your husband. At least he did send money for your passage. But I will keep an eye on him just the same. Tell him that Ms. Culbertson is expecting reports of a pious and good Christian life."

CHAPTER 26

Golden Lilies in Dai Fow 1891

Ming Jung was well known in Chinatown for her skills as a foot binder. Her profession had made her a wealthy woman with an unheard-of income of over $18,000 per year. She traveled up and down the coast of California to every Chinese enclave, but she lived and spent most of her time in Dai Fow. What she offered these families was a chance for their daughters to join the elite ranks of the golden lilies, the little foot women. Such women were highly sought after by rich husbands and lived a life of luxury, clothed in the finest silk garments and adorned with expensive Chinese jewelry. If you could afford Ming Jung's services, your daughter's life would be transformed, and she could be sold for a high bride price to a willing and wealthy Chinese suitor.

Ah Ying was busy tending to baby Ah Kay when she was startled by a loud knock at the door. She looked up from her infant daughter and felt her skin prickle.

"Who could it be so late in the evening?" she wondered.

Slowly opening the wooden door, she found an old Chinese woman, barely five feet tall with leathery skin. She was wearing a tunic with bulging pockets. The old woman stood there silently, as if she had been summoned. Ah Ying studied her face for a moment before she recognized the woman, instantly realizing why she had come. The hair on the back of her neck stood on end.

"Why are you here, Ming Jung?" Ah Ying demanded.

"I have been sent by Chin Shee's mother to see your baby

girl," she replied.

"I did not send for you!"

"No, but Lai Wah agrees that it is time. We must start the foot binding ceremony before your daughter's feet start to grow, and she is already three months old."

"She is only a baby! Let her be," Ah Ying exclaimed glaring at the old woman.

"It is up to you, of course. I have plenty of other business to attend to with mothers who appreciate my skills and want the best for their daughters."

Ah Ying was now a bit less sure of herself, but she did not like this old Chinese woman.

"Isn't Ah Kay too young to start the footbinding?"

"No, she is the perfect age. My results are best when I start the molding process at infancy. Some parents delay calling me until the girl is six or seven years old. By then, the foot has already started to grow and is much harder to shape. There is only so much I can do. With an infant, I can make the perfect lily-shaped foot that will attract the very richest husband. Let me see Ah Kay's foot," ordered Ming Jung.

Ah Ying was now clutching her baby protectively, but she slowly offered her baby's foot. Ming snatched the baby's foot and removed the tiny sock Ah Kay had been wearing. She gently held the supple little foot and kneaded it in her hands. She pressed the toes under and slightly flexed the little arch.

"See, the foot is very supple and easy to shape into the perfect lily." She then pulled out a roll of white tape from her bulging pocket, explaining, "This is the bandage that I use to mold the foot. She will not feel any pain. It will be very easy for your baby, since she is so young."

Ah Ying was still unsure about this old woman, but she was comforted that Ah Kay did not seem to mind the old woman manipulating her foot.

"I will need to discuss this with my husband. When can you come back?"

"Do not take long to decide," she warned. "The good fortune

time for my foot binding ceremony will not last much longer. We must start the ceremony within this week. Next week is not good, and I cannot guarantee the results."

With that, the old woman turned and stalked away. Ah Ying watched her disappear into the fog that was settling over the Chinese enclave.

"Where is Gee Sung?" Ah Ying sighed, peering down Commercial Street towards his cigar store.

Ah Ying and Gee Sung argued for days. But in the end, Ah Ying relented and agreed to let Ming Jung return to perform the foot binding ceremony. The potential to secure her daughter a rich husband and a life of luxury won out over her concerns. But she still felt a deep sadness knowing that her daughter would for the rest of her life depend upon other women—those with natural feet, no less—to take care of her every need and whim. For the independent and strong spirited Ah Ying, this seemed like a terrible sacrifice.

Ming arrived at sunrise. Her pockets were stuffed with tape and an assortment of other supplies.

"Today we must prepare the home for the foot binding ceremony," Ming explained, as she carefully lit the incense and scattered bits of curled lucky papers around the apartment. "You must burn the incense day and night for one week and recite these incantations. The evening before the ceremony, you must double your incantations so the good spirits will smile on Ah Kay and give her the perfect tiny lotus shaped feet."

When the day of the foot binding ceremony finally arrived, Ah Ying and Gee Sung waited impatiently as Ming arranged a little wooden table and lit the last of the incense.

"Come and sit on the floor in front of me!" commanded Ming, motioning for Ah Ying to bring Ah Kay with her into the front room.

Ming placed a pair of tiny wooden shoes on the stool and

placed a sprig of the Chinese good luck plant, *hovee-sin*, into each shoe.

"The *hovee-sin* in the left shoe will bring success to our binding treatment, and that in the right shoe is to give baby Ah Kay health, happiness and a rich husband. Now sit in front of me and place the baby in your lap," instructed Ming.

Ah Ying and Ming Jung sat on the floor, their knees interlocked so that the three-month-old baby rested partly on one lap and partly on the other.

Ming took Ah Kay's tiny foot in her hand and began wrapping the strip of half-inch white tape around the ball of the foot at the point of the great toe. The tape was securely fastened and then drawn around the heel, which was pressed forward towards the hollow of the foot near the instep. The wrapping was carried forward to the toes, which were neatly tucked under close to the foot, and bound together across the ends, making a sort of roll.

Ming next bound the feet with a stout cloth, which she wrapped across the foot and again around it lengthwise. She sewed it together with a strong thread, whipping over the seams again and again. With some difficulty, Ming then forced a wooden shoe onto each foot and covered it with a bandage of richly embroidered cloth.

"You must not remove the binding. I will return every week to inspect the binding.

Now you must pay me the fee for my work today," Ming demanded with her hand outstretched.

Lai Wah reached into his pocket and fished out the small red envelope, which he placed into Ming's hand.

"It's all in there, the entire $200."

Ming took the envelope without a word and stuffed it into her pocket.

"You will need to pay me $800 more to continue to visit Ah Kay every week for the next five years," Ming explained, as she gathered up her bandages and headed out the door to her next clients.

Ah Ying held baby Ah Kay closely. Her newly bound feet looked huge in their little wooden shoes. She softly hummed the Chinese lullaby, "O Little Lotus Flower," that Chun Fah sang to the girls every night at the Mission Home. A single tear ran down her cheek.

The moon is bright, the wind is quiet,
The tree leaves hang over the window,
My little baby, go to sleep quickly,
Sleep, dreaming sweet dreams.

The moon is bright, the wind is quiet,
The cradle moving softly,
My little one, close your eyes,
Sleep, sleep, dreaming sweet dreams.

The next two weeks were agony as little Ah Kay cried incessantly. Ah Ying held her baby, rocking her gently, but was unable to console her daughter. The crying and fussing continued day and night. Lai Wah retreated to his cigar store but felt guilty for deserting his wife.

Ah Ying removed Ah Kay's blanket exposing her legs.

"Your feet will be perfect my little one, and you will find a rich husband. Now shush."

Ah Ying looked up when she heard Gee Sung returning.

"How is the baby?" he asked, his face showing no sign of hope for a favorable response.

"No better. Nothing I do seems to help. She won't stop crying!"

"Ming Jung promised that it would not hurt her because she is so young," Gee Sung replied, clearly not really believing his own words. He looked at his exhausted young wife holding the crying infant.

Suddenly, both Ah Ying and Lai Wah were startled by the silence. Ah Kay had stopped wailing. But a single tear ran down her face as she continued to cry silently.

Ah Ying looked down at her baby and began to sob as well.

"Gee Sung we must stop this."

Lai Wah took the baby from his wife, and without a word he began to unwrap the embroidered cloth, exposing the little wooden shoes.

Ah Ying took her husband's hand.

"Are you sure?" she asked, equal parts hopeful and apprehensive. "It was so much money."

"Here, you remove the shoes," instructed Lai Wah ignoring his wife's question.

Ah Ying removed the wooden shoes, exposing the mass of bandages encasing her baby's feet.

"What if it is too late? What if the bones are already broken?"

"Don't worry, Ah Ying. We have decided and now must finish this."

Ah Ying took the mass of tape encasing her daughter's foot and began to slowly unwrap the long strips. The tape was wrapped tightly, but quickly unraveled into a pile on the floor. Ah Ying exposed the final wrapping, but then paused.

"I can't bear to look, Gee Sung."

"It will be alright, Ah Ying. Would you like me to remove the last bandage?"

"No, I will do it."

Ah Ying took a breath and slowly peeled away the layer.

Ah Kay's feet were white and crushed. The skin was shriveled and wrinkled with impressions from the criss-crossing tape. The crumpled toes were still.

"We are too late!" gasped Ah Ying.

Jaw set, Lai Wah took his daughter's tiny feet and gently began to rub them, massaging the blood back into them. He worked quickly without saying a word. After several minutes, the color began to return to the little toes as they uncurled for the first time in half a month.

Ah Ying choked back a sob of relief as Ah Kay began to curl her toes and move her foot. She quickly removed the right shoe and began to unwind the tape binding. Once exposed, the right foot looked and smelled just as bad.

"Quickly Gee Sung. Fix her other foot!"

Lai Wah took his baby's shriveled right foot and repeated the process of bringing it back to life.

"This is how we treated the frost bite in the ice and snow of the mountains when we built the railroad. Every day, our hands and feet were almost frozen in the bitter cold," he explained as he worked Ah Kay's little foot back and forth.

The ghastly white color and shriveled skin magically gave way to Lai Wah's attention, revealing ten pink, wiggling toes. Baby Ah Kay smiled and cooed. It was a wondrous sound, and one that her parents had all but forgotten.

Ah Ying held her baby close, smiling at Gee Sung as he stood in the midst of a pile of bandages and two overturned wooden shoes.

Suddenly, there was a loud knocking at the door.

"Knock! Knock!"

"Oh no! It must be Ming Jung coming back to scold us for undoing her work! How did she find out so quickly?"

Lai Wah slowly opened the door, revealing two White men. One was the tallest person Lai Wah had ever seen. He wore a clergyman's coat and white collar.

"We are here to see Ah Ying and the baby," he announced.

Hearing her name, Ah Ying came to the door and peered around Gee Sung tentatively. She immediately recognized the two men from years ago.

The shorter man piped up, "I am Nathaniel Hunter from the Society for Prevention of Cruelty to Children, and this is Rev. Vrooman—"

"I know who you are. Don't you recognize me?" Ah Ying interrupted. The two men were frequent visitors at the Mission Home, and Ah Ying had seen them at the Home and at in Judge Murphy's courtroom during the hearing.

“Yes, Ah Ying we remember you,” Rev. Vrooman said, smiling. “We have been keeping an eye on you for Ms. Culbertson since you left the Mission Home last year.”

“We received reports that Ming Jung the foot binder has been here and that she has bound the feet of your baby,” Mr. Hunter interrupted glumly.

“Please tell us this isn’t true or we must take the baby away, for we cannot allow such cruelty to children,” Vrooman explained.[64]

Ah Ying smiled and let out a sigh of relief. She was undoing Ah Kay’s blanket when the men spotted the tangled pile of bandages on the floor. Ah Ying stepped forward and held out Ah Kay’s pink little feet for the two men to inspect.

“See, everything is good now,” she assured them.

The two men ignored Lai Wah, who was busy pushing the pile of discarded bandages and the little wooden shoes into the dark corner.

"I am very glad to see that," said Rev Vrooman smiling broadly. “And while we are here… there is someone else who would like to meet your baby.”

The two men stepped aside, revealing Miss Cable and Sue Lee, and both women rushed forward immediately.

“Ah Ying! She is perfect! What a beautiful baby girl,” Sue Lee exclaimed as she hugged her long lost best friend.

Sue Lee! I thought I would never get to see you again!”

“Me too! But they brought me along to talk some sense into you. So many people saw that evil Ming Jung woman come to visit you. We were all afraid of what she must have done to your baby!”

Ah Ying smiled and could not stop looking at Sue Lee, whose friendship she missed so dearly. But she forced herself to look at Miss Cable and said “I did not think you or Miss Culbertson would want to see me again after I ran away from The Home.”

Miss Cable smiled and gently placed her hand on Ah Ying’s shoulder, replying “My dear Ah Gew, you will always be part of our Mission Home family and God's family. We pray for you every night."

Ah Ying felt her face flush but was silent. Then, remembering her manners, she quickly added, "Please come in. Our home is a mess but you, my friends, are always welcome."

She stepped aside as her guests entered their small apartment. Lai Wah who was finished pushing the bandages into the corner joined them in the living room as Ah Ying seated her guests on the wooden chairs. The six of them spent the afternoon catching up and reminiscing.

"Ah Gew, I mean Ah Ying, we want you to come back to the Mission Home to teach the younger girls to sew. You were always the best with a needle and thread, and when you are ready you can become an assistant teacher at The Home," suggested Miss Cable.

Ah Ying was surprised, and she replied, "I can't believe you want me to come back after all the trouble I caused you by running away, and the court hearing, and everything else!"

"Well, my dear. We have not given up on you and we could use your skills to teach the younger girls."

"Yes, Ah Ying! Please come back. All the older girls miss you and you would be a good teacher now that you don't have to worry about planning your next escape," Sue Lee added with a sly smile.

As the evening sun set over *Tong Yan Gai*, Ah Ying held her baby and felt truly happy, basking in the warm friendship of her guests from another, very different world.

[65]

CHAPTER 27

Rescue in Southern California March 6, 1892

Maggie Culbertson felt her pulse quicken as she gazed out the train window and saw the lights of Los Angeles against the darkening evening sky. The two-day train trip from San Francisco to Los Angeles was taxing under the best of circumstances. Maggie was glad that she had brought along Chun Fah to keep her company and to assist her in the rescue. Unlike rescues of slave girls in San Francisco, this time she would not have the cooperation of the local police. Maggie had no idea what to expect.

"By the grace of our heavenly father, we will prevail," she whispered.

Her pocket watch showed 9 p.m. It was March 6, 1892.

"Who are we going to rescue?" Chun Fah asked interrupting Maggie's thoughts.

"Her name is Ah T'sun. She is a bit younger than you. A year ago, she was sold in San Francisco for $2,000 to a Chinese named Ah Gow, who brought her to Los Angeles for illicit purposes."

The story was all too familiar to Maggie. Ah Gow beat Ah T'sun repeatedly and forced her to be a *baak haak chai* a hundred man's wife. Ah T'sun had sent word to friends pleading to be delivered from her abusive and shameful life.

The Southern Pacific train slowed as it passed through the orange groves that surrounded the Arcade Station at Fourth and Alameda Streets. Built in 1888 the massive wooden Victorian building and train shed had a roof that soared 90 feet above the platform. A fully-grown Washington fan palm welcomed arrivals to the subtropical paradise of Los Angeles.

Maggie Culbertson and Chun Fah gathered their bags and stepped down the three steps onto the wooden train platform.

"How will we find Ah T'sun?"

"She is being brought by our friends from the Presbyterian church here in Los Angeles. That is if everything has gone according to plan," Maggie explained hoping that they had successfully rescued the girl from the brothel and spirited her away without being accosted by her evil Chinese owner or the police."

Chun Fah looked out across the train yard worrying about how they would find Ah T'sun.

"What does she look like?"

"I really don't know. Hopefully, the missionaries will recognize us."

Almost on cue a horse-drawn carriage raced up to the depot stopping suddenly a few yards away. Two men jumped off the carriage before it came to a complete stop.

"Miss Culbertson! Come this way!" the taller man waved to Maggie and Chun Fah.

As they hurried towards the carriage, a woman dressed in a black dress and bonnet stepped out of the carriage holding the hand of a small girl.

Without a word Maggie took the girl's hand and pulled her trembling body close. Ah T'sun pulled away.

"No! No!" Ah T'sun cried out with tears streaming down her face.

Chun Fah stepped forward and spoke softly to the young girl in Cantonese.

"Ah T'sun, we are your friends. Don't worry, we are here to help you escape. Come. My sisters are waiting for you at our home in Dai Fow."

Chun Fah took Ah T'sun's hand comforting the frightened girl and whispering to her quietly out of earshot of the others.

The two girls continued to speak quietly as Ah T'sun calmed down and looked back at Maggie Culbertson.

"She is our mother and protects us all from harm. Miss Culbertson will give you a home and a new big family in Dai Fow."

The tall man approached Maggie.

"I am Reverend Jones, Miss Culbertson. It is an honor to meet you, but you must hurry. The local Sheriff is a man named Rogers, who is paid off by the Chinese. He is right behind us. If he catches us, we are all going to jail, and that poor girl will fall back into the clutches of the evil Ah Gow!"

Maggie thanked Reverend Jones for his assistance and looked down the tracks spotting the 10 p.m. Northbound Southern Pacific train approaching the station.

"Chun Fah! Hurry! Bring Ah T'sun and help me get her onto the train!"

The two girls followed Maggie up the steps onto the waiting train. Halfway up the steps Chun Fah stopped to look ahead towards the locomotive.

"Ah T'sun look at the smoking dragon!"

[66]

Both girls paused to gaze at the smoking and hissing black

locomotive.

"Hurry girls! Get inside before we're spotted!"

Maggie waved to Reverend Jones and the others as they spirited their carriage away from the station before the Sheriff arrived.

The three walked down the narrow aisle towards the back of the train. When they came to an empty car Maggie found a seat and motioned for the girls to take the seats across the aisle from her. She was not going to let the girls out of her sight.

Chun Fah and Ah T'sun whispered non-stop as they pointed out the window at the passing Southern California scenery. The train slowed as it climbed into the hills north of Los Angeles. It grew darker, and they left the lights of the city behind until there was nothing left to see.

Suddenly, it was pitch black. Ah T-sun sat bolt upright, "What's happening? We must have run off the tracks and into a cave! Stop the train before we crash!"

Chun Fah pulled her new friend close, "Don't worry Ah T'sun. We are in a tunnel that goes through the mountain. Chinese workers built his tunnel years ago. It took them over a year to complete because it's more than a mile long!"[67]

"That's right, Ah T'sun. Over 1,000 of your countrymen built this tunnel with hand tools and blasting powder. It is an engineering marvel. In fact it was not long after many of those same men completed the western section of the Transcontinental Railroad in 1869," Maggie added.

The train eventually came out the other end of the tunnel and continued on towards the Tehachapi Mountains and the Central Valley beyond. The girls were finally silent. They were exhausted from the day's events and the rhythmic movement of the train was making them drowsy. They both finally nodded off and slept head to shoulder.

---

[68]

Maggie Culbertson smiled to herself. *I am so glad I thought to*

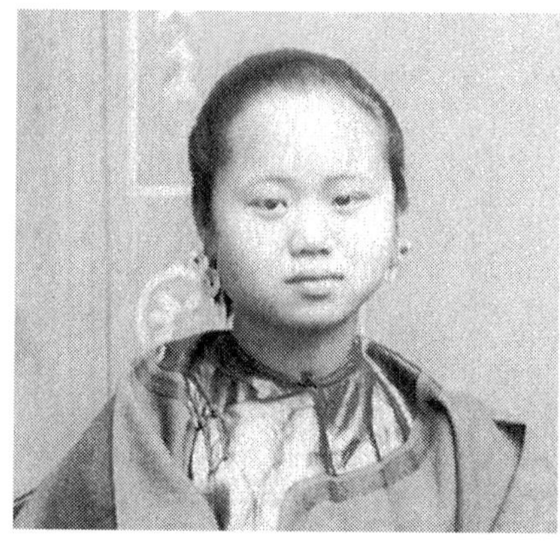

bring Chun Fah. She is the perfect companion for little Ah T'sun.

In truth, Chun Fah was like a real daughter to Maggie. Chun Fah had been with her in the Mission Home since she was five years old and had always been the light of the Home. She was indispensable as her interpreter doing battle in the courts to protect her girls. But it was her devotion to our Savior and her piety that made her a role model for all the girls. Maggie knew that Chun Fah's days at the Mission Home were numbered. She was engaged to Ng Poon Chew[69] a fine Christian man studying at the seminary in San Anselmo. The two were to be wed in May.

I am going to miss you dearly, my Spring Blossom.

As the train passed over the Tehachapi Mountains and began its descent to the San Joaquin valley below, it entered a long slow spiral known as the Tehachapi Loop. The 28-mile spiral controlled the descent to a manageable 2.2% and was a marvel of engineering. It had been constructed by over 3,000 Chinese workers in 1876 who used hand tools and blasting powder to create the 18 tunnels, 10 bridges, and 28 miles of track in less than two years.

Realizing that she had a mission to complete Maggie kept her eye out for trouble at every stop, fearing that some over-eager lawman would take them away in shackles! Maggie whispered a prayer.

"Dear God, please help me to deliver this innocent young girl back to the safety of your Mission Home."

Finally, she too fell into a light sleep as the train headed up the Central Valley on its way back to San Francisco. Maggie awoke with a start and realized that the train had stopped. Someone was shaking her.

"It's her! It's Culbertson! Where is the girl! You are in a lot of trouble for aiding a fugitive from the law!"

Maggie rubbed the sleep out of her eyes peering sleepily at the two men in uniform standing over her.

"Is this some kind of a joke? I have done nothing wrong!"

Maggie quickly looked across the aisle for Chun Fah and Ah T'sun. Their seats were empty. She turned and saw them hiding in the shadows in the back of the car.

They must have seen the police boarding the train, she thought.

"Are you Margaret Culbertson?" demanded the short policeman.

"Yes. You seem to know all about me! Who are you, and why are you molesting me?"

"We received a telegram from Sheriff Rogers in Los Angeles. The Chinese girl who is with you is wanted for grand larceny!"

"There has been some mistake. I am a good citizen of San Francisco just passing through your town. I know nothing about a Chinese girl. Now let me be so I can continue my journey."

"Where is the Chinese girl?"

"I have no idea what you are talking about. I am traveling alone. You can see for yourself. There is no one else with me!"

The officers looked at the other empty seats in the car and began to confer about what to do next.

While the policemen were busy Maggie motioned to Chun Fah and pointed at the train's exit.

From the back of the train Chun Fah slowly moved with Ah T'sun towards the exit and was about to slip out the door onto the platform when she heard the policeman call out, "Stop you two or I will shoot!"

The girls froze in mid step but did not turn around. They heard the footsteps of the men running down the aisle towards them. In the next instant the police roughly grabbed the girls and placed them both in handcuffs. The two policemen escorted the girls off the train with Maggie Culbertson trailing right behind.

"Where are you taking them?" she demanded.

"To the police headquarters where we will wait for Ah T'sun's husband to arrive."

[70]

"Husband! You idiots! Ah Gow is a despicable pimp! He is the lowest scum to walk this earth! And you are playing right into his hands, if you turn over this innocent girl to that monster!"

They ignored Maggie's impassioned pleas and continued to walk up Tulare Street away from the new red brick train station.

Maggie turned back towards the train and was about to return for their bags when she spotted a Chinese woman running towards her waving frantically.

"Miss Culbertson!"

When the woman caught up to her she was panting and trying to catch her breath. Maggie looked at her more closely and then broke into a relieved smile when she recognized one of her original ten girls from the early days of the Mission Home.

[71]

"Ah Mooie! My dear what are you doing here in Fresno?"

"My husband and I left Dai Fow, and we are now moving from Santa Barbara to Bakersfield to start a church. We heard about your troubles. Miss Cable sent us a telegram describing your rescue of Ah T'sun and Sheriff Rogers pursuing her with charges of grand larceny! We thought you could use our help, so we have been waiting here for the train to arrive."

"And I am so glad that you did, Ah Mooie! Where is your husband Ng Hon Kim?"

"He is with me, but right now he is headed for the court house. We must free Ah T'sun and Chun Fah. Don't worry, Ng Hon Kim has many important friends here in the Central Valley. Judge Harris is his good friend. I am certain he will help us!"

Maggie and Ah Mooie made their way to the courthouse and found Ng Hon Kim in Judge Harris' chambers. The men were inspecting a copy of the writ of habeas corpus sworn out to retrieve Ah T'sun from Margaret Culbertson.

"See! Just as I thought! They misspelled her name and used the wrong date! This warrant is invalid!" said Judge Harris with a smile. "I will invalidate this warrant and order them to release Ah T'sun into your custody. You will be free to take Ah T'sun wherever you please."

Ah Mooie and Miss Culbertson smiled from ear to ear as they inspected the flawed warrant.

"Judge Harris and Mr. Kim, thank you for your intervention! We are all indebted to your kindness!"

The two women and Ng Hon Kim hurried on to the police station where they presented Judge Harris' ruling.

The police inspected the writ of habeas corpus and were embarrassed by the obvious and simple error that had invalidated the warrant.

"Alright, Jones. Release the girls. We cannot detain them or Judge Harris will haul us before the court on charges of false arrest and imprisonment."

Back at the train depot Maggie and Ah Mooie were arguing about the next train to catch.

"The next train to San Francisco doesn't leave for several hours," Maggie lamented.

"You don't want to go on the train to San Francisco," Ah Mooie offered.

"Really? That's where the Mission Home is located. You remember, Ah Mooie. It has been a few years since you lived at the Home, but it is still at 933 Sacramento Street."

Ah Mooie smiled. "They won't give up Miss Culbertson. These agents will be waiting to arrest you and Ah T'sun when you arrive at the train station in San Francisco. Believe me, they won't make the same mistake on the next warrant."

"Then what do you suggest?" Maggie asked.

"Catch the next train to Sacramento instead. They will never think to look for you on that train. We can purchase your tickets all the way to Sacramento. But get off the train in Tracy. We will have someone waiting for you in Tracy who will secretly take you on to Dai Fow."

"Brilliant, Ah Mooie! I don't know how we can ever thank you."

"No thanks are necessary! Believe me. Any of your girls would do this for you, Miss Culbertson."

Chun Fah embraced her older sister Ah Mooie as the girls boarded the train with Miss Culbertson.

Once safely on the train to Sacramento Maggie and the girls took seats in their private compartment. Ah Mooie had insisted that a private compartment was best to avoid prying eyes. Looking out the window she was admiring the striking red brick depot with its black slate roof when she spotted Ah

Mooie waving at her.

Farewell, my dear Ah Mooie.

The remainder of the trip was exactly as Ah Mooie had planned. As far as the conductor knew, they were traveling to Sacramento. They secretly exited the train at Tracy and were met by friends who arranged for their passage back to San Francisco.

By the time they arrived at the at the San Francisco train depot at Townsend and 3rd, Chun Fah and Ah T'sun were good friends returning from an adventure.

"Miss Culbertson, we have to hide Ah T'sun. We can't take her back to The Home. The police will be waiting for us and will take my little sister back to her owner."

Maggie had been worrying about the same thing. Chun Fah was correct. They could not take Ah T'sun back to the Mission Home and any of the Christian homes of her girls here in San Francisco were off limits since the police knew them all.

"I have an idea! Follow me," Chun Fah instructed, as she led them up 3rd Street back into Chinatown.

CHAPTER 28

Hidden in Plain View

The knock at the front door startled Gee Sung who was worrying about the fires that had been occurring nightly in *Tong Yan Gai*. He slowly opened the door expecting trouble. One look at the woman was all it took.

"What are you doing here?" he demanded. "You cannot have my Ah Ying! The Judge set her free! Go away!" Gee Sung shouted, as he started to close the door.

"Lai Wah! Wait! This girl needs your help! Please, get Ah Ying," Miss Culbertson pleaded.

Maggie stepped aside as Chun Fah gently pushed Ah T'sun forward. Her head was bowed, as she was afraid to look at the towering Chinese.

"Please! You can't turn her away," Chun Fah pleaded.

Gee Sung silently looked at the meek Ah T'sun and slowly opened the door. "Come inside."

Inside Maggie explained their plight, "This poor child needs our help. We rescued her from a brothel in Los Angeles and have traveled all night by train and coach. The Sheriff is pursuing us with trumped up charges of grand larceny! They arrested her in Fresno, but we got away with the help of a friendly judge. Now they are hot on our heels and determined to get their evil hands on Ah T'sun!"

Ah Ying appeared carrying her infant son Bing.

"Gee Sung! Let my friends in! Miss Culbertson! I never expected to see you at my home!"

"My dear, Ah Gew, I mean Ah Ying! We need your help!"

"Of course. I heard your story. Please come in and have a seat," Ah Ying ushered her guests into her home.

Ah Ying spotted her friend Chun Fah and let out a joyous laugh, "Chun Fah, my sister! Oh, how I have missed you!"

The two sisters embraced as Maggie and Lai Wah smiled.

"Let me see your son, Ah Ying! Can I carry him?"

Ah Ying gently placed Bing into her sister's arms, "I hear that soon you will be married and will start your own family."

Chun Fah smiled as she held and gently cradled Bing rocking him back and forth. She softly sang the songs of their childhood.

The moon is bright, the wind is quiet,
The tree leaves hang over the window,
My little baby, go to sleep quickly,
Sleep, dreaming sweet dreams.

"Oh, Chun Fah! How I have missed your singing us to sleep at night!"

Maggie smiled seeing the love between her two girls, Chun Fah and Ah Gew. The two would leave the Home on very different terms, but the bond between these sisters was unbreakable and had nothing to do with religion.

"Ah Ying, we need you to hide Ah T'sun for a while. The police are searching everywhere for her and will take her back to her life of slavery in Los Angeles!"

"We can't take her to the Mission Home because I am certain the authorities are lying in wait," Maggie Culbertson added.

"Of course, we will hide her," Ah Ying reassured Miss Culbertson.

"Don't worry. I know just the person to help us keep her hidden," Lai Wah offered.

Later that morning Gee Sung led Ah Ying and Ah T'sun to Ho Boon Gai back to where they had met years ago. Ah Ying smiled remembering their first meeting in this very alley.

"You were young and fearless, Ah Ying," Gee Sung recalled smiling at his wife.

"But how will this place help us to hide Ah T'sun? She can't stay here."

"Just wait and hear out my idea," Gee Sung replied leading them into the barbershop.

Lai Wah approached his barber Ah Sun and explained what he wanted. The two men turned around as Lai Wah pointed at Ah T'sun. Ah Sun nodded and motioned for Ah Ying to bring the girl forward.

"Here little one. Sit on this stool and hold still."

Ah T'sun sat but was trembling.

"What is he going to do? Don't let him hurt me," she pleaded to Ah Ying.

Ah Sun picked up his razor and approached the girl. Ah T'sun pulled away.

"No! Don't hurt me!"

Understanding Gee Sung's plan Ah Ying held Ah T'sun and comforted her, "It's alright, Ah T'sun. I won't let him hurt you. Ah Sun will help us hide you."

Ah Sun gently shaved Ah T'sun's forehead and then brought out a long queue made from hair saved from his customers. He attached the queue to the back of Ah T'sun's hair and then stepped back to inspect his handiwork.

"Not bad! But we need some different clothes."

Ah Sun went into the backroom and returned with a mandarin jacket, black pants, and skullcap.

"These are my son's. Too small for him now, but perfect for you!"

Ah Ying helped Ah T'sun to dress and then presented her to the waiting men. The transformation was complete and pretty convincing.

"Meet my new son, Gum Dew." Ah Ying beamed.

Gee Sung and Ah Sun and the other customers inspected the disguise and nodded their approval.

"Not bad! Now you need to walk and act like a ten-year-old boy!" Ah Sun added.

"I think he needs some dirt and grime to make the transformation complete," Lai Wah observed.

As they exited the barbershop, Ah Ying turned to the right and headed up Sacramento Street to the Mission Home. She knew every store and street corner and had been coming back to the Home to teach sewing. As they walked, Lai Wah tried to show Ah T'sun how to walk like a boy. Gum Dew awkwardly copied Lai Wah's movements.

"Not too bad. It's OK to run and jump and hop off curbs."

Enjoying her newfound freedom Gum Dew followed Lai Wah's lead and ran a few strides up the street.

They arrived at 933 Sacramento on the left side of the street and ascended the ten steps to the front door, and Ah Ying rang the doorbell.

The door monitor opened the door and peered at the three guests. Ah Ying was disappointed that she did not recognize the inmate.

"Can I help you?"

"We are here to see Miss Culbertson," Ah Ying explained.

"Who should I say is calling?"

"Tell her that Ah Gew, Lai Wah, and their son Gum Dew are visiting."

When Maggie came downstairs she had a puzzled look. "I did not expect to see you at the Home, and what did you do with Ah T'sun?"

"Let me introduce my son Gum Dew."

Ah Ying stepped aside revealing the transformation.

Maggie laughed admiring their handiwork, "Pretty convincing!"

Just then there was a vigorous ringing of the doorbell!

Slowly opening the door, the monitor was immediately pushed aside by two police officers brusquely entering the Home.

Maggie's surprise was quickly replaced by a determined frozen expression as she led them into the parlor and quietly waited for the men to explain their errand.

"I am Detective Glennon, and this is Detective Cox, and this is Sheriff Rogers from Los Angeles."

"We are here for the girl," Sheriff Rogers interrupted. "Where is she? We need to take her into our custody at once and return her to Los Angeles to stand trial."

"She isn't here Mr. Glennon," Miss Culbertson replied tersely.

The men were clearly not surprised but were unsure of their next move.

Maggie interrupted their whispering, "What are the charges against this girl?"

Deputy Rogers replied, "She is charged with larceny by her owner, Ah Gow. She stole a pair of diamond earrings, a pair of gold bracelets, and a diamond ring."

"Oh, yes," responded Miss Culbertson. "It's the same old story!"

"It is our duty to search the house."

He went out the front door and returned with a burly Chinese man.

"This is Ah Gimm. He knew Ah T'sun in Los Angeles and will help to identify the girl."

"Be my guest!" Maggie replied coolly stepping aside so the men could ascend the stairs and begin their inspection.

Ah Ying had shrunk to the back of the room holding Gum Dew's hand. She couldn't believe their bad timing.

"Gee Sung! What should we do?"

Lai Wah pulled his wife and Gum Dew forward and whispered, "Don't hide. Let them see our son."

The three police officers and Ah Gimm circled the room inspecting the girls who had crowded into the room to see what the commotion was about.

As they passed, Ah Gimm paused reaching out to Gum Dew, "Who are you? There are no boys living here."

Lai Wah stepped forward grabbing Ah Gimm's wrist and twisting his arm backwards.

"If you touch my son, I will take your head off! We are guests in this home. You insult my family and you will answer to me and the Bing Kong Tong!"

The room was silent as everyone froze looking at the ferocious Lai Wah towering over Ah Gimm.

Clearly taken aback Ah Gimm pulled his wrist free and hurried through the rest of the room and then headed upstairs to the bedrooms.

"Hurry let's leave, Gee Sung, before they return."

"No. Stay here. That Ah Gimm is watching to see what we do."

A few minutes later the three police officers and Ah Gimm returned downstairs.

"She no here!" Ah Gimm announced.

"Of course, she is not here! Now leave us so we can continue with our evening service," Miss Culbertson replied showing the men to the door.

After they were gone the girls crowded around Ah Ying and Ah T'sun inspecting the disguise. Each wanted to check out her queue to see if it was real.

"Does it hurt if I pull on it?"

"How is it attached to your head?"

"Do you wear it at night?"

"Please girls, let Ah T'sun, I mean Gum Dew have some peace," Maggie said trying to shield the newest member of The Home from the inquisitive prodding of her family.

Turning to Ah Ying, "I think it is best if Gum Dew stays with you for a while until all this attention dies down."

Ah Ying nodded in agreement thinking, *It will be fun to have another woman in the house.*

As they were leaving, Miss Culbertson touched Lai Wah's sleeve, "Thank you, Gee Sung, for protecting Ah Ying's sister."

Lai Wah said nothing but smiled as they walked back down Sacramento to their home in Chinatown.

Sheriff Rogers and Ah Gimm continued their relentless search for Ah T'sun. Picking up the story a reporter for the San Francisco Call stopped by the next day to interview Miss Culbertson.

"That Chinese, Ah Gimm, claims he knows exactly where Ah T'sun is being hidden and that he can deliver her at any time. What do you have to say about that?"

"I don't believe a word he says. They always commence their attacks on us in just this manner, but when it comes to the test they fall short. I don't believe this man or any other Chinese knows where Ah T'sun is. I have taken good care to put her out of harm's way. They will proceed against me, of course, with a writ of habeas corpus, but it will do them no good. I don't believe they can compel me to tell where she is. It is enough that she is not in my keeping or custody. I expect to be served with the writ tomorrow."

Eventually, the interest in Ah T'sun subsided, and she was able to join her family at the Mission Home. She quickly became part of the family and lived with Miss Culbertson and the girls for several years. Although she never again needed the disguise, she always kept her queue and boy's clothing in the bottom of her chest just in case. Ah T'sun and Ah Ying remained good friends and sisters for many years and often retold the story of how Ah T'sun was transformed into a boy and was hidden in plain view.[72]

CHAPTER 29

Chinese Cigars April 1893

In 1859, Herman Englebrecht and H.L. Levy needed more workers to expand their small San Francisco cigar company. But most of the labor force had succumbed to the lure of the Gold Rush, leaving only 21 skilled cigar rollers in the entire city. Chinese labor—cheap and locally available—seemed like the perfect answer.

They posted help wanted signs throughout Chinatown, promising to teach a valuable new trade to new hires. Of the hundreds of Chinese who lined up outside their factory, Englebrecht & Levy selected 200. And despite the outrage of the local Segar Maker's Association, who opposed their breaking the traditional racial hiring barriers, Englebrecht and Levy taught the secrets of cigar making to the eager Chinese.

But what had seemed like a brilliant experiment to tap a new labor force instead unleashed a tidal wave of unwanted competition as these workers took their new knowledge of the industry and struck out on their own. A one-man cigar factory could be set up for only five dollars. A cigar store with twenty to thirty rollers could be set up for a little as three hundred dollars. A typical Chinese cigar store and factory could employ fifty workers. Soon, half of the four-dozen cigar factories in San Francisco were owned and operated by Chinese.

In the early 1870s, many of the 12,000 Chinese workers from the completed Transcontinental Railroad were making their way back to California in search of new opportunities for employment. Making cigars seemed like child's play to these men, who had survived the rigorous and dangerous work of building a railroad through some of the harshest landscape in North America. Within a few years, the Chinese were responsible for eighty percent of the cigars rolled west of the Rockies.

Lai Wah was in one of his rare thoughtful moments, in which he was willing to talk about his past. After putting three-year-old Ah Kay and one-year-old Bing to bed, he and Ah Ying were finally able to relax.

"Tell me how you came back to Dai Fow after you finished working on that railroad."

Lai Wah gazed out the window with a faraway look that took him back to his earlier life, and recounted, "My brother, Jick Wah, and I were sitting around camp at Promontory trying to figure out our next move. Jick Wah had heard talk of new opportunities in a place called Montana. I remember that conversation like it was yesterday."

'Jick, why do you want to go up there? Haven't you had enough of the snow and cold weather?' I asked him in disbelief when he told me about his plans.

'A man can make a lot of money up there from the miners. I can open a store or Chinese restaurant in a town called Kalispell. Our cousin opened up the Bong Tong Restaurant last year and says business is booming! Besides, it's too far to walk back to Dai Fow! My feet are tired, Lai Wah,' Jick Wah laughed and gave me a slap on the back.

'I have had enough of the cold weather and small towns, Jick Wah. Dai Fow and big city living are for me. There are plenty of jobs making cigars and shoes. No more hard labor with picks and blasting powder!' "

"For the first time in our lives we went our separate ways. I was 19 and Jick Wah was 21. It took me two years to walk back to San Francisco! I finally made it back in 1871. I got a job at Wee See Tong cigar factory on Jackson Street not far from where you lived," Lai Wah recalled.

"Ten years later there were 7,000 Chinese cigar rollers in Dai Fow. We were making over 100 million cigars that were shipped all over the world! Those were the days!" exclaimed Gee Sung proudly.

"What happened to all those men? There are only a handful of Chinese cigar stores left," commented Ah Ying.

"That's right, Ah Ying. Today there are less than 1,000 Chinese making cigars. In the early days I could make good money nine dollars per week making sixty cents for every 100 cigars. We had 34 men who each made about 150 cigars every day. When we got the cigar molds our factory really took off! But I soon figured out that the owners of the factory were making the real money. The poorest cigars sold for $16 per thousand and our best cigars sold for $60 a thousand. The White cigar makers pronounced them as good as those made by White men for $90 per thousand. Our cigars were a bargain!"

"I worked at other cigar factories like the Hong Sing Cigar Factory[73] on Sacramento Street near where you lived with the Missionary ladies."

"We had to go out on strike many times to demand better prices for our cigars from the White merchants. That was the beginning of the end. The White Cigar Union started a campaign to drive out the Chinese competition. And then there were those horrible blood feuds between the rival Chinese cigar makers!"

Suddenly, shouting from outside interrupted his thoughts. Lai Wah's eyes grew wide, and he jumped up when he heard the bells calling the fire brigade.

"Oh, no! It can't be another fire!"

A rash of suspicious fires had burned down many Chinese businesses in Chinatown. As usual, there was lots of finger pointing. The Chinese all suspected arson perpetrated by the White business owners trying to drive out the Chinese.

Without another word Lai Wah ran out the door, down the

stairs and then down Commercial Street towards his cigar store. As he approached 635 Commercial, he found his store in flames.

"Aiyaah! Who did this? I will find him and tear out his liver!" cried Lai Wah.

He tried to enter his store, but the flames were too intense. The smoke burned his eyes and choked his lungs. He felt his arm being pulled back.

"Gee Sung, don't go in there!"

Lai Wah turned around and found that Ah Ying had followed him from their apartment.

"We need you alive, Gee Sung. We can rebuild your store. Let it go."

Lai Wah looked on in dismay as his livelihood went up in flames. It took several hours for the fire company to extinguish the fire that night. In truth, they just let it burn out. It was nearly a total loss. The fire gutted the building and destroyed his inventory of cigars.

An exploding coal oil lamp had caused the fire. Captain Comstock of the fire patrol later found a desk saturated with coal oil. Two men were seen leaving the building just before the flames appeared. That night two other Chinese factories were burned down as well.

"We lost $1200 in cigars, Ah Ying!"

"Don't worry. You have insurance and we can all help you to rebuild the store and factory. Remember, my Gee Sung, we never give in. We never quit!"

After a long night, they walked back to their apartment in silence. The smell of smoke still filled the night air. In spite of his wife's encouragement, Lai Wah felt the darkness overcoming him. How could he support his family and rebuild his business by himself? It was too much for one man.

The next afternoon Lai Wah heard a knock at the door. Outside he found nearly 100 Chinese gathered together. Each came forward in turn, offering Lai Wah and Ah Ying food and money. Uncle Chan brought them dinner from the Hang Far

Low restaurant on Dupont.

"My Ah Ying, don't despair. Your friends will help you and Lai Wah to rebuild."

Chin Wah stepped forward and placed three cigar molds on the pile.

"These are from the Ping Song Tong Cigar Maker's Society. We must stick together, Lai Wah."

Lai Wah and Ah Ying were speechless as their friends and neighbors came forward offering their support and leaving behind a mound of food and gifts.

The job of rebuilding was a difficult one, but it was no match for the resilience that bound the community together. Within four months Lai Wah was back in business. It took a while to build back the previous volume of cigar production, but with his friends' help Lai Wah recovered. They never did find the persons responsible for the fire, but Lai Wah never stopped searching. [74]

CHAPTER 30

Dog Tags and Vigilantes in Chinatown 1893

Lai Wah felt the anger roiling up inside of him as he stared at his hands in the darkened room of their apartment.

"These hands built their railroad and now they treat me like a dog! I will never register for their dog tag! I have been in the country for thirty years and can never vote, but I will not submit to this humiliation!"

Ah Ying gazed at her proud husband and worried about the cost of his pride.

"If you do not register, they will deport you, Gee Sung."

"Let them try!" Lai Wah roared. "Besides, what is left here? So many of our friends have already left and gone home to China. Almost half the businesses in Chinatown are vacant or about to close. Their exclusion act is killing us slowly. The White devils wanted us gone, and now it looks like they are getting their way!"

"We can't leave, Gee Sung," Ah Ying replied softly. "Our life is here. Our two children were born in America. What would we do in China? This is our home."

Lai Wah finally looked up at his wife and saw the single tear on her cheek. Immediately feeling ashamed he replied, "I am sorry, Ah Ying. Of course, we can't leave. But staying here won't be easy."

Ah Ying wiped the tear from her eye and smiled, "We will not give in, Gee Sung."

Lai Wah pulled Ah Ying close and rubbed the spot on her

back where he knew she carried the scar from her childhood.

"You are the strong one in this family, Ah Ying."

Ah Ying looked up at her husband and smiled, "The children are with Sing Yee and Lun Chee tonight. Let's go out for a walk in the evening air."

Lai Wah frowned thinking about the White mobs he had seen with warrants to arrest unregistered Chinese without identity cards.

"We must be careful, Ah Ying. I think those men will return and cause more trouble."

"Don't worry so much, Gee Sung. Besides, don't you remember how I outran the Hop Sing highbinders?"

Lai Wah sighed and then smiled at the memory of his little Ah Ying outrunning and outwitting the highbinders.

"OK. But let's just go out for a short walk and then go to fetch Kay and Bing from Sing Yee."

Ah Ying already had her coat in hand and was headed out the front door and down the steps. She looked across the street and saw the kerosene lantern burning at the Six Companies headquarters at 728 Commercial Street.

"Come on, Gee Sung. Let's walk down Kearny towards Portsmouth Square."

She spotted King Owyang, the Chinese Counsel General, leaving the office of the Chinese Six Companies.

"Good evening, Lai Wah. Hello, Ah Ying. It is pretty late to be on the street. What brings you out?"

"We are going for a stroll and then heading over to Dupont to pick up Kay and Bing from our friends' apartment in the Spanish Building," Ah Ying explained while putting on her coat.

"Be careful tonight. I know you probably did not register. We are all in violation of the Geary Act. There are White men looking for Chinese to arrest. They are self-appointed vigilantes with trumped up arrest warrants. We were just discussing this danger at the Six Companies meeting tonight."

"What is your opinion of this Geary Bill[75], Mr. Owyang?" Ah

Ying asked.

Without hesitation Counsel Owyang replied," The Geary bill means that the Chinese are placed on the same level as a dog. If you have a dog, you buy a license tag and fasten it to the dog's collar. The number on the dog's tag is its immunity from arrest and impoundment. Under the Geary bill, the Chinese must carry their number in their pocket and anyone who so desires may stop them and demand to see their tag. Any unregistered Chinese without a tag will be served with an arrest warrant and deported."

"Please don't get Lai Wah started again," Ah Ying pleaded.

Unable to contain his anger Lai Wah sputtered, "Those White devils are meeting all over the city stirring up trouble against the Chinese! They are the self-appointed enforcers of this evil law. I saw them yesterday with the US Marshall at the Shot Tower[76] over on 1st Street threatening innocent Chinese with their arrest warrants. They hauled five Chinese away in the Police Wagon while the crowds cheered!"

UNREGISTERED CHINESE ON THEIR WAY TO PRISON.

[77]

"Yes, they call themselves the Anti-Chinese Law and Order League, but they are nothing more than sand lot agitators trying to whip San Franciscans into a frenzy of hatred against us." King replied. "They already have 20,000 members in this city alone. It is that evil Denis Kearney from the Workingman's Party spreading his hatred propaganda all over again. They are using this Geary Bill to pursue their racist agenda. Their slogan is 'The Chinese Must Go'."

"I will never register and will never carry their dog tag!" Lai Wah exploded. "They can try to arrest me, but they had better come with more than a piece of paper, and they had better be ready for a fight!"

"You are in good company, Lai Wah. Very few Chinese have registered.[78] The May 5th deadline has already passed but so far IRS collector Quinn has been sitting idle waiting to register the Chinese at his office. He threatened to hire 180 US Marshalls to go door-to-door throughout Chinatown to hunt down unregistered Chinese like animals and then deport them all back to China!"

"Well, the Chinese Six Companies has told all Chinese to resist and not register, and so far that is exactly what we are all doing," Ah Ying declared proudly.

"Yes, they hired my attorney Thomas Riordan to represent the Chinese against the government to show that the Geary Act is unconstitutional," Lai Wah added.

"They may have to go all the way to the Supreme Court to make their case. But the real dangers for us Chinese are these vigilantes and their mob violence. In the Central Valley a mob of White fanatics drove the Chinese out of Fresno and Selma and burned down their homes!" King sputtered in disgust.

"And it's no better in Southern California," he continued. "In San Bernardino White rioters with guns threatened to drive out 200 Chinese from Redlands, giving them 48 hours to leave. The Chinese barricaded themselves in their homes with shotguns and revolvers for protection. Even the National Guard may not be able to keep the peace"

"Tensions are going to explode, and we are right in the middle of it all," Lai Wah growled.

Remembering why they had come out of their home Lai Wah changed the subject; "Ah Ying wants to take a short walk to Portsmouth Square. We will be quick, and I will keep a close watch for trouble."

"Good night, then. Be careful. Tonight, the Law and Order League is holding a monstrous convention at the Metropolitan Temple. The whole city is going and they will be in a frenzy." King waved to his neighbors as he entered their building, making his way up the dark stairwell to his third floor apartment.

As Ah Ying and Lai Wah walked up Kearny Street, they passed boarded up storefronts with "For Rent" signs.

"This area used to the bustling heart of manufacturing in Chinatown. Now it is dark and deserted," Lai Wah lamented. "Even the brothels are deserted."

Spotting a bulletin board covered with papers, Lai Wah walked over, found an official looking notice, tore it from the wall, and ripped it into a dozen pieces. "Those devils! We will not register!" Lai Wah exclaimed as he stomped on the bits of paper kicking them into the gutter.

Ah Ying kicked the remaining bits of paper into the gutter. She had seen Lai Wah and other Chinese men do this many times, destroying the official government notices ordering the Chinese to present for registration at the IRS office. She then pulled out a stack of papers from her tunic and tacked one up on the bulletin board.

"There, now that is much better, don't you think, Gee Sung?"

Lai Wah squinted at the Chinese characters and then let out a hearty laugh as he read the notice out loud,

> *"Notice from the Six Companies to all Chinese: Do not to comply with the Geary Bill. It is an unjust law. No Chinese should obey it. It is a cruel and bad law. The law degrades the Chinese and if obeyed will put them lower than the meanest of people. They have disregarded our rights. Pay no attention to their promises. They make a law to suit themselves, no matter how unjust to us. Let us stand together. Secretary Tone, Chinese Six Companies."*

"Where did you get these notices, Ah Ying?"

"My sister Chun Fah from the Mission Home is married to Rev. Ng Poon Chew. He had these notices printed and Chun Fah gave a few to me to spread the word. She says Rev. Chew is a fierce advocate for Chinese civil rights and dreams of publishing a Chinese newspaper someday."

Lai Wah shook his head and smiled, "Let's plaster Chinatown with your notices, Ah Ying." For the next thirty minutes Ah Ying and Lai Wah posted the Six Company notices on every bulletin board and lamppost they could find.

"Come, Gee Sung. Let's enjoy the evening air. Forget about these problems for a while," Ah Ying implored, pulling Lai Wah's sleeve as she led the way up Kearney Street.

As they approached Portsmouth Square, Ah Ying heard the Chinese men still playing mahjong late into the evening. She saw their dark shapes huddled around a makeshift table and then spotted Uncle Chan as he looked up and smiled at her.

"*Maahn on*[79], Ah Ying and Lai Wah. How are you, my friends? Have you eaten?"

"Hello, Uncle Chan," beamed Ah Ying at her favorite Uncle. "I see you are still trying to feed me. How many bowls of noodles did you sneak to me and Sue Lee when we were children?"

"Just a few, Ah Ying, and I would do it all again for you and Sue Lee," he laughed.

"No, Uncle it was many, many more than a few bowls of noodles. You kept us alive and gave us hope and something to look forward to every day. Without your kindness..." Ah Ying paused and let the words trail off into the night air.

"No thanks needed, Ah Ying. You and Sue Lee were like my daughters, and you gave this old man something to look forward to as well."

"We are walking over to Dupont to pick up Kay and Bing. Do you want to join us?" Ah Ying asked.

"No, No. You two young lovebirds go on your stroll without your old Uncle Chan," he laughed and waved them on their way.

The two walked along Clay Street away from Portsmouth Square. As they approached Dupont Gai, Ah Ying paused deep in thought.

"What is it, Ah Ying? Why are you stopping?"

"I am remembering all those years I walked these same

streets as a *mui tsai*, working for those horrible people on Jackson Street," replied Ah Ying softly.

"Don't think about those times now. That part of your life is finished," Lai Wah reminded her.

"No, Gee Sung. It is part of who I am. I don't want to forget. Seeing Uncle Chan tonight made me stop and think about how hard our life was. I was always hungry and tired, and they never tired of beating me. But it taught me to never ever give up. I whisper those words to Kay and Bing every night."

"I will protect you now, Ah Ying," Lai Wah offered as he pulled her closer.

"Yes. I know. But you may not always be here, Gee Sung."

"What do you mean? I am not going anywhere," Lai Wah protested.

Ah Ying was about to explain, when they both heard the noise in the distance and stopped. It was the sound of men yelling far behind them. Not one or two men, but dozens of men, and the noise was growing louder.

"We have to go, Ah Ying. I know that sound. It is Kearney's mob out looking for blood." I saw them last week after their meeting. They wanted to arrest some Chinese for not having his *chock chee*[80]. They probably would have done worse than arrest him, but the police showed up and put a stop to it."

Ah Ying heard the concern in her husband's voice, "Let's get the children and go home, Gee Sung."

They hurried along Dupont past their old apartment, when suddenly they came to Commercial and stopped. Looking to their left, they saw the group of hollering White men, their faces lit by torchlight. A poor Chinese man was huddled on the ground as they taunted him and demanded to see his certificate.

US Marshall Long stood over the man. "We have a warrant issued by Judge Morrow to arrest Ah Hing for the offense of unlawfully coming in, now being, and remaining within the limits of the State of California."

Men in the crowd called out, "Show us your certificate. I bet you never even registered!"

"Arrest him!" the men screamed.

"Send him back to China!"

The frightened man did not stand a chance. Even if he had a certificate, this crazed mob was not going to let him go free. Marshall Long was barely in control.

Lai Wah stepped out of the shadows to help the man.

"Let him go! He has done nothing wrong. You have no authority to arrest him or anyone else in our colony. Leave us alone!" Lai Wah boomed.

The crazed men stopped and looked up at the tall Chinese man.

"Well, John. Then we will arrest you! This here warrant says any Chinese without a certificate is an illegal alien and needs to be arrested and deported!" yelled their ringleader.

"Yeah! Get him. Get the tall Chinaman! He's asking for it. Arrest him!"

As the mob started to move towards Ah Ying and Lai Wah, a small figure that moved like lightening darted out of the pack sprinting towards them.

"Quick, Ah Ying! Follow me!"

Ah Ying was puzzled. But as the boy approached, she spotted the sandy hair and the freckled face.

"Billy! What are you doing here?"

"No time for that now! We have to get moving. Follow me!" Billy ran down Dupont Street past Sacramento with Ah Ying and Lai Wah following right behind.

"Ah Ying was breathing hard and having trouble running in her wooden sandals, "Where are we going, Billy?"

Billy, still running, yelled out, "The church!"

Ah Ying spotted St Mary's Cathedral as Billy leapt up the steps to the huge wooden door. It was late but the door opened easily, and the three slipped inside closing the door behind them.

"Are we safe here, Billy?"

"Yes, those men are all good Irish Catholics. Well, actually, they're bad Irish Catholics, but they won't risk the wrath of their god or wives by bringing their mob into a house of worship."

In the dimly lit church Ah Ying looked more closely at Billy's face. He was now a young teenager, but he still had the same freckles and mischievous grin.

'What were you doing with those men, Billy?" Ah Ying asked her friend.

"My Pa got caught up in this Anti-Chinese League, and he can't give it up. I tried to talk some sense into him, and my Ma forbid him from coming to the meeting, but he wouldn't listen. He's a good Pa, but he is out of work and blames the Chinese," Billy explained.

"It's not your fault, Billy," Lai Wah offered.

"Anyway, he made me come to the meeting. There must have been 1500 men crammed into the hall. They handed out badges with an American eagle to all the men. They pinned on their badges and strutted around like peacocks! Marshall Long and a few men left with the arrest warrants and headed up Market Street towards Chinatown. But then more and more men joined in. The crowd kept growing and someone brought out the torches. It got really crazy!"

"Last week I saw them doing the same thing. They want to send us all back to China," Lai Wah added.

"I was shocked tonight when I saw you and Ah Ying. And then you started yelling at the men. I thought you were crazy to take them on!" Billy exclaimed. "I knew I had to do something or you were in for a rough time. My Ma takes me to church, and I remembered this church from when you sent me to find Gee Sung with your letter, Ah Ying. Anyway, I think we will be safe here," Billy finally finished.

Lai Wah went to the front door and opened it a crack to look out. Most of the men had left, but a few of the diehards were still roaming around outside the cathedral with torches in hand.

"We will have to wait a bit longer for the rest of the men to give up."

"No worries. I have all night," Billy laughed.

Ah Ying, Billy, and Lai Wah spent a couple of hours reminiscing on the church pews before they finally parted in the early hours of the morning, heading to their homes in opposite ends of the city.

"I never thought I would ever see Billy again," Ah Ying later confessed.

"Well, I'm glad that we have a friend like Billy. His friendship helps me to remember that there are still good people in *Dai Fow*."

CHAPTER 31

Chinese at the World's Fair – June 17, 1894

The pandemonium and violence of the prior fall began to recede as Chinese were given another seven months to register.[81] Chinese embraced the registrations when they realized that there was a black market for the Certificates. They could sell them for $100 apiece to Chinese trying to enter the country. It took a while for officials to realize that the Chinese were obtaining dozens of duplicate certificates for resale. As life returned to normal, city officials hoped that the planned Midwinter Exposition would bring the city together and would show the world the best of the multicultural city by the bay.

Chinatown had been buzzing with excitement for weeks. After a delay caused by rain, their big day was finally upon them. Today they would show the world the very finest Chinese culture and beauty. The Midwinter Exposition of 1894 was the brainchild of Michael H. de Young, the editor and sole proprietor of the San Francisco Chronicle.[82] This World's Fair highlighted the latest in technology and showcased San Francisco's cultural diversity. After much public debate, the Chinese Pavilion, a two-story building modeled after a pagoda, was approved to be part of the Exposition. Today the Chinese planned a parade for the fair goers complete with handsome floats, gorgeous costumes, and a Chinese band. They had been working non-stop for months in anticipation of Chinese Day at the Midwinter Exposition. Chinatown was deserted as all the residents of the Chinese Quarter were at the fair on Sunday. The cable cars were packed with Celestials. Even the notorious highbinders put down their hatchets and pistols to take part in the festivities.

"Come along Ah Kay."

Mama took her daughter's little hand as she helped her up onto the cable car. Papa was right behind carrying three-year-old Bing on his shoulders as he hopped up onto the cable car in one easy stride of his long legs. Looking up and seeing the car packed with Chinese all dressed in their finest clothes, Ah Kay's eyes grew large.

"Mama, where are they all going today? Look there is Uncle Doc Wah!"

"We are all going to the fair in Golden Gate Park," explained Mama. "Today is Chinese Day at the exposition. We want to arrive early to see the Chinese parade."

Ah Kay jumped at the sound of the *Clang! Clang!* and felt the car lurch forward as they started their journey along California Street towards the park. Holding her mother's hand tightly, four-year-old Kay felt the cool San Francisco breeze on her face as the car rumbled along from stop to stop. She rarely adventured outside of Chinatown and marveled at the sights and sounds of The City. The streets were crowded with horse-drawn wagons and carriages and throngs of San Franciscans making their way to the Fair. As they approached the end of the line, the cable car slowed to a stop and all the Chinese in unison clambered off the car, rushing on to the park.

"Come along Kay. Hold your mama's hand tightly. Don't get lost," admonished Papa looking back with Bing still on his shoulders.

Ah Ying took Kay's hand tightly as they walked along to the fair entrance. Her childhood friend Sue Lee was right behind carrying Chun Ngou, Ah Ying's one-year-old daughter.

"Sue Lee, you should not carry my baby! She will become too heavy."

"Don't worry Ah Ying. She is much lighter and a better baby than those children we used to have to carry around when we were *mui tsai*." laughed Sue Lee. "Besides you're pregnant again! We have to take care of you."[83]

Ah Ying smiled. *This baby will be another son*, she mused to herself certain that the gods would bless her family with another heir. She hadn't yet told Gee Sung about the baby. He would know soon enough.

[84]

As they came up over the rise, they all looked down on the most magnificent spectacle imaginable. The Midwinter Exposition covered 200 acres with more than 100 buildings erected just for this World's Fair. The fabulous Electric Tower dominated the landscape looking like the Eifel Tower of Paris.

The Chinese and White fair goers lined up at the entrance all eager to pay the fifty-cent admission fee. Lai Wah returned with their tickets in hand and led them through the gates and onto the Midway.

"Let's head to the Chinese Pavilion right away. We don't want to miss the parade," Papa said, leading the way through the crowds. Lai Wah knew the way to the Pavilion, since he had helped with its construction. "Come along, it's right over here just past the Electric Tower."

Ah Kay and Bing wanted to stop and look at everything.

"Bing, look at those men on the funny horses!" laughed Kay to her little brother.

"Those are camels, Kay," explained Papa. "Those men are from Egypt. They live in the desert where their camels are just like horses. Except they can go across the desert for days without drinking water."

Kay was amused by the funny shapes of the camels but was already off looking at the circus performers on the Midway. Elephants, clowns, and acrobats were putting on a show for the newly arrived Chinese guests at the fair.

"Come, let's take this short cut," said Papa, as he took Bing's hand and headed between two buildings. The others followed behind closely not wanting to get lost in the crowded alleys. As they turned the corner, the magnificent Chinese Pavilion came into view.

"Papa, it looks like Chinatown!" said Bing.

"That's right, Bing. We wanted the building to show off the best Chinese design. Let's get ready to watch the parade coming down the Midway."

In truth, every Chinese artist, painter and carpenter had taxed his ingenuity and perseverance in preparing and building the Pavilion in time for the fair's opening. Red, green, and purple paint was ordered and used in unlimited supply for the project as well as tinsel and golden paper.

"Look, Papa! Here comes the dragon!" shouted Bing.

The dragon shook his scaly coils in the wind with a score of bright yellow flags. He glared at the visitors as he wound his way around the Midway on the way to the Central Court. The dragon was resplendent in all his glory with his red and green painting, golden tinsel and variegated trimmings. This was a great day for the dragon and for the Chinese.

"Hold on tightly, Bing. We don't want the Dragon to take you away!" admonished Papa with a smile at his first-born son.

Kay overheard her father's joking and held onto Ah Ying's

hand with a four-year-old's death grip.

The parade was more than gorgeous. It was iridescent with a glittering array of rainbow hues that bewildered the spectators lining the midway. The parade was led off by a platoon of Midwinter Fair guards and the Cassasa's Band. Next came two dignified Chinese officials on horseback representing civil officers of the Flowery Kingdom. Next came several hundred Chinese schoolboys from the Chinese Public Schools laughing and yelling with delight. Leong Lang, the President for the day, rode in a horse-drawn carriage with beautiful embroidered Chinese coverings.

The Chinese beating on their big brass gongs followed in colorful costumes carrying decorated lanterns. Beautiful Chinese maidens followed next on horseback, riding sidesaddle. The Chinese band of 24 musicians was not to be forgotten by anyone who heard the sheer magnitude of their raucous music. Each band member seemed to be trying valiantly to make even more noise than his neighbor. The result was beautiful music for the Chinese and an ear-splitting discord for the Caucasians.

The real hits of the parade were the multicolored Chinese

floats covered with natural flowers. Their design and themes had never been seen before in any American parade. The first was an immense dragon ship made of gaudy red material formed in the shape of an immense dragon with open mouth and glaring eyes. Next came floats that represented a Chinese Joss House, the famous Lok Yung Bridge over the Yeung Gee River[85], and the Chinese Goddess of Peace Gwoon Yum, upon which rode a Chinese maiden and her court. All the floats were decorated with beautiful garlands of fresh flowers.

Not to be left out thirty Chinese merchants rode in fine carriages in the midst of the parade. At the end of the parade was a handsome float representing the return to the homeland of a Chinese in exile.

"Come, let's enter the Chinese Pavilion to see the opera," encouraged Papa.

The ten-cent entrance fee was waived for Lai Wah's family since he was well-known to the Pavilion staff. Inside the Pavilion, Chinese banners waved everywhere, and strings of colored lanterns were stretched from the galleries. Colored paper fish with enormous eyes and crimson-hued dragons hung from poles, staring down at the guests.

Kay and Bing loved the colorful paper fish and dimly lit lanterns. They watched the Chinese opera with fascination, but Bing soon tired of the play and fell asleep on Lai Wah's shoulder.

After the performance, Papa said, "I have a surprise for you, Kay and Bing. Follow me quickly."

He walked the family down the midway towards the carnival. Kay looked up and spotted the giant Firth Wheel spinning around and around. The 100-foot wheel had sixteen glass cars with ten riders in each car.

"Papa, can we go on the ride?"

"Of course, we can, Kay. You ride with Mama, and Bing will go with me in the next car," replied Lai Wah.

"Sue Lee, do you want to ride the Firth Wheel with Chun Ngou?"

"Not on your life! That thing is too big and doesn't look safe to me." said Sue Lee as she clung to baby Chun Ngou.

"Suit yourself, but thank you for watching our little girl."

Sue Lee pulled Ah Ying aside, "Do you think you should go on that thing in your condition?"

"Oh don't worry, Sue Lee. I will be fine," promised Ah Ying with a smile.

Kay and Ah Ying stepped onto the platform and watched the Firth Wheel slowly come to a stop. The attendant raised the bar and motioned for them to step forward and take a seat in the glass car. Ah Ying took Kay's hand and gently hoisted her up onto the seat. The door was closed, and the car began to slowly move them up into the air.

"Mama, we're flying!"

Ah Ying looked down and saw Lai Wah and Bing seated in the car below them.

"Bing, look up! See your Mama and sister!"

Once the Firth Wheel was loaded with passengers, it began to turn in earnest, picking up speed as they spun around and around. Kay felt the rush of the wind on her face as the Firth Wheel went up and down, around and around showing her a view of her world that was new and exciting.

"Mama, look! I can see the Electric Tower lights and the water and even Chinatown!"

"Yes, Ah Kay, we are flying like birds," laughed Ah Ying as she pulled Kay a little closer for protection.

On the ground again, the Hung family laughed about their great adventure. Their day at the fair was one they would remember for years. As young slave girls, Ah Ying and Sue Lee could never have imagined such a fine day in their futures. Before they left the World's Fair, Ah Ying spotted Mr. Taber, their friend from the Mission Home , with camera in hand.

"Hello, Ah Ying, what a fine family you have now. Let me take your photograph so you can remember this day," smiled Mr. Taber. "Stand in front of the carnival signs. Now look this way and smile!"

With a flash and a puff of white smoke, the photograph was taken and the moment was captured for all time.

"We will call this one 'Chinese at the 1894 World's Fair.' I will make sure you get a print!" Isaiah Taber then disappeared into the crowd.

Ah Ying sighed to Lai Wah, "What a perfect day. Let's go home now."[86]

CHAPTER 32

An Unpaid Debt - October 4, 1896

Lun Chee forced his eyes open trying to block out the horror of the image seared into his fleeting consciousness. *Tong Yan Gai* was blurry and turned sideways. Everyone was running about and shouting in Chinese. The back of his neck was wet, and his head throbbed with pain. Touching his right hand to his neck,

felt the warm sticky blood oozing from the wound in his back. Trying to stand, Lun Chee's legs were limp and motionless. Rolling to his left he looked up as the sign on the drug store came into focus, 'Ting Wah Hung – 722 Jackson Street.'

It had all happened so fast but was replaying in his mind in slow motion. He had come to collect a debt from Chin Kim Leon and had found him outside the drug store with two other men. He recognized the short man as Ah Wah, the assassin.

As he approached the trio, Chin Kim pointed at him, "He is the one! Shoot him! Hurry! Shoot him now!"

Lun Chee saw Ah Wah running towards him in slow motion with his right hand in his coat pocket. He tried to duck behind a barrel on the sidewalk, but it was too late. Ah Wah grabbed Lun Chee, spun him around, pulled out the revolver, and pulled the trigger in one practiced and deadly maneuver. The explosion was deafening, as the deadly bullet shattered Lun Chee's spine.

[87]

As he collapsed to the ground, Lun Chee recalled Ah Wah's sneering face framed by a black flat-brimmed hat that seemed too small for the man's head. In that instant total chaos erupted. Jackson Street was crowded with Chinese, who were now shouting and running for cover. Lun Chee saw a police officer running towards him and then turning and giving chase as Ah Wah and his partner ran up Jackson Street.

Officer Freel ran after the fleeing assassins, following them into the building at 720 Jackson Street. Chasing the men up the dark stairway, he had them cornered in the kitchen at the rear of the building. He saw Ah Wah hurriedly pass the revolver to the tall Chinese, who threw it into the fireplace. Freel grabbed Ah Wah, spun him around, and handcuffed him in one motion. Seeing the tall Chinese bolting for the door, Freel pulled out his gun.

"Halt! You are both under arrest! Stop or I will end this for you right here!"

The fleeing Chinese froze in his tracks, and Freel handcuffed him to Ah Wah.

"Come along, you heathen scum!"

Freel led the men to the City Prison where Ah Wah and the taller man identified as Ah Chan were held pending the result of Lun Chee's injuries.

Meanwhile, Lun Chee was taken in the patrol wagon to the Receiving Hospital, where Freel found him a little after one o'clock about ninety minutes after the shooting. Sergeant Colby, the officer on duty, approached Lun Chee to take his statement through the translator, Joe Chang Tone.

"I believe I am going to die from the gunshot wound I received today at 722 Jackson Street. My name is Gin Lun Chee. I am 51 years of age and was born in China. I am not strong enough to tell all the circumstances of the shooting."

"Chin Kim Leon told the two men that were arrested to kill me because he owned me money. I asked him to pay me, and for this reason he told them to kill me."

"Just before I was shot, I turned my head and saw Chin Kim Leon standing by those two men. I heard the tall man tell the short man Ah Wah that I was the man to shoot, pointing his finger at me. The short man Ah Wah is the one who shot me in the back of my neck."

Too weak to write his name Lun Chee made a cross as his mark on the written statement.

Colby turned his head in the direction of a commotion in the entryway to the police station. A pretty Chinese woman with a little baby in her arms rushed into the room.

"Where is he? Where is my Lun Chee?" she demanded with tears streaming down her face.

"My dear Sing Yee! I am so sorry!" sobbed Lun Chee, as his young wife rushed to his side.

"Lun Chee, are you alright?"

"I am afraid I will not survive to see our children grow up," Lun Chee whispered with tears in his eyes reaching to stroke the face of his infant son. "Where are the other children?"

"Qui Fong is watching her little brother and sister. I wanted to ask Ah Ying to check on them. But I did not have time. They will be fine. It is you we must take care of right now," sobbed Sing Yee.

"All of our friends and many of your customers are outside the hospital. They want to know if you will be alright."

Colby pulled up a chair for Chin Shee to sit by her husband's cot.

"Here, Miss. Please sit down."

Sing Yee smiled weakly at the officer but was unable to speak. Sitting next to her husband she whispered, "I am so sorry I made you go and collect the money Chin Kim Leong owed you."

"Do not be sorry, my dear wife. It is I who let you down. I do not have the money, and now I will not be here to support you and the children."

"Sing Yee, you must be strong and take over my business in the Chee Sang Tong drug store. It is yours now. Do not let them bully you and steal the money in my business," implored Lun Chee, knowing that his partners would try to cheat his young wife.

"Don't talk like that, Lun Chee! You are going to recover. Besides, what do I know about your business?"

"You must be strong, Sing Yee!" Lun Chee exploded. "My share of Chee Sang Tong is worth $1,000. It is yours now. You must take over my business for the sake of our children!"

Sing Yee continued to sob. As she silently nodded her head in agreement, tears streamed down her face.

Ah Ying quietly entered the police station holding room. Without saying a word, she slid her arm around her grieving friend, comforting the one person who had been her friend in her brightest and darkest moments. The two women sat quietly at Lun Chee's bedside, while he drifted into a restless sleep.

Lun Chee clung to his precious life for 10 days before finally succumbing to his fatal injuries on October 14, 1896. Chin Ah Wah was charged with murder. The first trial in March, held in Judge Trout's court, ended in a hung jury to the dismay of all of Chinatown. After deliberating for nine hours, ten jurors voted for murder and two for manslaughter.

The retrial in Judge Dunne's department of the Superior Court took place in late May and early June. District Attorney

W. S. Barnes conducted the prosecution for the state assisted by Thomas D. Riordan and Walter S. Hinkle. The Chinese Six Companies offered to pay $600 to their special counsel if a conviction of murder in the first degree was secured and $400 for a verdict of murder in the second degree. The retrial concluded on June 5, 1897 with a conviction of first degree murder. Ah Wah was sentenced to life imprisonment in San Quentin Prison. Chin Ah Wah contended that he acted in self-defense, but the jury did not believe him.

To care for her family Chin Shee kept her promise to her husband and assumed his role as part owner of the firm Chee Sang Tong & Company at 710 Dupont Street, across from the Hang Far Low Restaurant. Having a woman as a partner in the company was a novel concept for the other sixteen partners of the firm. But Chin Shee found a strength she did not know she possessed and became a force to be reckoned with in her business dealings. The other partners soon came to accept her and to respect her fierce determination to protect her family's interest in the business. The family continued to live right above Chee Sang Tong, allowing the 28-year-old widow to keep a sharp eye on the business dealings.

Uncle Gin Lun Lum was Lun Chee's younger brother who had been with Chee Sang Tong & Company for 25 years. He now succeeded Lun Chee as the new business manager. Uncle Lun took Chin Shee under his wing, teaching her the business and warning her about the less scrupulous partners in the firm. In less than a decade Chin Shee would learn the hard way that her trust in Uncle Lun was greatly misplaced.

[88]

CHAPTER 33

Growing Up in Chinatown – 1900

Six-year-old Kim sat quietly at his desk in the Chinese Primary School at 916 Clay Street in Chinatown, not knowing what to expect on his first day of school. All of the students were Chinese, and all were boys, as the girls stayed home with their mothers learning to sew and cook. Kim's friend Wei Gin was seated in the next row. Kim couldn't wait to learn about everything. He was always pestering his parents with questions they couldn't answer. His thoughts were interrupted.

[89]

"I am Mrs. Greer, your teacher. What is your name?"

Kim looked at the White woman for a few seconds. She was tall with her hair pulled back behind her head. She was wearing a blue blouse with white buttons and a long black skirt that reached the wooden floorboards.

"I am Hong Kim Sung," he replied tentatively unsure how to address this English-speaking woman.

"Well, let's see. Kim is easy, K-I-M. But your other name is a bit odd. We will spell it S-E-U-N-G. Alright then. You will be Hong Kim Seung." Mrs. Greer declared as she wrote the words in bold letters on the chalkboard.

With that pronouncement, Kim's name was firmly established in written English. He had never seen his name written in English letters. He liked it and practiced it for the rest of the morning, writing Hong Kim Seung on his papers. It looked very official.

When Mrs. Greer pulled out a map of the world, Kim was enthralled, imagining all the places he would visit as an explorer. Kim was hooked as a life-long student by the time school ended at 3 p.m.

He rushed home to tell Mama about his first day at school and to show her how to write his name, HONG KIM SEUNG. *She will be so proud.*

"Mama! Look at my paper from Mrs. Greer! I wrote my name!"

"That's very nice Kim, but you need to get ready to go to Chinese School. It starts at 5 p.m. every day. Here, have something to eat and then find Bing so you can both go to school to learn Chinese."

"But Mama, this is America! Why do I have to go to school to learn Chinese? I need to learn American things. Chinese is a waste of time!"

"You go to school anyway, for your mother!"

Well, Kim never disobeyed Mama, but he knew this was

going to be a big headache. He went to Chinese school with Bing. The school was over on Commercial Street on the third floor. It was not far from where he was born at 711 Commercial. His father's cigar store was nearby. But learning Chinese was harder than anything he had ever attempted. What a headache! Gradually, he got the hang of it. Fifty years later he would receive a letter from the Ming Sung Company in Chun King China offering him a job to build their big ships. That letter was written in Chinese!

Kim's later words were, "I could read it, so my mother wasn't so wrong after all!" *Don't forget to follow Mama. Your Mama is always right!*"

Every morning Kim and Wei Gin, Chin Shee's youngest son, walked to school together dressed in their Mandarin robes and skullcaps. The boys had become best friends, which was convenient since their mothers were also the other boy's godmother.[90] After school, Kim ran back to his home on the corner of Sacramento and Stockton Streets with his queue flying behind him He was eager to have some free time before Chinese School. Sometimes Mama had other ideas.

"Kim, here is five cents. Go down to Lung Chung grocery store and buy ingredients so I can make dinner. You are a good boy, Kim."

Kim clutched the five cents and ran back down Sacramento Street, to Dupont Gai, where he passed Mama's friend, old Uncle Chan.

"Hi Uncle Chan!" Kim shouted out as he raced by on his way down Dupont.

"Hello, Kim! Say Hi to you mama for me! She was always my favorite!"

At Lung Chung, Kim bought one cent worth of bean sprouts, one cent of bean cake, one cent of pork, one cent of bok choi, and one cent of something else for flavor. Then he got a packet of cornstarch and a piece of ginger or garlic for free.

"Five cents for dinner! Can you believe it?" Kim marveled.

Kim's mouth watered just imagining the taste of the Chinese stir-fry dinner that his mother would make with these simple ingredients. Kim suspected that there wasn't a lot of money, but they never wanted for good food and a warm place to sleep at night.

Kim and eight-year-old Bing played outside in the streets and alleys of *Tong Yan Gai*. Gum Toon was only four years old, and sometimes they let him tag along. They played kick-the-can and hide-and-seek with the other children in the neighborhood. Chin Shee's two boys, Wei Seung and Hong Seung, were about the same ages and often came over from their home at 710 Dupont to play with the Hung boys. On rare occasion, Kim's sisters, Ah Kay and Chun Ngo, would escape the house and join them for some fun and games.

Just like when Ah Ying and Sue Lee were young *mui tsai*, the children were looked after and pampered by their many Uncles, the aging bachelors in *Tong Yan Gai*.

"Here, Kim and Bing! Have some candied ginger and coconut!"

"Thank you, Uncle!"

"Say, hello to your mother! Did I ever tell you about the time she outsmarted the Hop Sing highbinders? No? Well, she was really something special when she was your age!"

Gradually, the boys came to learn of their mother's exploits. Even they were in awe of the young Ah Ying, who the old bachelors loved so much.

"Mama, are those stories about you true?" Kim asked with a disbelieving but hopeful look.

"That was a long time ago, Kim, and you can't believe everything you hear!" Ah Ying replied with a little smile.

Lai Wah walked in just in time to hear the exchange. "Your mother was a force of nature, Kim. No one got in her way once she had her mind made up! Not her owner. Not the missionary ladies. Not the highbinders. And certainly not the Judge!" Lai Wah laughed.

"Fortunately, she took a liking to your old father when I was a younger man!"

"Lai Wah! Stop filling their heads with such inflated nonsense. I am just a meek and innocent Chinese mother You can ask anyone, Kim."

Kim and Bing smiled at their mother's modesty. They didn't have to ask. They had heard the stories for years. What a grand old lady their mother was.

Bing looked up from his Chinese homework, "Mama, will I get a chance to have my own adventures before I grow up?"

"Don't worry, Bing. There will be plenty of adventures in your life. It is in your blood. Your father was the real adventurous one in this family. Tell them, Lai Wah. Tell them about when you were a young boy doing the work of two grown men in the mountains of California!"

The boys had heard the tale of the great railroad many times, but they never tired of hearing it again and again. They sat closer to Lai Wah as he looked out the window recalling his boyhood in Dai Long Village.

"My father took me and Jick Wah to the Hong Family Temple to ask our ancestors for their protection before we began our journey to Gum Saan. I was fifteen years old and Jick Wah was sixteen. Our mother See Too Shee was crying but wouldn't show us her sadness. We were among the first men to leave Dai Long, but many more would follow us. Some would die in Gum Saan. Jick Wah was almost killed. To this day he carries the scars of that horrible explosion."

"But let's eat dinner. I will continue this long story after dinner, and after you finish your Chinese lessons."

"Papa! We want to hear the story now!" Bing and Kim cried out in unison.

"Let you father rest now, boys. He will tell you the story later so you will always know where you come from."

With those words, the Hong family sat down together for dinner. Lai Wah never did get back to his story, but the boys knew most of the story by heart. As their Mama said, 'it was in their blood.'

[91]

CHAPTER 34

Early Morning in Dai Fow - 1904

As Kim opened his eyes, he rolled over and bumped into his older brother, Bing. Kim hadn't slept all night, thinking about their trip to Montana with Uncle Jick Wah. But there was Bing sound asleep. Across the room, he saw the outlines of the rest of his family in the dim morning light. There was little brother, Gum Toon, and his older sister, Chun Ngou. Instinctively he looked for his oldest sister, Kay, but he knew she wouldn't be there. Kay had married and left for Salem, Oregon. She was ready to start her own life and family. He missed her, although, she was a little bossy at times.

Uncle Jick Wah had arrived from Kalispell, Montana just last week. They called him Uncle, but Kim had never seen him before. Unlike Father, Uncle was a small man but full of energy. The patch covering his right eye fascinated the boys, but they hadn't yet found the nerve to ask Uncle about it. Besides, he was always moving about and had so many stories to tell about his home in the mountains of Montana.

At first Uncle had been reluctant to take the boys back to Montana. He was a bachelor. What did he know of taking care of young boys? But Ah Ying had insisted. The boys were nearly grown. Kim was ten years old, and Bing had just turned twelve. It was time for them to go off on their own, and Uncle Jick was just the person to help them. After all, he did need help watching the store in Kalispell. He wasn't getting any younger, and his new business, selling lingerie to the "ladies of the night" kept him away from the dry goods store more and more. So it was settled. Kim and Bing were going to Montana!

Kim listened out the window for the familiar sounds coming from the streets of Chinatown. It was just getting light outside, but already he heard the stirrings of the merchants and peddlers getting ready for business. In the distance he heard the clip-clop of a horse pulling its heavy cart up the steep cobble stone streets.

Kim would miss his family but was excited with anticipation as he thought about the train ride to Montana. He rarely ventured outside of the Chinese quarter. His mother had always warned him to stay within the twelve blocks of Chinatown. The taunts and occasional rocks were not to be taken lightly. But Kim yearned to see the rest of this great city and the world beyond. He knew from his teachers at McKinley school that there was so much more to see.

As his thoughts drifted far away from his home, he heard his brother stirring.

He poked him and whispered, "Bing, wake up! It's time to get ready!"

Bing grunted and pulled the covers up over his head.

Unable to contain his excitement, Kim sat up and swung his bare feet onto the cool wooden floor. He stood and heard the familiar creek of the wooden planks. He quickly got dressed in the traditional Chinese clothes a colorful mandarin robe and silk vest, and of course, the skullcap. He wrapped his queue neatly behind his head. Mother had insisted that the boys wear their finest Chinese clothing on this special day.

Kim was almost finished getting dressed when Bing sat up, rubbed his eyes and looked sleepily around the room.

"What's your rush?" he groaned. "It's too early, and Uncle won't be up for hours!"

But Kim was not to be delayed. He tiptoed out of the room and found Mother already preparing breakfast for her two sons. He saw the steam rising from the pot of rice and smelled the delicious aroma of cha siu bow warming on the stove.

When he saw the feast his mother was preparing Kim's eyes widened in amazement. Food was scarce, and he was used to being a little hungry.

"Mama, I have never seen so much food!" exclaimed Kim.

After they had finished their meal, Ah Ying reached into her pocket and pulled out six Chinese coins. Each coin had Chinese characters around a square hole in its center. She handed three coins to each boy and looked at them earnestly.

"When you cross the bay, you must drop the three coins into the water for good luck. Promise me you will do this!"

The look on her face told them to nod in agreement as each boy placed his coins in his pocket for safekeeping

Ah Ying sighed as she absent-mindedly cleared the table. She remembered when her mother had given her those three coins in the village home so many years ago. The years had passed too quickly. Her boys seemed so young to be leaving home! Had she made a mistake by insisting that Jick Wah take the boys to Montana? But she herself had only been nine years old when she had been brought to Gum Saan 24 years ago. She trembled slightly at the memory of how she had been kidnapped, taken on the steamer to Gum Saan, and forced to work as a servant for that dreadful family on Jackson Street.

Ah Ying often thought of her early days in Gum Saan. The missionaries had given her a new life. She remained close to the Mission Home. In fact, the family home on Sacramento and Stockton Streets was only a block away. She taught sewing to the young girls at the Home. But with a family of her own to care for, finding time to visit the Home was becoming more difficult.

After Judge Hebbard married Ah Ying and her Gee Sung in 1889, the five children were born in rapid succession between 1890 and 1896. Now her first-born daughter Kay was married and gone to Salem, and her two boys were about to leave home for Montana. She looked at Kim and Bing eagerly waiting for Uncle Jick Wah to get up. Where had the time gone?

Kim opened the door to their flat and crept down the rickety wooden steps to Sacramento Street. The cool morning air was mixed with the delicious smells coming from the restaurants and street vendors preparing food for the neighborhood. In the alley he saw the familiar orange glowof the outdoor stoves and the steam rising up from the woks. He wondered if they had such good food in Montana.

Kim looked down towards Dupont Gai, hoping to see father coming back from the Hang Far Low restaurant where he worked as a cook. He turned around and saw Bing at the top of the stairs. "Where's Father? It's almost time to leave! We can't go without seeing him!"

[92]

Just then Kim looked up and saw Lai Wah's tall silhouette striding towards them. He reached down, and in one practiced motion scooped up one boy in each arm, carrying the delighted boys up the stairs!

"Gotcha!"

Sitting at the top of the stairs, Lai Wah placed one boy on either side. He looked down at his sons with pride and remembered the twenty years he had spent alone in Gum Saan as a bachelor. Now his two older sons were going off on their own.

"You must be good and must always obey Uncle," he said sternly. "You must work hard and make your family proud."

The boys nodded in unison as Lai Wah gave each of his sons an awkward hug. He hoped they knew what he really meant to say.

Lai Wah looked at his swollen hands as he took the red papers from his pocket. His face and hands were already showing the swelling he had seen in other men in Dai Fow. His strength was not what it once was. But today he felt the power of his ancestors and a surge of pride as he sat with Kim and Bing. Lai Wah handed the boys a red paper on which he had written Chinese characters.

"Now, you tell me what it says. Did you study hard in Chinese school like you promised your mother?"

Kim stared at the Chinese characters, wrinkling his nose, as he struggled to make sense of the characters.

"Like a spring of water, remember your source..."

CHAPTER 35

Lai Wah's Story

Lai Wah looked out across the streets of Chinatown, and then across the ocean, and the many years that had passed since his boyhood days in Toishan.

"I was only a young boy, not much older than you, Bing, when the foreign devils came to my village promising work and a chance to make a fortune in Gum Saan. The White ghosts were building a great road of iron rails across the country for their steam-breathing dragon. They wanted all the young Chinese men to sign up to work on their railroad."

Lai Wah paused a moment looking at Bing and Kim with pride.

"Don't stop, Papa. Tell us the part about the village," Bing implored.

Lai Wah smiled at his sons and continued, "Our village was called Dai Long. Later it would be called the *Village of the Foreign Chinese*, because so many of the men went off to Gum Saan to work. Many returned years later as wealthy men. Others like me are still waiting to go home. Dai Long is in Sunning[93] near Hoiping in the Kwangtung Province. That is where the Hung family is from, boys. You must remember your roots and always pay respect to our ancestors."

[94]

The boys nodded in unison, as Lai Wah continued, "My father, Long Yin, was fortunate to have five strong sons to help him and to bring honor to our family. My brothers' names are Doc Wah, who is the oldest, Wing Wah, Jick Wah, and Fun Wah. I am the fourth son, Lai Wah.

"My four brothers and I worked on our father's ten mow of farmland, growing sweet potatoes, yams, rice and beans. But years of drought and wars made for meager harvests. Many of the villagers were hungry, and most were poor. Some winters the stores of food ran out, and we only had roots and beetles to eat."

Kim and Bing frowned at the thought of eating beetles.

"Go on, Papa," they encouraged.

"That night, after I had seen the foreign devils, our family was gathered for dinner. I wanted to tell my father I was going to go to Gum Saan to work on the railroad. After all, I was already fifteen years old by Chinese counting. I was ready to leave home to find my fortune."

"How did you tell your father you were leaving home?" Kim interrupted.

"I remember our words like it was yesterday."

Lai Wah looked wistful as he told the story.

"I am big and strong. Look! I am a head taller than any other man in the village!"

"You are tall and strong, and your heart is big. But you must watch out for the White ghosts. They are dirty and crude and pay no respect to their ancestors. They will trap you in their foreign land and not let your return to your village," Father said.

"I will be careful, Father. I will work hard and send home money to help the family. There is no work here in the village, and already so many men from other villages have left for Gum Saan."

Long Yin was resigned, "You may go, but not alone. Doc Wah is the oldest and must stay to take care of the family. Jick Wah will go with you to Gum Saan."

Jick Wah was surprised. He had not heard the railroad man speak and knew nothing of the steam-breathing dragons in Gum Saan. Jick Wah was also smaller than his younger brother. He was always looking for a way to make money and was very enterprising. He probably thought he would go to Gum Saan and find gold nuggets on the ground to fill his pockets.

There was no further discussion. Jick Wah and Lai Wah were going to Gum Saan to work on the railroad. It was 1864, the second year of Emperor Tongzhi's reign, and both were young and eager for adventure. They had no idea what was in store for them in the mountains of Gum Saan. They would endure bitter cold, exhaustion and pain that they could not yet imagine. Lai Wah would survive, but Jick Wah would not come home whole.

Within the week Jick Wah and Lai Wah were saying goodbye to their family. Their mother's eyes were filled with tears as she held them close one last time. They all gathered around the family altar upstairs. Jick Wah and Lai Wah bowed three times while holding the burning incense sticks. Doc Wah clearly wanted to be going with them, but he was strangely silent. As the oldest son, he knew he was much too important to the family to go and live with the barbarians.

Father took them to the Hung family shrine at Quen San Temple to pay respects to the ancestors. They burned incense, made an offering, and read the inscription on the tablet.

[95]

The foundation of our prosperity was laid by our forbearers' virtues: kindness, goodness, honesty and loyalty.

After they left the temple Father said farewell one last time. Walking through the gate to Dai Long, the two boys both turned and looked back at the village that had been their home for their whole lives. Long Yin was still standing on the path as the village disappeared around the first bend in the road. They had no idea how big and different their world was soon to become, or that they would never see their father again.

Jick and Lai Wah walked for almost a day to reach the coast and then found a fishing boat that took them to Hong Kong. The railroad men from Gum Saan met them at the docks on Connaught Street and took them to the Pacific Mail Steamship

Company. They boarded the great steamer, Alaska, and went below deck where they spent the next two months with 1000 other young Chinese men and boys. The trip to Gum Saan was stifling. It was crowded and hot, and everyone got sick.

Lai looked down at his two sons.

He recalled, "We were afraid to eat the barbarian's food, but it was not long before the food Mother gave us was gone. The little barbarian food we did eat made us sick. It was unlike the good Cantonese food we were used to."

"What did you do on the boat for two months, Papa?" Bing asked.

"To pass the time, Jick Wah and I watched and listened to the barbarians, trying to guess the meaning of their strange words and gestures. Slowly, their odd words became more familiar and we understood them, while the other Chinese only shook their heads at the strange foreign tongue of the White ghosts."

Lai Wah continued on with his story.

"Finally, after almost two months, the steamer arrived in Dai Fow. We gathered our few belongings, tied them to a bamboo pole and lined up to leave the steamer. We were full of excitement and a little fear."

The boys were weak and hungry and their legs wobbled as they walked down the gangplank onto the docks. Men were shouting to them in Chinese and in the foreign devil's tongue. Jick Wah and Lai Wah stayed together looking around anxiously until they found a man speaking Sze Yup, their dialect of Chinese. He told them to climb onto the horse-drawn cart, which was their ride to the ferry docks. The ferry would take them to Yee Fow, the second city, which the White ghosts called Sacramento.

Lai Wah's reminiscing was suddenly interrupted, by a tugging on his sleeve.

"What was the ferryboat ride like, Papa?" Bing asked.

"Well, we boarded the ferry named Rio Vista with all the other Chinese railroad workers. They were crowding us below deck when I spotted an opening and grabbed Jick Wah, pulling him towards the rail. We squeezed through the men and grabbed hold of the ferry's smooth painted wooden rail.

"The cool salt air felt good on my face. I looked down and saw the dark water of the bay lapping against the side of the boat. Suddenly, there was a horrible noise, and the ferry belched smoke from its top. The giant paddle wheel slowly began to turn, churning up the water, and the ferry pulled away from the dock. Jick and I watched, as Dai Fow grew smaller in the distance. Neither of us said a word. We both knew that Dai Long Village was growing further away as well."

The trip up the Sacramento River to Yee Fow took most of the day. As they went further inland, the air became warm and dry. It was April, the middle of spring in Gum Saan. Late in the afternoon they arrived at Yee Fow where the railroad men met them. They were hairy men like all the other barbarians Lai Wah had ever seen. They waved and pointed, speaking in their foreign tongue. Lai Wah watched them closely and listened to their strange words. Already he had come to understand a few of their phrases. Simple ones. The game that Jick Wah and Lai Wah had played on board, guessing what the barbarians were saying, really paid off.

"Tell us the part where you became the gang boss, Papa," Kim implored.

"Well, I understood the barbarians, so I turned around and spoke to the Chinese men in Sze Yup."

Lai Wah could still picture it all these years later.

"Get in a line and be quiet!"

The men were silent, but they listened and got in line behind Jick and Lai Wah. They walked up to a barbarian and a Chinese man sitting behind a wooden desk covered with papers and an opened logbook.

The Chinese worker asked, "What is your name and where are you from?"

"I am Hung Lai Wah, and this is my brother Jick Wah. We are from Dai Long Village in Sunning District, Kwangtung Province."

"Lai Wah, you understand some of the barbarian's tongue. That is good. You will be in charge of these thirty men. Tell them to stay in line and to pay attention. They will sign their name and be given supplies. We will pay each man one dollar a day, from which we'll take out money for food and supplies."

Lai Wah turned around and explained to the Chinese men what he had said. They nodded but stood silently as they waited in line. Each man in turn came up to the table, and gave his name and village, which was recorded in their logbook.

As the men were saying their names in Chinese, one barbarian looked up and scowled, "The Chinese all look alike! We don't need their names. We will just pay the tall one, Lai Wah, for all his men and he can take care of paying them. Otherwise, we are likely to pay some Chinaman twice!"

That is how it worked. Lai Wah became the gang boss for these thirty men.He was paid once a month, from which was taken out money for each man's supplies and all of their food. Then he paid each man what he had coming.

"Lai Wah! Take your men to the supply tent!"

Hearing his name, Lai Wah turned around. The barbarian was pointing at a large tent across the field. Figuring he meant for them to go there, he walked his men single file to the white tent.

"Hey! He understands good English for a Chinese" said the pleased barbarian. "We need more Chinese like Lai Wah. Stro will be pleased with this group."

"We will work them till they drop and then get more. Where is Kwangtung anyway?" another barbarian laughed.

At the supply tent they gave each man a shovel and pickaxe. The gang was supplied with three white tents, a rope, poles, a cart and two axes.

Lai Wah turned to the Chinese worker who had spoken Sze Yup.

"The men need to eat. We have had nothing to eat since we got off the steamer yesterday."

He motioned for them to go to a large tent where the barbarians were gathered. They followed him, and he brought out a pot with more disgusting barbarian food.

"We cannot eat this! It made us sick on the boat!"

Lai Wah turned to the men and asked in Chinese, "Who can cook?"

A small man named Lum Chew[96] came forward, "I was a cook in my family restaurant."

"Good! Tell him what you need to prepare us a good Cantonese meal."

Well, Ah Chew rattled off the most amazing list of ingredients; dried pork, oysters, shrimp, bok choi, bean sprouts. He went on and on, and the men became more and more hungry listening to their cook's demands.

It took awhile, but they eventually found Ah Chew all the ingredients and cooking implements that he needed. Over a small fire, he made a feast the likes of which they had not seen for months. From then on, Ah Chew prepared all the meals. Every month they had to send to San Francisco for his list of food, but the men were well fed and happy. Even though they had to pay for their own food, unlike the barbarian workers, the Chinese were better fed and worked harder.

The next day they got their first look at the railroad that was to become their lifeline. A great steam locomotive was sitting quietly on the tracks. It had huge iron wheels, some as large as a man stood tall, and a great funnel-shaped smoke stack on its top. They all stared at the locomotive, unable to take their eyes off it. It was the most powerful beast they had ever seen. Behind the locomotive were four flatbed cars loaded with iron rails, railroad ties and other supplies. The railroad men took them to an empty car at the back of the train and motioned for them to climb up onto the car.

They had all just climbed aboard when the locomotive began to hiss and then roar as steam and smoke came billowing from the smoke stack. There was a rhythmic hissing sound as the train began to move slowly down the track. Picking up speed, the train pulled away from the wooden platform. What a sight they must have been to the barbarians of Yee Fow, a trainload of Chinese with their queues flying behind them in the breeze! The train ride was fun, but it was the last fun they would have for some time to come.

Lai Wah looked behind and spotted the Chinese man he met yesterday in Yee Fow.

Approaching Lai Wah with a grin he said, "I am Jow Kee,[97] but the Whites call me Jim King. I am from Sun Chung Village in Chungsan. The barbarians trust me, and I will show you how to stay out of trouble with the White ghosts."

His friendly face was a welcome change from the barbarians. These men did not yet know the Chinese, but some of the White ghosts had hatred in their eyes.

"Where are they taking us?"

"We are going to the end of the line, and then you and your crew will begin clearing trees ahead of the graders. Enjoy the ride. It will be your last for some time to come. From now on, you'll walk everywhere, and work twelve hours a day, six days every week."

Sometime later, Lai Wah looked out from the train, which had picked up speed and was rushing past the trees alongside the tracks. The warm wind was blowing in his face, and his loose blue tunic was flapping in the breeze. It felt like they were flying down the track. He looked back and saw Jick Wah with his arms spread out to the side, as if he truly were flying down the track! Up ahead, Lai Wah spotted some buildings.

"What is this village called?" he asked Jim King.

"They call this place Newcastle. I call it the place of the great wooden centipede."

Just as he was about to ask him what he meant, they came upon a huge wooden structure that took the rails across a deep ravine. The wooden bridge had hundreds of paired legs supporting the track. It looked just like a giant centipede! As the train crossed over the wooden bridge, they all looked down into the ravine. The bottom of the ravine was far below. No one said a word, but they were all hoping that the structure would hold up under the weight of the locomotive.

Jim King shouted above the noise, “The Whites call this a trestle. Hold on! It is a long way to the bottom.”

They had been slowly going up into the foothills east of Yee Fow. The trees were beginning to change, and the air was becoming a little cooler. A few miles ahead the train slowed as it approached another village of wooden buildings.

“This is the town the White ghosts call Auburn,” answered Jim King before Lai Wah could ask the question. “The first Chinese to work on the railroad came from this town, including one of your cousins. They worked so well that the boss man Strobridge now wants more Chinese workers to build his iron road. They want to have 7,000 men from Kwangtung working on the railroad by the end of the year.”

“Who is the man named Strobridge?”

“He is the head boss man. The White ghost workers call him ‘Stro.’ He lost one eye in an explosion, so we call him ‘One-eyed Bossy Man.’ He is strict and will work you hard, but he is fair.”

Looking down the track, Lai Wah asked Jim King, “Where does this iron road go? Does it go past Auburn?”

“Right now, the tracks end here, short of Auburn.[98] From here we walk. But we are going to lay their iron tracks up into the mountains they call the Sierra Nevada. It will be very cold with snow on the ground for much of the year. Strobridge says we must go through the mountain and meet a railroad coming from the east. These White men are always in a rush.”

In the distance Lai spotted horse-drawn carts being loaded with rocks by Chinese men from Kwangtung. He looked at Jick Wah. They both knew that the free ride was over.

Bing’s eyes were wide open hearing his father’s story. He couldn’t imagine life in a railroad camp.

He turned to his brother and said, “You be the boss man and I’ll be the cook!”

He ran over to grab some apples for their lunch.

CHAPTER 36

Central Pacific Railroad
Working in the Mountains of California

Lai Wah felt a tug on his sleeve. Looking down, he saw Bing, still wide-eyed and bursting with questions, as he munched on his apple.

"Papa, tell us about the centipede! Did its legs move?"

"No, Bing," laughed Lai Wah. "But once I did have quite a scare on another monstrous centipede!"

"Tell us, Papa. What happened?" both boys pleaded wanting to hear the stories they knew by heart.

"Well, it was about a year later in the spring of 1866. We had built another longer trestle and had been clearing trees and rocks ahead of the graders, going up into the mountains. We were young and strong, but it was exhausting work. We worked from before sunrise to sundown, usually eleven hours a day. The days are shorter in the mountains so we often worked past sundown. Every night my muscles were sore and my back ached."

"But tell us about the centipede, Papa," Bing interrupted.

"Ah, yes. That was an adventure! We were working past Secret town about sixty miles from Yee Fow. They had warned us about walking on the trestle, you know, the centipede. But I had gone back to the camp to pick up an extra axe and needed to get back to work quickly. So, being young I figured a quick run across the trestle was the fastest route.

[99]

"Well, I made it across just fine and picked up the axe. I started back, and halfway across the trestle I felt the trestle shaking and heard a rumbling noise. Turning around, I was faced with a monstrous steam-breathing dragon of a locomotive bearing down on me! It wasn't more than fifty feet away! I thought about running to the other end, but knew I would never make it. And that locomotive was never going to stop for a Chinese. The engineer was looking to run me down! This was sport for him!"

"What did you do, Papa? "

"Well, I looked down, saw the ground far below, and realized that jumping was a bad idea. So, I climbed out to the edge, grabbed onto the railroad tie, swung down and hung on with both hands, while that train rumbled overhead! The whole trestle was shaking and I could smell the oil and steam from the locomotive. By the time the train had passed, my arms were aching. But I was alive!"

"What happened to the axe, Papa?" Kim asked with a puzzled look.

"When I climbed back up after the train passed, I looked around for it. Lo and behold, it was still laying on the track where I had dropped it in my mad scramble. It was lucky for me, because Stro would have made me pay for it out of my wages if I had lost it!" laughed Lai Wah. "Stro liked me because I could speak his language, but he was a stickler and demanded a full day's work with few breaks."

"What did you do at night after work, Papa?" Bing asked. "Did you see any wild Indians?"

"We did come across native Indians from time to time. They seemed to like us. They sure looked a lot like the Cantonese people. I think they saw the resemblance too. Once near the summit I met an Indian who had worked for the United States Army as a scout. He could speak English and told me about his land and people in the flatlands beyond the summit."

"Did he come from Montana where Uncle Jick lives? Can I visit his tribe?" asked Bing hopefully.

"He said he was a Shoshone. I don't know about Montana, Bing. You can ask your Uncle Jick."

Lai Wah was lost in his thoughts, remembering life in the camp like it was yesterday. After work, all 28 men returned to camp dirty and exhausted. Every day Ah Chew had ready a huge boiler tub of water set over the campfire. First thing they did was to wash with hot water. That warm sponge bath was a luxury beyond belief. Layers of dirt and grime came off. They washed down from head to toe and undid their queue to clean their hair every night. They changed into clean clothes and braided their queue, while Ah Chew served them the most delicious dinner of Cantonese food. The men squatted around the campfire with rice bowls and chopsticks in hand. The food was divine. They had fish, bamboo shoots, oysters, clams, pork, vegetables, rice and hot tea.

"Eating outdoors in the mountains after a full day's work is the best way to enjoy Chinese food, boys!"

"Where did you sleep, Papa?"

"They gave us tents, but we turned them in once we learned that we had to pay to use the tents. That was a waste of money. In the good weather we slept under the stars. Later we made shelters from materials we found, and sometimes we found caves to live in."

Once they reached the high mountains, the snow started to fall, and the men slept in crude cabins that were quickly buried under the snow. They had to dig a tunnel from the cabin to get to the summit tunnel where they were working. They were like moles living underground. They never saw the sun for months that winter. The snowstorms were non-stop for days on end, and afterwards there was the constant threat of avalanches. One winter an avalanche wept away an entire camp of Chinese. They searched for days but never found any of them until the following spring.

"Papa, tell us the story about Uncle Jick's eye! Have you ever seen what it looks like?" Bing interrupted unable to contain his questions any longer.

"Jick Wah wears that eye patch with pride, but how he got it was not a pretty story nor one for the faint of heart. Your Uncle Jick has the heart of a lion and sees more with one eye than most men see with two!"

"Yes, but how did he lose it? What happened?" Bing protested impatiently.

"It was in the spring of 1867. We had been drilling and blasting at the Summit Tunnel for over one year. The work was dark, dirty and very dangerous. We had three crews of Chinese working on each of the four faces of the tunnel on eight-hour shifts. Our progress after working for 24 hours was only ten inches on each face!"

"How did you have four faces, Papa? You can work from both ends but that makes only two faces," Kim observed with a puzzled look.

"You are right, Kim. But we drilled a huge shaft down the middle of the mountain so Chinese could work from the inside of the tunnel in both directions. So, two from the inside, and one from either end makes four faces."

Crocker and Strobridge were growing impatient. They had been struggling to build their railroad through the mountains for almost four years. After a while, they brought in Cornish miners to speed things along.

"But, you know boys we Chinese beat the pants off those miners in no time. We blasted out more tunnel in a shorter time! The Cornish miners threw down their tools in disgust and quit after just one week!

"Anyway, your Uncle Jick and I were working on the west face farthest from Donner Lake. We were deep in the bowels of that tunnel. It would have been pitch black except for the dim light of the kerosene lanterns. The third member of our crew was Lun Chung. Jick was smaller but agile, so he held the star drill and rotated it while Lun and I took turns striking the drill with our twelve-pound sledgehammers. It was non-stop pounding, all so we could drill a hole in the solid granite deep enough to pack with black powder. The hole had to be 18 to 24 inches deep for black powder but only 12 inches deep for nitroglycerine."

"I vote for using nitro. It would be a lot less work making smaller holes in the granite," offered Bing.

"Yes, but that nitro was nasty stuff! It was much more powerful than black powder but it kept blowing up before we were ready!"

Because the nitroglycerine was too dangerous to ship on the trains without exploding, they had a chemist mix it up at the Summit Tunnel. They started testing the nitro early in 1867. The powerful nitroglycerine blew up the granite, making smaller debris that was much easier to remove. Progress on the faces improved from 10 to 24 inches per day. But the accidents with nitro started happening the very first day. A crew was using it on the interior face, and it exploded too early. Fortunately, no one was hurt that time, but it made everyone nervous.

"Did the nitroglycerine blow up in Uncle Jick's face?"

"Actually, Bing, we had stopped using nitro after those early accidents proved it was unsafe. We switched back to using black powder."

The men had been working for several hours that day and had finally drilled a hole deep enough to pack with powder. Packing the black powder into the hole, inserting the fuse and lighting the fuse was Jick's job. The men stayed with him until he was ready to light the fuse, and then they ran out of the tunnel. They usually had about fifteen seconds to make their escape before the explosion and the rain of rocks and debris and smoke choked the tunnel. Jick was always right behind. He was so fast and wiry that sometimes he passed them running out of the tunnel.

"What happened that day, Papa?"

"Well, we never did find out. All I know is that Jick never made it out of the tunnel that day. The explosion seemed to happen too soon. We kept waiting for Jick to come through the smoke and debris. But the seconds passed and the smoke started to clear, and Jick was nowhere to be seen!

"Jick didn't make it out! I called out frantically to Lun and the other men.

"We all ran back into the tunnel."

The air was still choked with dust and smoke, and it was dark even with their lanterns. They frantically searched for Jick, fearing the worst. They had all seen these accidents before, and the results were pretty horrifying.

"He's over here!" Lun called out.

"I ran towards the light of Lun's lantern, and found him bent over Jick's crumpled body. We gently turned Jick over, certain that he was dead. What we found was Jick's bloody and mangled face covered with soot and debris. It must have blown up right in his face. It was hard to look at him.

"We were trying to make a stretcher to remove Jick's body from the tunnel when I heard a noise coming from Jick! Looking closer with the lantern I could see Jick's bloody lips moving!"

"Jick! You're alive!

"I had to strain to hear his whispered reply. 'Of course, I am alive little brother! Don't give up on me. We Cantonese don't quit! Now get me out of here!' "

"Did he really say those words, Papa?" Bing asked with pride.

"Yes, your Uncle is a tough and proud man who refused to die in that tunnel."

They took him back to camp, and Ah Chew cleaned and patched him up as best he could. It was clear that his right eye was destroyed. They had the Chinese doctor attend to his wounds. Later Stro brought Jick one of his eye patches to wear. Jick wore that eye patch with pride. He said it reminded him that life can be tough, but you always have to always get back up and never be afraid.

"I think your Uncle Jick and your mother both have that spirit, Lai Wah observed."

"Did Uncle Jick help you to finish the tunnel?" Kim wondered.

"It took Jick a couple of weeks to recover. But soon enough he was right back at it working in the tunnel, and Jick was there when the Chinese finally broke through in August that summer. Seeing the light streaming through the hole in the granite face, after fifteen months of backbreaking work, was miraculous.

"You can't imagine the cheers from all the workers, Chinese and Whites alike! The whole mountain came alive! It was a moment of celebration that I will never forget!"

"Was it easy work after the summit tunnel?" Kim continued questioning.

"Actually, Kim, we had another nine tunnels on the eastern side to complete before we reached Reno the next June. But those tunnels were no match for the Chinese railroad men. Our boys had become the best railroad men the world had ever seen! Those other tunnels were a piece of cake compared to that monstrous tunnel at the summit."

[100]

The men also had to finish building the snow sheds to protect the new railroad from snow and avalanches. The Chinese built 37 miles of those massive wooden sheds. After the Summit Tunnel, Jick and Lai Wah switched to working on the snow sheds.

"I think we both had earned a break from those dangerous tunnels. It was also harder for Jick to see with only one eye."

"Papa, did you see the railroads meet at Promontory, Utah? I learned about Utah in school from Mrs. Greer!" beamed Kim.

"Yes, Kim. Jick and I watched the final rails being placed by the Chinese. We honored our best workers that day to take part in laying the final rails. Ging Cui, Wong Fook, Lee Shao and five other Chinese brought up the last two rails. They let the big shots try to pound in the final golden spike, but they were pathetic! Stanford missed entirely, and Durant was not much better. Strobridge had to finish driving in the final spike through a special tie made of laurel wood. As soon as the big shots left, the pocket knives came out and that wooden tie was chopped into a thousand pieces for souvenirs."

"But Papa, in school I saw a photo of that moment at Promontory when the railroads met, and the Chinese are not in it. Where were you and Uncle Jick?" asked Kim clearly puzzled by the photo and his father's story.

"That photo was staged for the photographer hours after we Chinese laid the final rail!" huffed Lai Wah. "It is a fake!"

Actually, Jick and Lai Wah were miles away in Strowbridge's private rail car at Victory. When they entered that car Strobridge introduced them as the Hung Wah brothers, who had been his trusted foremen for all those many years. He toasted the Chinese workers and declared that the Central Pacific Railroad owed a great debt to these men, who built that railroad through the mountains of California and Nevada.

"You must have been surprised, Papa!"

"You have no idea! And when the soldiers and reporters stood and gave three hearty cheers, I felt like my chest was going to explode from pride! I think in the many years since then most of this country has forgotten what we did in those mountains. But on that day, in that railroad car, they knew that what the Chinese had accomplished was nothing short of a miracle."

"Was it a miracle, Papa?" asked Kim with a smile of pride.

"No, Kim. It was just the Chinese spirit of *gong keung*, you know, tough spirited and determined. Chinese also know how to bend like a willow, adapting, persevering, but never breaking. Like Uncle Jick says, *little by little we will get the job done.*"

CHAPTER 37

Bing and Kim Depart for Montana 1904

Slowly, the glaze in Hung Lai Wah's eyes cleared. The railroad, the blasting, and the horrible biting cold of the snow-covered mountains faded into his past. Lai Wah looked down and saw Kim and Bing staring back at him, listening intently to the story they had heard so many times before.

Kim had been trying to memorize his father's face, not knowing when they would see him again. "We will remember your story, Papa."

Just then Uncle came bustling down the steps, two at time. "Where are they?" he exclaimed. "I hope Bing and Kim did not leave without their old Uncle Jick!" he joked.

The boys smiled. They had just met Uncle but already liked him and thought of him as family. Mother came to the door with little Kim Toon clinging to her dress. She had two bundles neatly packed with all the boy's possessions. There was clothing, a little food for the long train ride, and a photo of the family taken just last year. Somehow she knew that it would be the last time they would all be together. She pulled each boy close, barely able to see them through her teary eyes.

[101]

"Work hard and obey Uncle. Remember to go to the American school and study hard. Always think of your family and come home to me soon. And Bing, you watch out for your brother!"

Bing and Kim hugged their mother and then scrambled

down the steps chasing after Uncle, who was already waving at the cable car coming down the steeply inclined street.

Kim and Bing jumped up onto the cable car and took seats on the outside. It was still early so there weren't many Barbarians riding on the car. Suddenly, the car lurched forward with a rumble and headed down the street away from Chinatown. The driver reached up and rang the bell *Clang! Clang!* Kim thought what a glorious adventure this was! He watched the driver work the two levers at the front of the car. Looking down at the tracks, he wondered about the great engine that pulled the cable and the cars through the whole city.

As the cable car turned the corner and headed down the steep street, both boys stood in unison holding on to the pole with both hands. Uncle Jick smiled as he saw the glow of excitement in their faces with their queues flying in the wind.

"Kim! Bing! Hold on tight! We don't want you to fall off. The demons would have you for breakfast! What would I tell your Mother?"

The boys smiled and grabbed on to the pole more tightly.

"Bing! Look at the view!" Kim exclaimed. "There's the bay and Alcatraz, and Angel Island and Goat Island!" He had learned of these places in the American school but had never seen them himself. Looking out over the wooden houses of Dai Fow he saw the fog sitting like a fluffy blanket covering the opening to the bay. He knew that was where the great steamers arrived from China. Father had told him of his journey from Dai Long Village in China to Gum Saan in 1864. Someday he too would travel on a great ship and see the world.

At the bottom of the first hill the cable car slowed down as it passed a horse-drawn cart filled with fruits and vegetables. Bing looked at the driver and immediately recognized Uncle Doc Wah, their father's older brother!

"Uncle!" cried out Bing. "We are going to Montana!"

Uncle Doc Wah looked up while holding the reins and waved at the boys going by.

"Be good! Watch out for the demons and the grizzly bears!"

Kim looked at Bing and asked, "What did he mean about bears?"

"Don't worry, Kim. The bears are big, but they won't bother us. I'm more worried about the Indians!" replied Bing with a smile.

"There aren't any Indians in Kalispell! Mother wouldn't send us to a place with wild Indians would she?" asked Kim.

"Yes, there are too Indians in Montana! Don't you know about Custer and Little Big Horn? That's in Montana," replied Bing.

Bing liked studying about the Indians the same way machines, gears and wheels fascinated his younger brother.

Kim sat quietly, hoping that Bing, as usual, was kidding about the Indians. He did recall something about Little Big Horn.

As they approached the wharf, Kim and Bing could smell the salt air and hear the gulls flying overhead. Kim spotted a group of sea gulls squabbling over scraps of food and thought to himself, *That's just like the Tang people in the Chinese market*! He recalled the day the fishmonger dropped a box of fresh fish, scattering hundreds of fish over the market floor. All the Tang people scrambled for the fish. Reaching his short arms between the legs of the Chinese men, Kim snared the slippery fish. That day he came home with pockets stuffed full of smelt. He was so excited to show Mama his "catch" that that he didn't notice the smell!

The cable car came to a stop and Uncle jumped off with the boys right behind. Kim and Bing ran over to the wharf and looked between the railings. Trailing behind, Uncle Jick laughed to himself at the sight of the two boys dressed in their mandarin robes with their heads stuck out between the rails and their queues dangling down behind them.

"Look at all the boats! There must be hundreds!" Kim exclaimed.

Bing looked out and saw the bobbing boats with their fisherman bringing in the morning's catch.

"Those fishermen must get up as early as Father. Come on, Kim. Let's go explore the docks!"

Just then the both boys looked up and saw the white ferryboat approaching the dock with smoke billowing from its stack. It was making its first trip of the day across the bay from Oakland to San Francisco. EUREKA was written in big block letters on its side. The ferryboat slowed as its captain began to maneuver the boat in towards the dock. Kim spotted the paddle wheel slowly churning up the dark bay water. He knew that he would have to take a closer look when they got on board.

The ferryboat Berkeley was already moored at the dock. Kim knew it was the first propeller-driven ferry to be used on the bay. Father had told him all about the ferryboats they might ride on. He secretly hoped they would ride on the Eureka so he could throw his Chinese coins into the paddle wheel.

"Kim, Bing! Let's go! They are going to board soon and we need to buy our tickets." called out Uncle, as he hurried off down the wharf towards the Ferry Building.

Forgetting their plans to explore the dock, the boys jumped up and ran after Uncle Jick.

"He sure does have a lot of energy." said Kim. "Do you think he ever rests?"

"In Montana you have to move fast so the grizzly bears don't catch you!" responded Bing with a grin.

As the boys caught up with Uncle, they found him in line at the ticket counter. The man selling the tickets looked down quizzically at Bing and Kim. His handle bar mustache almost touched his ears and looked like giant furry tails to Kim.

"What kind of a git-up is that?" he asked suspiciously inspecting the boys' Chinese robes and skullcaps. "They can't get on the ferryboat dressed like that!"

Without missing a beat Uncle responded, "These boys are descendants of the great Emperor of China. This is the official dress for the royal family. They are going to meet the Emperor in Montana and give him a tour of this great country. They must dress in the royal clothes or bad luck will come to you and this ferryboat company!"

"Well, why didn't you say so? Come on aboard!" replied the demon with a wink as he handed Uncle three tickets.

Kim looked at Bing in disbelief, "Uncle talks fast too!"

"Hurry up! Let's get on the ferry before he changes his mind!" hissed Bing.

The boys followed Uncle around a corner and down a dark passageway. When they came out into the sunlight Kim was delighted to see the Eureka with her huge paddlewheels waiting for them at the dock. Kim and Bing walked down the gangway, they both felt the up and down motion of the wooden planks giving way under the weight of the passengers.

Once on board the boys rushed over to the side of the ferry and looked out over the railing. Suddenly Kim realized that he was surrounded by demons! He tried to look out at the bay, but he knew they were staring at him. Mama had warned him about these "White ghosts." Perhaps someone had overheard Uncle's tall tale about the Emperor and they were now going to make them get off the ferry. Turning around, he spotted Uncle talking amiably to a demon man and he felt much better.

Seeing the worried look on Kim's face, Uncle came over to

the railing and looked down at his nephews.

"Well, boys, are you ready to start the journey to Montana?"

"Yes, Uncle!" Kim and Bing chimed in unison.

"Will we sleep on the ferry?" asked Kim.

"Oh, no!" laughed Uncle Jick, "The ferry ride to Oakland is very short. We will be there in thirty minutes. Now, when your father and I came to Gum Saan so many years ago, that was a real journey. It took us almost two months to cross the great ocean from Kwangtung to Gum Saan! 1000 Chinese slept and ate and got sick in the hold of the ship. We rarely went on deck. Compared to that wretched trip, this ferry ride will be a luxury cruise."

A sudden blast from the Eureka's horn announced that they were ready to depart. Kim and Bing looked down over the railing and saw the gap widen between the dock and the side of the ferry. Slowly they pulled away from the dock and then picked up speed as the Eureka headed out into the Bay.

Kim felt the wind blowing on his face. He hoped that his skullcap wouldn't fly away. He looked back and saw the wharf and the buildings of Dai Fow growing smaller in the distance. Now he knew for sure that they were leaving Mama and Father. He wondered when he would see them again. Perhaps going to Montana wasn't such a good idea. He didn't much like the thought of having grizzly bears and Indians as neighbors.

"Kim! Come and look!" cried out Bing.

Kim looked up and saw Bing leaning over the rail. He scrambled over to the edge of the boat. "What's the big deal, Bing?"

"Look at the foam coming off the boat!" replied Bing. "Uncle said the foam comes from the breath of the sea dragons guarding the boat."

"Look Bing! There's Alcatraz!" shouted Kim, as he peered at the outlines of the buildings on the island. "I wonder if they have any Tang people on that island."

"I doubt it. And if there are any, they're never getting off that island, unless the sea dragons carry them back home!" said Bing with a smile.

Just then Kim placed his small hand into the pocket of his robe and felt the three smooth, cool coins with the square hole in their middle.

"I guess it's time to keep our promise to Mama, Bing!"

With that he went to the side of the boat with the three Chinese coins clutched in his hand. He looked at the sea and then looked back towards Dai Fow, just in case Mama was somehow watching. Forgetting his plan to throw the coins into the paddlewheel, he closed his eyes and then dropped them into the dark blue waters of the bay.

Opening his eyes just in time to see the coins break the surface of the water and disappear into the depths, Kim sighed, "I hope Mama was right about the coins bringing us good luck."

Bing watched Kim intently and then threw his three coins as far out into the bay as he could!

"There! That should appease the sea dragon and keep the evil spirits busy looking for my three coins!"

Sometime later Uncle Jick came up to Bing at the railing and asked, "Where's your brother, Bing? You are supposed to watch out for him."

"He was just here, Uncle! Honest!" pleaded Bing.

"OK. Let's go and find him before the demons throw him overboard." said Uncle, as he headed off in the direction of the cabin deck.

Suddenly, Bing spun around and exclaimed, "I know where he is, Uncle Jick!" Remembering his brother's fascination with wheels and gears Bing headed down the narrow stairs marked "Engine room."

As they went lower into the dark bowels of the ship, the rhythmic chugging noise of the engine grew louder and louder. The fresh salt air was replaced by the warm oily smell of the ferryboat's innards. Just as they climbed down the third ladder they spotted little Kim in his mandarin robe staring transfixed at the great walking beam steam engine that drove the Eureka's twin 27-foot paddle wheels.

Turning around as if he expected to see them Kim purred,

"Isn't she beautiful! Someday I will make an engine like this for a great ship!"[102]

As they emerged from below deck, Bing and Kim felt the ferry slowing down. They raced to the railing where they both spotted the twin towers guarding the entrance to the mooring at the Oakland pier. The wooden pilings lining the passageway with the small dark opening of the ferry building at its end made Kim think of being swallowed into the gullet of a giant serpent.

"Goodbye sea dragons!" called out Kim, as he turned around for one last look at his home now far off across the bay. He was glad to have had their protection and wondered if the train to Kalispell had such friendly dragons.

The ferry bumped into the dock, and two demon men threw ropes to workers on the dock while other men lowered the gangplank.

"Bing and Kim, let's go! It's time to find our train to Montana." called out Uncle Jick as he hustled towards the gangplank with the boys trailing behind.

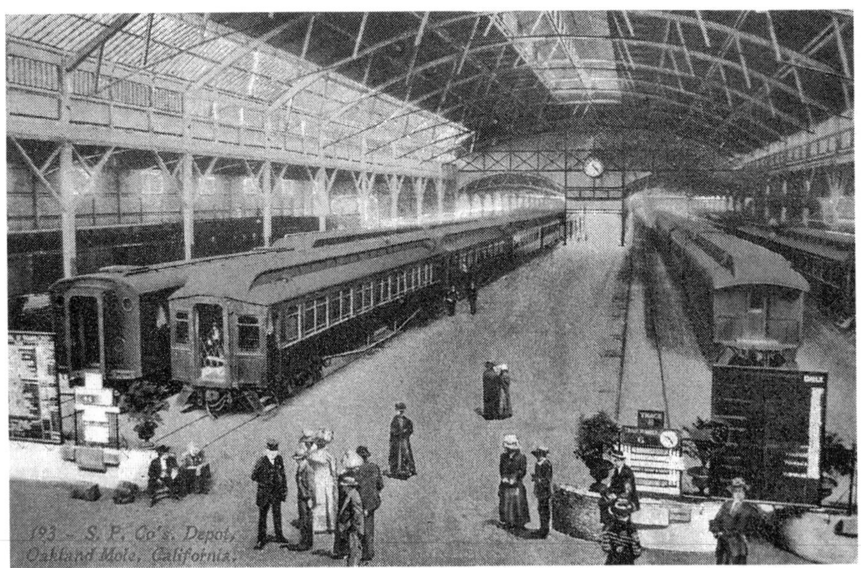

[103]

As they disembarked, they entered a long wooden building with a curved roof that was filled with passengers and trains.

"They call this building the Oakland Mole," explained Uncle Jick.

"Maybe it's because it feels like we're underground."

Kim and Bing stared silently at the rows of trains. There were red trains, green trains and yellow trains. The cars were lined up in long rows with the locomotive at the front. They looked like they were ready to race out of the station at a moment's notice.

Bing wandered over to the nearest train. "Kim, look! This is the caboose with a smokestack on the roof. I'll bet we could ride up there on top! What a great view we could have!"

Uncle Jick laughed, "That would be a pretty cold trip to Montana, Bing. The mountain passes are full of snow. For this trip you had better sit inside with me and Kim."

Bing followed Uncle and Kim towards the front of the train but couldn't help looking back at his caboose. "Someday," he thought to himself, "I will travel on this train and see the West."

[104]

Back in Dai Fow, Ah Ying looked out the window of their apartment on Sacramento Street imagining Kim and Bing on their journey to Montana. At least they had Jick Wah to watch over them. But the home was too quiet without her boys, and she felt a loneliness that only a mother can understand.

Stop your sniveling, Ah Ying! You taught your boys to survive. Now let them go and have their adventure. At least Uncle Jick can feed them. With those thoughts Ah Ying turned her attention to Gee Sung whose illness had slowed him down.

I will need all of my strength and that of little Chun Ngo to see us through.

CHAPTER 38

Supporting the Revolution
The Manchus Must Go!

The knock at the front door at 834 Sacramento was soft at first and then grew to a loud incessant rapping.

"Ah Ying! Open up! We can't be late for the meeting. Dr. Sun is speaking!"

Ah Ying opened the door to find her friend Sing Yee waiting impatiently.

"*Nei hou*, Sing Yee. What is this meeting you have been pestering me about?"

"It is the Toong Mung Wui[105]. You remember we demand a free and independent China. Free of the yoke of oppression that we Han Chinese have endured for almost 300 years at the hands of the Manchus and their evil Qing Dynasty!"

"Ever since you returned from China last year, you have had this patriotic fire burning in you, Sing Yee. I am afraid that it is going to consume you."

"Don't worry, my Ah Ying. I hate the Manchus, but I love China. In China for three years I was surrounded by intellectuals and students all agitating for change, to overthrow the Manchu Dynasty and to establish a democratic China," Sing Yee replied as she absently pulled out a pouch of tobacco and began to roll a cigarette.

"What did the Emperor ever do to hurt you? And since when did you start smoking?"

"Don't get me started, Ah Ying. The Manchus invaded our

Kingdom almost 300 years ago and have subjugated us and taxed us into submission. Our men must wear their hair in a long queue as a symbol of subservience or be threatened with beheading! Enough! It is time for us to overthrow these foreign invaders! And I can smoke if I want to. This is the 20th century, Ah Ying!"

Ah Ying was quiet as she thought pensively about her life, and how in a very real way the Manchus were responsible for the poverty in her village that had forced her parents to do the unspeakable, to sell their own daughter for a few measly yuan.

"You are right, Sing Yee. They took away my family's dignity. What can we do as women?"

“We are women warriors in this revolution! Just like the legendary Mook Lan[106], who as a young girl, took the place of her elderly father when he was conscripted into the army to defend China against invaders. In China today women are rising up, and their voices are being heard!”

“But Mulan is only a legend from over 1500 years ago. What about today?”

“Women are joining the revolution in China and overseas. Qiu Gin[107] is a young woman from our Gin family, who is a leader in the movement against the Manchus. She is younger than you, Ah Ying, but she is already a force that strikes fear into the heart of the dynasty. She wears Western men’s clothing, is an expert in martial arts, and writes and speaks passionately on women’s rights and her Anti-Manchu ideology.”

“Where do we start?”

"Come to the meeting in Portsmouth Square. Hear Dr. Sun Yat-sen speak, and then join us in this revolution! Dr. Sun is the spearhead of the revolution, but the party needs all of us to carry forward the fight for China's independence."

"Alright. Chun Ngo can stay to take care of her father."

Lai Wah appeared in the doorway, his face swollen from Beri-Beri. "Go, Ah Ying. We Chinese must drive out the Manchus and cast them back into the hole they climbed out of. And while you are gone, I may cut off my queue to defy the emperor!"

Ah Ying smiled at her Gee Sung. "Get some rest. I will be back soon. If I don't go, Sing Yee will never stop pestering me."

As the two friends walked down Sacramento Street, they passed the shops and stores she knew from her childhood. The sidewalks were crowded with barrels, crates and baskets packed with every imaginable Chinese vegetable and fruit, seafood, meats and dry goods for sale. Live chickens were clucking in their wooden pens. Rows of roasted duck hung by their feet in the storefronts, and the aroma of steaming dim sum wafted from the steamers positioned over wood-burning stoves lining the alleyways. They passed horses waiting patiently on the cobble stone street still hitched to their two-wheeled carts while Chinese merchants readied their shops for the day's business. The world and China might be changing, but the sights and sounds of San Francisco's Chinatown had changed little in the past three decades.

Turning left on DuPont Gai, they came to 710 DuPont where they found Sing Yee's daughter Suey Fong waiting for them outside the Chee Sang Tong drug store.

"Hurry, mama! We are going to be late for the meeting!"

"Where is your brother?" Sing Yee asked looking up at their apartment above the drug store.

"Uncle Lun says that Hong Theung must work in the store today."

"The revolution is more important than making a few yuan in the store." Sing Yee replied.

"Come on, Mama. We don't have time to argue with Uncle. Brother can come to the next meeting."

The three women made short work of the two blocks to Portsmouth Square walking briskly along DuPont and turning right on Commercial and left on Kearny. At the corner of Commercial and Kearny, Ah Ying stopped to look at her old home at 711 Commercial where each of her five children had been born.

"Do you remember delivering my first baby, Sing Yee?"

"I remember running from the Spanish Building on DuPont to your apartment. I was gasping for breath by the time I arrived."

"You were a perfectly calm and controlled midwife."

"It was a show. Believe me I was out of breath! It was an easy delivery, but then you started to complain about the sitting month. What a baby you were!"

"Yes. It's a good thing you brought out Uncle Chan's gingered pig's feet!"

Both women laughed enjoying their shared memories, while Suey Fong looked on with a puzzled expression.

"But now we women must do more than have babies and sons for our families," Sing Yee offered, turning serious.

"What do you mean? Isn't having a baby difficult enough?"

"We must raise our children to support the glory of a free China. You see, Ah Ying, I have a plan. Someday soon we will have grandchildren and I will give each child a patriotic Chinese name. The first will be *Hing Wah*: to raise a new China! The next grandchild will be named *Cherk Wah*: to make China supreme! I have a whole long list of names just in case I am blessed with many grandchildren!"

"How many names have you come up with?"

"Don't get me started. *Jerng Wah*: to contribute her best to China, *Jook Wah*: to construct a new China. I have more!"

"No, that's enough. I think you should be giving the lecture today for the Toong Mung Wui, my friend," Ah Ying laughed.

As they approached Portsmouth Square, they could see that the grassy square was packed with dozens of Chinese men dressed in their finest American suits. The three women stood out conspicuously.

"Mama, there are no other women here," Suey Fong whispered.

Just then Ah Ying and Sing Yee felt a hand on their shoulders. Both women turned around and found themselves face-to-face with a middle aged mustached Chinese man.

"Welcome sisters. Thank you for joining our revolution. We

need all Chinese to restore the glory of China, both men and women." he proclaimed.

"Thank you, Dr. Sun," Sing Yee began.

[108]

"No thanks are necessary. You two women have struggled more than any of these men. We are honored to have you join us as warriors in our fight for the freedom of the motherland," Dr. Sun assured them, as he gestured for them to take a seat in the front row.

Ah Ying listened intently to every word. Dr. Sun Yat-sen was an impassioned advocate for a free and democratic China. She had never heard such words. The Principles of the People: nationalism, democracy, and the right to a decent livelihood awakened in Ah Ying an awareness of a new and better life that she had never imagined. By the end of the hour she too felt the patriotic fire burning inside of her belly. She glanced at Suey Fong and Chin Shee. Both women were entranced by Dr. Sun's words.

"The world is changing, and China is changing. We must restore the glory of China. Not to the glory of the past but to its rightful place as a democratic nation at the center of a modern world. The 20th century is upon us and we must overthrow the Manchu Dynasty that has subjugated the Chinese for nearly 300 years. The time for action is now. Change must start here with each of you. I need you to be soldiers in our revolution. Not to bear arms but rather to raise funds to support our cause!"

After the pledges for money to support the revolution were committed Ah Ying looked up and saw her friend Isaiah Taber with his camera and tripod.

"Hello Mr. Taber!" Ah Ying called out waving at her friend from so many years ago.

"Hello, Ah Ying! You haven't changed a bit since your days at the Mission Home!"

Ah Ying smiled and blushed, as she gave a wave to her friend, "It has been a few years Mr. Taber!"

Isaiah and his assistant then began the task of herding the throng of Chinese, arranging them for the group photo. After a few minutes of milling about, the group was set. Dr. Sun was in the middle of the second row surrounded by dozens of Chinese men. In the back row on the right Ah Ying, Suey Fong, and Sing Yee stood proudly as the newest member in the Toong Mung Wui. At the invitation of Dr. Sun Yat-sen, they were equal partners and warriors in this fight for a free and democratic Republic of China.

[109]

CHAPTER 39

Wednesday April 18, 1906 5:12 am

Ah Ying lay awake in bed with the image of her Gee Sung reaching out to her. It was not yet light outside. She knew it was 5 am. Gee Sung always haunted her in the predawn hour. In her dreams he was young and vibrant. The end of his life had been different.

Please, Gee Sung. You must leave us!

It had been over four months since he had died in their home at 830 Sacramento Street. In truth, he had been ill for over two years, but the last few months of his life were the worst. Swollen and disfigured from Beri-Beri[110]her Gee Sung was a shadow of the man she had fallen in love with so many years ago. Thirteen-year-old Chun Ngo had become her father's caregiver, until he passed on December 8th of last year. But now Ah Ying had to move on and care for her two remaining children. With little money or food, this would be difficult to manage. Ah Ying had taken on more seamstress work to make ends meet. There was the occasional call to perform midwifery, but life in *Tong Yan Gai* was darker than at any time she could recall.

We have always survived. This will be no different. Besides, Kim and Bing are safe in Montana with Uncle Jick Wah and are sending money home every month. They are good boys.

As she sat up on the edge of the bed, her worried thoughts were interrupted by a strong jolt, as the bed jumped up from the floor. Twenty seconds later at 5:12 a.m., the house shook violently with the floor pitching and rolling sideways. The bed slid across the room with Ah Ying clinging to the railing. Pots and dishes crashed to the floor in the kitchen. Plaster and dust filled the air as the ceiling and walls crumbled from the violent quake. The sharp sounds of breaking glass mixed with the rumblings from deep within the earth. The quake seemed to last an eternity. In truth the magnitude 8.0 earthquake that destroyed much of San Francisco lasted a terrifying 42 seconds.

Jumping off the bed, Ah Ying ran to the bedroom doorway. Feeling a sharp pain in her right foot, she looked down and saw glass shards and her bloodied foot. 'Aiyaah!' Finding her shoes, she hurriedly slipped them on her feet and ran towards the other bedroom.

"Chun Ngo! Gum Toon! Are you hurt?"

The silence that met her pleas was terrifying.

"Where are you, my children?"

The dust was thick, making it difficult to see anything and even harder to breathe.

"Cough! Cough!"

"Mama, I am fine. But I can't find sister," Gum Toon reported.

The bed was lopsided on the floor with one leg broken and parts of the ceiling plaster littered on top.

"Quick, lift up the bed. Maybe she is crushed underneath!"

Ah Ying and little Gum Toon heaved the heavy bed up into the air with a strength that only a panicked mother can possess. She looked under the bed. There was only more dust and debris.

"Where is Chun Ngo? She must be dead, crushed by the falling wall!"

"Look, Mama! The door is open!"

In the confusion she had not noticed that the front door was wide open. Running through the front room, Ah Ying reached the opened door overlooking Sacramento Street. What she witnessed was a scene from another world. Bricks from fallen chimneys littered the street. Up the street the entire front wall the old Mission Home at 933 Sacramento Street had collapsed, exposing her old room to the world. Dazed Chinese and San Franciscans were already starting to mill about.

"Look, Mama! There is Chun Ngo!" exclaimed Gum Toon pointing up the street.

Her daughter was standing in the middle of the street looking towards the waterfront. The billowing smoke was already darkening the sky from the dozens of fires which followed the devastating quake.

[111]

Running up to her daughter, Ah Ying grabbed Chun Ngou and held her tightly. "Aiyaah! What are you doing out here? I thought you were dead! Come inside quickly!"

Chun Ngou stood silently staring at the smoke and chaos unfolding on her street. "It may be safer out here, Mama."

"Don't argue! Come back inside at once!"

They made their way back towards their apartment. As they passed the now collapsed building at 933 Sacramento, Ah Ying wondered if her daughter's caution was warranted. She looked up at the exposed walls and marveled at how the wallpaper was the same as when she arrived there twenty years ago. They passed the new Mission Home on the opposite side of the street at 920 Sacramento. Except for the crumbled chimney, the five-story brick building was remarkably intact. She spotted Miss Cameron shepherding her girls away from the windows as they all stared at the devastation on Sacramento Street. They passed Miss Ferree carrying a large basket of bread.

[112]

"Ah Ying! What are you doing out on the street? It is chaos everywhere! Here, have a loaf of bread to feed your children. The local bakery donated it for the Mission Home. As our sewing teacher, that includes you and your little ones!"

"Thank you Miss Ferree," replied Ah Ying, grateful for her friend's kindness.

"Of course, Ah Ying. You are part of our family. Be careful using gas for your stove. People are reporting broken gas lines. It could be dangerous. And the water main broke, so there is no running water," Minnie cautioned over her shoulder as she hurried off to feed the girls at the Mission Home.

Ah Ying and her two children cautiously entered their home, stepping over and around the fallen furniture and debris to reach the kitchen table. Ah Ying and Chun Ngo prepared a quick breakfast of bread and cold cha siu from last night's dinner. The three were famished and ate the simple meal like it was a feast. They were terrified as the table shook suddenly for a few seconds.

Minnie Ferree was correct about the water main. There was no running water, and they heeded her warnings about the gas lines, eating the breakfast cold rather than risk a gas explosion.

Refugees from the lower parts of the city were quickly filling the streets on the hillside as they sought refuge and a better view of the rapidly spreading fires.

Later that afternoon Ah Ying looked out the window and saw Miss Cameron leading the fifty girls and children from the Mission Home, walking two-by-two up Sacramento Street towards Van Ness.

"The fires are getting closer! We need to go, Mama! The soldiers are making everyone leave and are setting up barricades. They have guns!" exclaimed Gum Toon.

"Alright! Get some clothes and whatever food you can find. We can follow Miss Cameron and the Mission Home family!"

Loaded with clothing, blankets and a food basket, Ah Ying, Chun Ngo and little Gum Toon gathered outside their home. Ah Ying spotted Sing Yee and her three children coming up from Dupont Gai.

"*Nei hou*! Sing Yee! Why are you coming this way?"

"Hello Ah Ying! The fires have blocked the streets in *Tong Yan Gai*! We can't get through! The whole Chinese quarter is in flames!"

"Come with us! We are following Miss Cameron!"

With that the two families joined forces and began the long trek up Sacramento to Van Ness Avenue. A sudden violent explosion shook the ground followed by another.

"Mama, is it another earthquake?"

"Don't worry, Gum Toon. We saw soldiers trying to stop the fires by using dynamite to blow up buildings," explained Chin Shee.

Gum Toon joined the other boys. "I am not afraid!"

Sing Yee smiled at Ah Ying, "I see this one has your spirit."

The whole city seemed to be fleeing at once. They were rich and poor, Chinese and Whites, men, women and children. They were all the same today, refugees from an earthquake. The events of this day had for now become the great equalizer.

They eventually arrived at the Old First Presbyterian Church at Van Ness and Sacramento Streets, where they spent the night with the Mission Home family. They were exhausted more from the events of the day than the one-mile walk through the rubble-strewn streets.

After a restless sleep on the church pews, the early morning prayer was interrupted by shouting from the back of the church.

[113]

"You have to leave immediately! The fires are approaching us from three sides. It is not safe to stay here a moment longer. Hurry! Gather your belongings and head out towards the Ferry Building!"

Outside, the early morning light was orange from the reflected glow of the approaching fires. Ah Ying looked back towards *Tong Yan Gai*. The whole city was ablaze with flames leaping from the tallest buildings and billowing smoke filling the sky.

Come on Ah Ying. You must keep moving to save the children.

"Sing Yee, we can't head back into the city to reach the ferry. That would take us right into the fires. We should head west away from the fires!"

"Yes. The other Chinese are heading towards the Presidio. I heard they are setting up tent camps with hot food and water."

With that, the two families bid farewell to Miss Cameron and the girls of the Mission Home.

"Good luck, my Ah Ying. We will all meet again someday soon," shouted Donaldina as she led her band of girls east on

Broadway towards the Ferry Building at the foot of Market Street.

Ah Ying and Sing Yee led their children west on Broadway towards the Presidio. Men in dark suits and bowler hats walked about as if they were going to work. Some cable cars were still running along Broadway. However, the threat of the approaching fires had everyone on edge as they stared at the smoke-filled sky to the east.

Approaching the County Jail on Broadway, they came upon a most unexpected sight. The jail had been severely damaged by the quake. Sixty National Guardsmen with rifles and fixed bayonets were escorting 176 prisoners down Broadway towards the Presidio. The prisoners were handcuffed to a long chain. Gum Toon, Wei Seung and Hong Seung Gin were fascinated by the spectacle.

One of the guardsmen called out to Ah Ying and Sing Yee, "You better get going Ma'am. We are going to dynamite the old jail as soon as these prisoners are evacuated to Fort Mason."

"Hurry children and don't look at those bad men!" cautioned Sing Yee.

Later that morning, as the families trudged along towards the Presidio, Sing Yee remarked, "Your daughter Chung Ngo and my son Hong Seung seem to be flirting. Maybe we should separate them."

Ah Ying had noticed the same thing as well. The two of them were laughing, oblivious to the surrounding chaos. "No, let them be. A little light-hearted fun is what they need right now."

"I will keep my eye on those two!" cautioned Sing Yee.

"Chun Ngo refused our match last year. Her father was furious. She said that she would only marry for love! How silly these young people are!" sighed Ah Ying.

"Finding love in an earthquake seems like a crazy idea." Sing Yee added with a smile, "I remember what a crazy and stubborn young girl you were with your Gee Sung!"

"Yes, but I was older. I do hope her sister Ah Kay is happy.

She was so young when she married Low Sun Fook. She never objected to the match because she knew we needed the money to feed the other children. Still I worry about her in Salem," confided Ah Ying. "She already has one child and is expecting another in September."

The families plodded uphill on Broadway, finally reaching the crest at Divisadero Street. Ah Ying stopped to catch her breath and enjoy the view of San Francisco Bay on the right. Even through the smoke and haze from the fires, the Bay was spectacular.

Further up Broadway, they approached a group of men and boys waiting in a long line that snaked down the street.

"Mama, I smell something good," Gum Toon said.

As they drew nearer, they spotted a man sitting in the middle of the street in front of a small oven made from fallen chimney bricks. He had a brisk little fire going with an iron skillet balanced on top. A wonderful aroma emanated from the golden-brown waffles he was preparing for the good citizens of San Francisco. It was a bit of culinary paradise in the midst of the chaos and destruction. Yesterday's millionaires and the downtrodden were all equal as they waited patiently for their turn to sample the delectable hot waffles. Business was booming! The hand-written sign proclaimed, "High Sierra Waffles! Pay What You Can!"

Ed Toon looked longingly at the waffles and was disappointed by his mother's words, as she looked ahead on Broadway, spotting the greenery of the Presidio where they hoped to find shelter and some food.

"Let's keep going. We're almost there!"

They had to step over the twisted wreckage of a home whose wall had fallen into the street. Piles of bricks and debris slowed their progress as they picked their path along Broadway. Suddenly, the ground shook from another aftershock. This one was by far the strongest.

Ah Ying darted into the alcove of the nearest building. "Quickly, come stand in the doorway of this building. This is the safest spot around here," she instructed, as the five children and Sing Yee huddled with her in the entryway to the three-story brick mansion.

The shock wave passed, and they let out a sigh just as the next tremendous jolt struck. Wave after wave continued shaking the ground and buildings.

Gum Toon cried out, "Mama, make it stop!"

Ah Ying was about to reassure her son when the building began to creak and crumble. It had been weakened by yesterday's quake, and the added stress was too much for the old structure. She looked up just as the walls caved in around them. Bricks and debris and dust crashed down, completely blocking the doorway. And then there was silence and darkness.

"Gum Toon, Chun Ngo! Are you alright?"

The silence terrified her. *Come on Ah Ying! Get up! Find your children!*

"Ah Ying! Where are you?" Sing Yee coughed weakly.

"I am over here and I am alright. But where are my children?"

"We are over here, Mama!" Gum Toon and Chun Ngo called out in unison.

Ah Ying moved towards the sound of their voices, feeling her way in the semidarkness. Finally reaching her children, she grabbed Gum Toon, holding him so tightly that he called out, "Mama, I can't breathe!"

"Are you alright?"

"Yes, Mama. We are both OK. I think the entryway saved us but the brick walls collapsed and have trapped us in here!"

Sing Yee and her four children crawled through the debris and found Ah Ying and her children.

"We are trapped in here! The whole building must have collapsed around us!"

"Don't worry, Sing Yee. We can dig our way out. Just be very careful not to make the rubble collapse and bury us completely!"

Sing Yee and Ah Ying began to gingerly remove a few small bricks, then realized that their task was impossible.

"There is too much debris piled up. We can't remove it all," Sing Yee lamented. "We may never get out of here."

The children pitched in and removed some bricks. "There is too much, Mama, and it is wedged in too tightly!"

The seven of them were sitting in the darkness when Ah Ying heard some voices beyond the rubble. They all began to cry out, "Help! We are trapped in here! We are alive! Please help us!"

"Do you think they can hear us, Ah Ying?"

"I hope so, because they may be our only hope," she replied.

"Help us! Help!"

The dust in the air made it hard to breathe, but they kept yelling to their rescuers.

Please let them hear us! Ah Ying prayed silently.

They stopped and heard more men and the sounds of digging, as men slowly removed the piles of debris entombing them.

After twenty minutes a shaft of light broke through the darkness. It was a glorious light and the answer to Ah Ying's silent prayers.

As the opening enlarged, a hand reached in to help them to safety. Ah Ying looked up into the bright sunlight. She expected to see a policeman in a round bowler hat. Instead she saw a sandy haired young man with freckles. She instantly knew it was her old friend Billy. He had grown up, but it was indeed Billy, and he had the same mischievous smile!

"Billy! Do you remember me?"

"Of course, I remember you, Ah Ying! You're the little girl who escaped from the highbinders!" Billy grinned.

"And you are the boy who outran the hungry Chinese!" Ah Ying laughed without hesitating.

"Are you alright, Ah Ying?"

"Yes, I think so. We are really dusty and dirty but glad to be alive!"

Before long both families were out on the street. Ah Ying and Sing Yee looked back at the collapsed building that had almost become their tomb.

"Billy, what are you doing here?"

"I am trying to get to the Presidio. Our house was destroyed during the night. All of Irish Hill is gone. I passed Chinatown on the way here. There is nothing left, Ah Ying. Where is Lai Wah?" Billy asked looking at the children and Sing Yee.

"My Gee Sung passed away last December, Billy," Ah Ying replied softly as her eyes moistened at the thought of her beloved husband.

"I am sorry, Ah Ying. My mom died last year too, from consumption."

"I am sorry as well, Billy," Ah Ying replied looking at Billy. "I remember you standing next to your Ma on Powell Street as the police wagon took me back to the Mission Home.

"We were just a few minutes too late," Billy lamented.

"Yes, but then you followed me to the Mission Home and took my letter to Gee Sung at his cigar store!"

"We need to keep moving Ah Ying," Sing Yee interrupted. "You two can reminisce while we walk."

Both mothers inspected their children. They were dirty and Wei Gin had a swollen and bruised right ankle. It was a miracle that no one was hurt more seriously.

Sing Yee put Wei Gin on her back carrying her son along Broadway towards the Presidio.[114]

"Put me down, Mama. I can walk!"

"Not with that swollen ankle!"

"Here, let met carry him," offered Billy, as he hoisted Wei Gin into the air and onto his broad back. "We will be there in no time at all even without highbinders chasing us!"

[115]

Early that afternoon, they arrived at the camp set up on the Presidio. Hundreds of canvas tents stretched as far as one could see. Gum Toon made a beeline for the mess tent with a huge sign announcing in bold letters: "Free Hot Meals."

It was the first real food they had had in two days, and they were more famished then they realized. It wasn't Chinese food, but there were no complaints from the appreciative refugees.

Ah Ying found Billy sitting next to Gum Toon at the table.

"Billy, come with us. We are going across the Bay when it's safe."

"I think I will stay in San Francisco and try to start over here. My people are still up in the Portrero. But don't worry, Ah Ying. I seem to find you whenever you need me," Billy grinned holding out his hand.

"Thank you, Billy. Come to find us in Oakland someday," Ah Ying took Billy's hand and bid farewell to her friend.

The staff set up Ah Ying and her two children in a tent near the center of the camp with Sing Yee and her three children in a larger tent next door.

Life in camp was not as comfortable as their home on Sacramento Street, but Ah Ying knew that by now the fires had probably destroyed their home. They were fed regularly from large wagons which provided bread, corned beef and coffee. Donations of food and supplies from every community on the West Coast and across the country kept the thousands of homeless San Franciscans fed. Relief trains from as far away as Omaha, Nebraska arrived carrying food, medical supplies, groceries, cattle, hogs and sheep. However, it was the arrival of a ship filled to the brim with rice from the Emperor of China that was met with jubilation by the Chinese.

The Chinese refuges were rounded up and shuffled off to other camps. They were forced to move several more times, from Fort Mason to the golf links on the Presidio, and then on to the barren wind-swept parade grounds at Fort Point. The racial division between the Chinese and the White San Franciscans once again became evident, as the effects of the great equalizer quickly faded.

The fires that destroyed eighty percent of San Francisco finally burned themselves out by April 23rd. Ah Ying's decision to head west, away from the fires was probably correct. Although Miss Cameron and the girls boarded a ferry that took them to San Anselmo, 20,000 refugees were trapped by the fires at the foot of Van Ness and needed to be rescued by the USS Chicago on April 20th.

All told, 3,000 people perished in the earthquake. The real number was likely much higher, as the thousands who died in *Tong Yan Gai* were never fully counted. 225,000 were left homeless out of a population of 410,000. Overall, the cost of property damage from the earthquake was $400 million, the equivalent of $10.5 billion today.

Golden Gate Park, the Presidio, the Panhandle, and the beaches between Ingleside and North Beach were covered with makeshift tents. More than two years later many of the refugee camps were still in operation.

[116]

A few days after the earthquake, Ah Ying and Sing Yee and their children left the camp and made it down to the ferry, which took them to their new life in Oakland. Ah Ying would never return to San Francisco. From the ferry looking back at the receding city, she thought of all that had happened since she arrived here as a nine-year-old *mui tsai*. In those 26 years, she had escaped from her life of slavery, lived with Miss Culbertson at the Mission Home, fallen in love with her Gee Sung, been kidnapped by highbinders, started a family in Gum Saan, joined the Revolution, and now lived through the earthquake and great fire. This chapter of her life was complete, and once again she had survived.

Now I must visit my grandchildren, she smiled to herself. Reaching into her pocket she pulled out three Chinese coins, which she absently handed to little Gum Toon as the ferry churned through the waters of San Francisco Bay.

EPILOGUE

Ah Ying and her two children, Chun Ngo and Gum Toon, started a new life in Oakland along with thousands of other Chinese uprooted by the devastation of the 1906 earthquake. The flirtations of Ah Ying's daughter, Chun Ngo, and Chin Shee's son, Hong Seung, as they fled the fire and earthquake, blossomed into a young romance. This was not surprising, since the families were next-door neighbors on 6th Street in Oakland.[117] The two were married in May 1910. Kim and Bing remained in Kalispell, Montana until 1910 faithfully sending their entire monthly earnings home to mama to support the family in California. By the time Ah Ying reconnected with Kim in 1913, he had cut off his queue and swapped his Chinese Mandarin robe for an American suit and tie. Kim's fascination with the mechanical world became a lifelong passion. He was the first in the family to attend an American university graduating with a degree in engineering in 1917. It was Ah Ying's proudest moment when she took the streetcar up Telegraph Avenue in Oakland to see her son graduate from the University of California at Berkeley. Bing continued his fascination with the West, hitching rides on top of caboose cars while exploring the world. He remained in Montana where he learned to cook and bake, a profession that kept him employed at resorts and hotels.

Ah Ying's grandchildren included some of the earliest Chinese women to attend an American university in the early 1900's. Kay's daughter Elsie was the first Chinese to graduate from Willamette University in Salem, Oregon, Ella attended UC Berkeley, and Mei Gill, aka Isabel, became a physician, a rare accomplishment for Chinese American women in the early 1900's. Chung Ngo's daughters, Hilda and Jeanette, graduated from college, and her , Carol, became a missionary nurse in India. She served the same Presbyterian Church that had rescued Ah Ying as a young *mui tsai* in 1886, and from which she fled with her Gee Sung three years later. Kim's daughter Arabella studied voice at Julliard and starred in the Broadway production of the Flower Drum Song in 1958.

Gwunde's restless and adventurous spirit led him from Salem, Oregon to the South Pacific in WWII where he was awarded a Silver Star for bravery in combat. His younger brother Stanley followed him and served as a tail gunner on a B24 Liberator based in New Guinea. Stanley gave his life for his country in January 1943. The B24 and its crew were never found. After the war the Army Air Force returned Stanley's belongings to his mother Kay in Salem, Oregon. In the box she found the Air Medal he had been awarded for downing five Japanese zeroes, the pair of gloves she had sent him, $1.28 in spare change, and the three Chinese coins she had given her son when he left home to go overseas.

Today there are over 100 descendants of Ah Ying and Hung Lai Wah. All of us can trace our roots back to a Chinese slave girl rescued by missionaries and a Chinese teenage boy, who came to build a railroad that united our country. Their story of triumph over hardship and exploitation is not only a Chinese story. It is truly an American story.

[118]

AFTERWORD

Oral history has a way of blurring the edges and covering up the bumps and scrapes. A century after Ah Ying's arrival in America as a mui tsai, my family believed, inaccurately, that missionaries had brought her here as a child. Even her given name had been forgotten. Her husband had worked on a railroad and made cigars. This was all that remained of the rich and romantic story of Ah Ying and Lai Wah.

In Three Coins I wanted to tell the story through the eyes of Ah Ying, a nine-year-old mui tsai, whose defiant spirit allowed her to survive and take control of her life. To recreate a world that existed 140 years ago, and to see it through her eyes, was no simple task. I utilized a variety of sources. Books about Chinese immigration to America and the Chinese experience once in Gum Saan, provided a backdrop with important facts and figures. Interviews with relatives provided recollections but few details. Ah Ying's son Kim, who was born in 1894 and lived to be 100 years old, was an articulate spokesman for the Chinese and left a series of videotaped interviews. I poured over these recordings, noting the details of his life growing up in San Francisco's Chinatown and his journey to Kalispell, Montana. Kim adored his mother, Ah Ying, whom he remembered as a "grand old lady."

Understanding and recreating the world of Tong Yan Gai from 1880 through 1906 required an on-the-scene perspective. To this end, I found contemporaneous newspapers provided the most accurate and sometimes colorful account of the world in which Ah Ying and Lai Wah lived. The newspaper articles were an endless resource to learn about relevant subjects such as Chinese New Year celebrations in 1884, the slave trade, Presbyterian and Methodist rescue homes, the effects of the Chinese Exclusion Act, the devastation of the 1906 earthquake, and court proceedings of the day. Indeed, the very story of Ah Ying and Lai Wah was chronicled in the newspapers.

The photographs of Arnold Genthe, Isaiah West Taber, and Thomas Houseworth showing San Francisco's Chinese community and the West are treasures that capture the imagery of this world in black and white. Charles Weidner's colorized photographic post cards and the wonderful paintings of Robert Frederick Blum, Charles Graham, Theodore Wores, Jake Lee, and Mian Situ add the color that brings this world to life.

Today one can walk the same streets in San Francisco's Chinatown where Ah Ying and Lai Wah's story unfolded. Remarkably, the buildings today look very similar to old photographs taken before the 1906 earthquake. I hope that Three Coins has provided you with a rich glimpse into Ah Ying's and Lai Wah's lives and the world of Tong Yan Gai.

ABOUT THE AUTHOR

Russell Low is a physician with a passion for discovery and story-telling. His discoveries in the medical field have changed the way that his colleagues world-wide practice medicine and image disease. Discovery of his own roots began thirty years ago through the stories of his parents and their siblings. Growing up in Central California, more American than Chinese, his connection to Chinese culture and history was limited and incomplete. Discovering the 1903 Hong family photograph among the belongings of 100-year-old great Uncle Kim sparked a decades-long search for the stories behind the photograph. These are the stories presented in Three Coins. In his searches, Russell came across a 130-year-old newspaper notice describing a "Villainous-looking Chinese after a Chinese Girl." In the article, he recognized his great-grandparents' names, but the romantic drama it uncovered shook the core of his family's belief in who they are and how they came to be Americans. Russell frequently lectures on Chinese-American history, and his family's story has been featured on the History Channel, National Public Radio, and the Voice of America.

Russell lives with his wife Carolyn Hesse-Low, an avid and well-known plein air artist, in La Jolla, California where they raised their two sons Ryan and Robert.

BIBLIOGRAPHY

Wong, Kristin & Kathryn. Fierce Compassion. New Earth Enterprises, 2012.

Marin Mildred Crowl. Chinatown's Angry Angel: The Story of Donaldina Cameron. Palo Alto, Pacific, 1977.

Wilson, Carol Green. Chinatown Quest: One Hundred Years of Donaldina Cameron House 1874-1974. California Historical Society 1974.

McDonald Julie. Donaldina "Dolly Cameron: Rescuing Chinese Girls from the Sex Slave Trade in 1900's San Francisco. Kindle. 2019.

Jorae, Wendy Rouse. The Children of Chinatown. The University of North Carolina Press, 2009.

Hom Marlon K. Songs of Gold Mountain. University of California Press, 1987.

Chang, Leslie. Beyond the Narrow Gate. Penguin Group, 2000.

Steiner, Stan. Fusang The Chinese Who Build America. Harper and Row, 1979.

Miller, Stuart Creighton. The Unwelcome Immigrant. University of California Press, 1969.

See, Lisa. On Gold Mountain. Random House, 1995.

Lee Erika. At America's Gates. The University of North Carolina Press, 2005.

Ling, Huping. Surviving the Gold Mountain. A History of Chinese American Women and their Lives. State University of New York Press, 1998.

Hoobler Dorothy and Thomas. The Chinese American Family Album. Oxford University Press, 1994.

Choy, Phillip. Canton Footprints Sacramento's Chinese Legacy. 2007.

Pfaelzer, Jean. Driven Out. The Forgotten War Against Chinese Americans. Random House, 2007.

Chong, Denise. The Concubine's Children. Penguin Books, Ltd, 1994.

Tong, Benson. Unsubmissive Women. University of Oklahoma Press, 1994.

Pascoe, Peggy. Relations of Rescue. The Search for Female Authority in the American West, 1874-1939. Oxford University Press, 1990.

Yung, Judy. Unbound Feet. A Social History of Chinese Women in San Francisco. University of California Press, 1995.

Jung, Judy. Unbound Voices. A Documentary History of Chinese Women in San Francisco. University of California Press 1999.

Chang, Iris. The Chinese in America. Viking Penguin, 2003.

Xinran. Message from an Unknown Chinese Mother. Stories of Loss and Love. Scribner, 2010.

Dicker, Laverne Mau. The Chinese in San Francisco. Dover Publications, 1979.

Hsu, Madeline Y. Dreaming of Gold, Dreaming of Home. Transnationalism and Migration Between the United States and

South China, 1882-1943. Stanford University Press, 2000.

Xinran. The Good Women of China. Hidden Voices. Pantheon Books, 2002.

Peffer, Gregory Anthony. If They Don't Bring Their Women Here. Chinese Female Immigration Before Exclusion. University of Illinois Press, 1999.

Yep, Lawrence. Dragon's Gate. Harper Trophy, 1993.

McCunn, Ruthanne Lum. Thousand Pieces of Gold. Dell Publishing Company 1983.

McCunn Ruthann Lum. The Moon Pearl. Beacon Press, 2000.

Tchen, John Kuo Wei. Genthe's Photographs of San Francisco's Old Chinatown. Dover Publications 1984.

Davies, Peter Ho. The Fortunes. Houghton Mifflin Harcourt, 2016.

Ambrose, Stephen. Nothing Like it in the World. Simon & Schuster, 2000.

Griswold, Wesley. A Work of Giants. McGraw-Hill Book Company, Inc.,1962.

Bain, David Haward. Empire Express. Building the Transcontinental Railroad. Penguin Books, 1999.

Chew, William F. Nameless Builders of the Transcontinental Railroad. Trafford Publishing 2004.

Mckay, Kathryhn L. A Guide to Historic Kalispell. Montana Historical Society Press. 2001.

Bonnett Wayne and Linda. Isaiah West Taber. Windgate Press, 2004.

Genthe, Arnold. As I Remember. The Autobiography of Arnold

Genthe. Reynal & Hitchcock, 1936.

Lee, Sue. Finding Jake Lee. The Paintings at Kan's. Chinese Historical Society of America. 2012.

Hart Alfred A. Waiting for the Cars: Alfred A Hart's Stereoscopic Views of the Central Pacific Railroad. Nevada State Railroad Museum, 2012.

---

[1] *Neih hou* means "hello" in Cantonese

[2] Grandma Hong with Mei Gil and Gwunde in Salem, Oregon. Low Family Collection.

[3] Jou sahn means "good morning" in Cantonese

[4] joong is Cantonese word for zhongi in Mandarin

[5] Grandma Hong's name is Tom Gew Ying aka Ah Ying. She later assumes the name Ah Gew.

[6] 1 mou equals 0.165 acres

[7] Gum Saan is Cantonese for the Gold Mountain as they called California

[8] Baak haak chai which literally means "100 men's wife is the Chinese word for prostitute.

[9] Dai Fow is Cantonese for First City or San Francisco

[10] Isaiah West Taber – 1882 Landing San Francisco. Public Domain

[11] Tai Tai is Cantonese for madame

[12] Mui Tsai Ah Ying 1880's - San Francisco. Cameron House Collection

[13] Dupont Street was renamed Grant Avenue in 1908. Chinese today continue to call it Dupont Gai.

[14] Mui Tsai 1800's. Public Domain

[15] Bartlett Alley is now Beckett Street

[16] Sik faan – Cantonese word meaning: eat rice

[17] Joi gin – Cantonese word meaning good bye.

[18] Yellow dragon adorned flag is the Imperial flag of the Qing Dynasty

[19] Robert Frederick Blum (1857-1903) - Street Corner in Chinatown San Francisco c. 1890. Public Domain. The building decorations and flags are in celebration of Chinese New Year.

[20] Jake Lee (1915-1991) - Chinese New Year c. 1959 – Chinese Historical Society of America

[21] Hung Lai Wah 1903. Low / Hong Family collection.

[22] *Gio Mo Soon* or "Chicken Feather Letter" is an urgent plea. A letter with three feathers indicates the greatest urgency.

[23] Jackson Street. Public Domain. 611 Jackson Street is on the South side of the street between Grant and Kearny Streets. Current building is still a 3-story structure.

[24] The Presbyterian Church founded the Occidental Mission Home for Girls in 1874. Moved to 933 Sacramento Street in 1877 where they remained until their new building at 920 Sacramento Street was completed in 1893. The 920 Home was destroyed by the earthquake and fires in 1906 and re-

built in 1908. It is now called the Cameron House in honor of Donaldina Cameron who succeeded Margaret Culbertson after her death in 1897.

[25] Run by Mrs. Turner 933 Sacramento was the most fashionable boarding house in San Francisco and a meeting place for Southerners. Public Domain

[26] Margaret Culbertson. San Francisco Chronicle August 1, 1897. Public Domain

[27] Register of Inmates Presbyterian Mission Home. Courtesy of Doreen Der-Mcleod

[28] Ah T'sun laid the cornerstone for the new Mission Home at 920 Sacramento Street on July 4, 1893.

[29] Chun Mooie (1863- 1940) brought to America as a child slave she was rescued by Presbyterian missionaries May 21 1878. In March 1883 she married Ng Hon Kim another convert to Christianity.

[30] 1897 - Charles Weidner (1866-1940) Photographs of Presbyterian Mission Home. Published 1897 San Francisco Wave. Public Domain.

[31] 1897 - Charles Weidner (1866-1940) Photographs of Presbyterian Mission Home. Published 1897 San Francisco Wave. Public Domain.

[32] Thomas Houseworth - (1828-1916) The Christian Stairway. The Kimm Family Collection.

[33] Chin Shee – c. 1895. Gin Family Collection.

[34] 1897 Charles Weidner (1866-1940) Photograph of Presbyterian Mission Home. San Francisco Wave. "Women's Holy Work." San Francisco Chronicle April 9, 1887. Public Domain.

[35] Tong Yan Gai – Tang People's Streets was the original Cantonese name for San Francisco's Chinatown

[36] Isaiah West Taber – (1830-1912) Chinatown SF, CAL - Miss Cable's class of Chinese girls and boys. ca.1880's Public Domain.

[37] Piedmont Springs Japanese Tea Garden – Postcard published 1910 Public Domain

[38] San Francisco Chronicle July 21, 1887

[39] Chin Shee - by Chinese custom a married woman is called by her maiden name followed by Shee.

[40] Spanish Building was at 712 Dupont Street between Sacramento and Commercial Streets.

[41] Little red envelopes, called "**lai see**" (利是), are packets that contain good luck money.

[42] Pow Fah Gow is a Chinese poisonous bark.

[43] Isaiah West Taber (1830-1912) Dupont Street, Chinatown, San Francisco 1880's. Public Domain

[44] Bagnio originally meant bathhouse but came to mean brothel in 19th cen-

tury San Francisco.

[45] Charles Weidner Post Card. Dupont & Clay Streets . Hang Far Low Restaurant. 1880's. Public Domain.

[46] Today 821 Dupont (Grant Street) is still a 3-story residential building.

[47] Charles Weidner. Portsmouth Square and Hall of Justice, San Francisco, CA Public Domain

[48] geuhng fu – Cantonese "husband"

[49] Dupont Street by night, Chinatown, San Francisco, CA. c 1890. Public Domain.

[50] Gwoon Yum is Cantonese for Guanyin

[51] Register of Inmates Presbyterian Mission Home. Courtesy of Doreen Der-Mcleod

[52] Daily Alta California Volume 80, Number 132, May 10, 1889

[53] Margaret Culbertson From McNair Family Collection of photographs.

[54] San Francisco Chronicle. Thursday May 9, 1889 Highbinder's Work

[55] San Francisco Chronicle. Sunday May 12, 1889 Mrs. Sung's Age.

[56] San Francisco Chronicle Thu May 16, 1889 – Gee Sung's Wife.

[57] Daniel J. Murphy – The San Francisco Call. September 25, 1900. Public Domain

[58] Hon. J.C.B. Hebbard – History of Bench and Bar of California. 1889. Public Domain

[59] Register of Inmates Presbyterian Mission Home. Courtesy of Doreen Der-Mcleod

[60] San Francisco Chronicle Sunday May 19, 1889. Li Wo's Girl.

[61] Photograph of Kay and her children in Salem, Oregon. Low Family Collection.

[62] 711 Commercial Street is a three-story building on the corner of Commercial and Kearney Streets.

[63] San Francisco Chronicle July 14, 1891. Chasing a Chinese Beauty. Public Domain

[64] The Society for Prevention of Cruelty to Children often investigated reported cases of foot binding of infants and children but only rarely could prove pain and suffering in court.

[65] Arnold Genthe (1869-1942). Ah Ying and baby c. 1895. Public Domain

[66] Southen Pacific locomotive at Arcade Station, Los Angeles, CA 1891. Public Domain.

[67] The San Fernando Tunnel is almost 7,000 feet long and was completed by over 1,000 Chinese railroad workers in 1876 connecting Los Angeles with points North.

[68] Chun Fah. Kimm Family Collection

[69] Ng Poon Chew (1866-1931) was an author and advocate for Chinese American civil rights. In 1892 he became the first Chinese Presbyterian minister on the West Coast. Starting in 1900 he published the daily Chinese language newspaper Chung Sai Yat Pao.

[70] Fresno train terminal 1890's. Public Domain

[71] Chin Ah Mooie (1863-1940). Brought to America as a child slave and rescued by the Presbyterian missionaries in 1874. Kimm Family Collection. Courtesy of Gregory Kimm

[72] Hung family oral history describes a mysterious older brother who appeared one day and was later adopted out, never to be seen again. This brother's name was Gum Dew.

[73] Hong Sing Cigar Factory was located at 723 Sacramento Street in 1882.

[74] Jake Lee (1911 - 1991) Chinese Cigar Makers c. 1959. Chinese Historical Society of America

[75] The Geary Act passed on May 5, 1892 extended the Chinese Exclusion Act for an additional 10 years with added requirements that all Chinese laborers register with the IRS and carry a Certificate of Residence at all times or face deportation.

[76] Shot Tower at the corner of 1st and Howard Streets was for years the tallest building in San Francisco.
A shot tower is designed for the production of small diameter shot balls by freefall of molten lead, which is then caught in a water basin.

[77] San Francisco Chronicle August 19, 1893. Kearney's Move – Five Chinese Arrested. Public Domain

[78] By the May 5, 1893 deadline 97% of Chinese in America had not registered.

[79] Maahn on – Good evening in Cantonese

[80] Chock Chee – Cantonese word for Certificate of Residence.

[81] The McCreary Amendment passed in October 1893 gave the Chinese until May 4, 1894 to register.

[82] In Oriental Attire. How the Chinese Celebrated Yesterday. San Francisco Chronicle June 18 1894.

[83] Ah Ying is pregnant with her 4th child and second son Kim Seung.

[84] Charles Graham - 1894 California Midwinter International Exposition in Golden Gate Park. Public Domain

[85] Yeung Gee River is Cantonese for Yangtze River

[86] 1894 Hung Family at Midwinter Exposition – San Francisco, CA. Hong Family Collection.

[87] The San Francisco Call October 5, 1896. Public Domain

[88] Charles Weidner (1866-1940). Chee Sang Tong Chinese Drug Store 710 Dupont, San Francisco, CA. Destroyed by earthquake and fire April 18, 1906.

Gin Lun Lum on right holding hand scale. Gin Seung Chung (middle) and Gin Yic Too (left). Public Domain

[89] Chinese Primary School 920 Clay Street. Chinatown, San Francisco. Principal Miss Rose Thayer. Public Domain.

[90] Qui Fong in an immigration interview in October 1907 stated that her brother's godmother was Tom Shee aka Ah Ying.

[91] Arnold Genthe (1869-1942) Library of Congress. Father and Children on Dupont Street. Public Domain. Lai Wah, Chun Ngo and Ah Kay.

[92] Hang Far Low Restaurant 733 Dupont Street c 1900. Public Domain

[93] Sunning is the prior name for Toishan

[94]Dai Long Village in 1970's. The Hong ancestral home is on the right. The taller buildings in the back were built with money sent home by overseas Chinese. Hong Family Collection.

[95] Hong Family Temple in Dai Long Village. Low Family Collection

[96] Lum Chew (1842-1906) was born in Chung Shan, Learng due Shar Peng Har, Guangdong province. He came to America when he was 19 years old. After the TCRR he worked building the levee system and then was a tenant farmer and a skilled orchardist in the Sacramento Delta for over 40 years. He died in Courtland, CA at the age of 64 years.

[97] Jow Yook Kee aka Jim King (1840-1902) came to America in 1855 and worked for some gold miners as a helper and then later for an American mining company. He became a labor contractor. Jim King was one of the first Chinese hired to work on the TCRR as a translator, foreman, and labor contractor.

[98] CPRR reached Auburn in May 1865.

[99] Alfred Hart (1816-1908) Secret town Trestle was 1100 feet long. Within 12 years of completion of the TCRR Chinese crews had filled in the entire ravine with dirt from the surrounding hills. Public Domain

[100] 1867 photograph from the summit with view of Donner Lake and the snow sheds on the right. Public Domain.

[101] Kim and Bing 1903 a few months before they left for Kalispell Montana wearing the same Mandarin Robes and guapi mao or Chinese skull cap. Hong Family Collection

[102] As the first Chinese American Chief Engineer in California Kim kept his promise and designed and built many large ships for Moore Dry Dock Company and later for Ming Sung Company in China.

[103] Oakland Mole postcard published by the Newman Post Card Co. of Los Angeles. Public Domain

[104] The Great Northern Train. Public Domain.

[105] Tong Mung Wui was a secret society and underground resistance movement founded by Sun Yat-sen in Japan in 1905

[106] Mook Lan is Cantonese name for Mulan.

[107] Qui Gin (1875-1907) was a Chinese revolutionary, feminist and writer who today is celebrated as a national heroine in China. Qui was executed after a failed uprising against the Qing Dynasty in 1907.

[108] Dr. Sun Yat-Sen. Public Domain

[109] Tung Meng Hui at Portsmouth Square in San Francisco, CA. Gin Family Collection.

[110] Beri Beri is caused by dietary deficiency of Vitamin B1 (thiamine). It is seen in people who eat predominately polished rice since the husk is the source of B1. Its cause was unknown until the end of the 19th century. Symptoms include edema, weight loss, weakness, impaired sensory perception, and an irregular heart rate.

[111] Arnold Genthe – photograph April 16, 1906. Looking down Clay Street/ Library of Congress. Public Domain.

[112] Arnold Genthe - photograph April 16, 1906 looking down Sacramento Street/ Library of Congress. Public Domain

[113] April 1906 San Francisco Fires. Public Domain

[114] Wei Gin told his children how their grandmother carried him on her back through the streets of San Francisco as they escaped the earthquake and fires.

[115] Free Hot Meals, San Francisco Presidio Refugee Camp April 1906. Public Domain

[116] San Francisco Refugee Camp, Presidio East of Letterman Army Hospital, 1906. Public Domain.

[117] Ah Ying lived at 318 6th Street and Chin Shee at 317 6th Street in Oakland near the current day Chinese Garden Park. After the earthquake the Presbyterian Mission moved from 920 Sacramento Street in San Francisco to Oakland at 447th 11th Street – 5 blocks from Ah Ying and Sing Yee.

[118] September 1903 - Photograph of Hung Family in San Francisco, CA. Hong Family Collection.